Malcolm: Volume Zero

Mike Greenhough

At this point many authors declare that all events and
characters in the work are 'entirely fictitious'. This though
would suggest that there has never been a person called
Malcolm or a mountain range known as the Alps. And,
moreover, that airports, discos, ducks, glaciers, yodelling,
prime numbers, sandwiches, the sun and moon, etc. are all
my inventions. I reluctantly concede this is not the case.

mikegreenhoughwriting.co.uk

I am grateful to Literature Wales for the award of a
mentorship and in particular to Catherine Merriman
for her valuable advice.

Cover Design and Illustration: Rose Horridge
www.rosehorridgeart.co.uk

FOREWORD

I suppose I might have written about abuse and addiction, blackmail and corruption, death, disease, disaster, destitution, deformity, depravity, despair, incarceration, mutilation, murder, oppression, pain, pestilence, poverty, sadism, sleaze and/or squalor. But 10^7 authors got there before me. So this is from what was left. Constraints? Bring 'em on. And eat your heart out Georges Perec!

Chapter 1

Three on a Match

It was getting late. Any minute the girls would be gone. It was all or nothing. There were no intermediate strategies open to Malcolm. No grey areas, half-way houses, or common-ground. No handy common-room with pool and ping-pong – neutral territory, where an invitation could be rejected without hurt, or accepted without commitment. Their respective studies and residences were probably miles apart.

It was make or break. Now or never.

My place, or yours?

Fat chance! And even granting that slim possibility, exactly *whose* would be *yours*, anyway? They were all three rather nice. As well as being bold, it would be pretty arbitrary of him to ask any one of them "out". Why, for example, Helen (or was it Ellen?)? Just because she was sitting closest? (Though by no means close.) Why Jenny? Because he'd lit her cigarette, rather fumblingly and only with the third from a soggy book of matches left on his table? (A bad omen he'd dimly felt.) Or why Angela? Just because she'd laughed (albeit with a captivating mouth) at his joke about the relentless, maddening jukebox?

Malcolm slumped back in his chair. That really had been the extent of their interactions. Not much. But still rather better than on most of the evenings he'd spent in the Union Bar, pretending to read and trying, genuinely and desperately, to ignore Bob Dylan (something only his fans seemed able to manage fully). Mr D. was even now in the terminal stages (a man could hope) of a lament about the sorry state of the world. It was a Forth Bridge of a song; the master tape, so Malcolm had suggested, spliced into an endless loop by mischievous recording engineers – a seamless, themeless, whining Möbius strip. The Students' Union jukebox itself seemed indestructible, having soldiered on for so many years in spite of beer, or worse, spilled, or thrown, by the gallon. Not to mention the scores of punters' kicks delivered to its nether regions when it ate their sixpences, then sat there blinking mutely for a while before finally treating them to its own choice of record. What chance had Malcolm's silent, hateful curses of penetrating its metal hide and irreversibly shorting all the valves?

How many times must I sit through this song,
Without comprehending a word?

The answer *my friend* (what a patronising poser) was always the same: too bloody many!

The pickup finally lurched towards the hole in the music. A window in the wall of sound. Malcolm's last chance. He looked across at the trio. In principle he could always ask 'would any one of you like to go out with me?' But what kind of person would say a thing like that? Apart from a perfectly rational, honest one.

And suddenly it was all over.

'*What?*' said Malcolm, a bit more brusquely than he'd meant to.

'I said, would you like to come to my birthday party, tomorrow night? It's my twentieth! We're starting about nine,' said Angela.

Trilemma resolved by a quirk of the calendar. And it wasn't even a Leap Year.

'I'd love to,' Malcolm tried, and failed, to say coolly, wondering when he'd last got an invitation as promising and unsolicited as this. In the back of his mind there arose another Angela. One whose glossy tresses had dangled within caressing distance, before his very eyes, through every hot, sticky biology lesson of that long summer term. Sixteenth-birthday parties for such peaches had heavy parental supervision, though one little lapse during a seemingly innocent game had allowed one little intimacy – undreamed of, unreferred to ever after. And quite unforgettable.

Through a wild and delicious extrapolation into the present – the late but still fully swinging 'sixties – Malcolm conjured up the scene. *Her* games would be overtly erotic; *her* folks, absent, in Cowes, or

Cannes, or somewhere further (academic anyway, as the three girls clearly shared a flat); *her* tresses, routinely caressable. Heaven. Unless, of course . . .

He was brought back to earth by the flashing of bar lights. Dregs were drained, handbags fumbled in, noses powdered. Minutes passed. The management administered the *coup de grâce* to the jukebox, arresting it in mid beat. Malcolm leapt in with the crucial, parting, confirmatory question.

'Where do you, er, live, Angela?' He was more nervous at speaking her name for the first time than anything else.

'Why?' She sounded suspicious, and in the reigning silence everybody was tuned in.

'Er, you asked me to your party. You know. Your twentieth?'

Angela brightened. 'Oh. No! It's at *Dingles*.'

'Well, where does *he* live?'

'Who?'

'Dingle.'

'No, no, *Dingles* is a club!'

His gravest fears confirmed, Malcolm managed, if only by considerable effort, to affect even greater disappointment than he actually felt. 'Not that damp cellar with the ear-splitting music and beer at ten bob a pint?'

'That's *Bundles*,' chorused the trio.

'You must know *Dingles*,' said Helen, 'it used to be *Spindles*.'

'What happened?'

'They changed its name.'

'Never!'

'Had to, people were always confusing it with the other one.'

'What, *Bundles*?'

'No, *Rumplestiltskins*.'

'That's nothing like it!'

'It is when you get inside.'

Malcolm trudged out after the three just far enough behind so that no-one would know whether he was with them. He certainly didn't himself.

Look, why don't you just come over to Gray Hall. It's free. Quiet too. We could play ping-pong in the basement, which isn't at all damp. Quite cosy, actually. There's a TV there and a long, grey continuous sofa, where intimacy can grow or fade quasi-statically, an infinitely variable dimmer switch offering softening lights, sweetening music (with not a demisemiquaver of you-know-who) – subliminal seduction, if you so choose, stretching for hours or postponed for the replay. Or forever.

This was exactly what Malcolm didn't say next. By the time he'd half formed the words the girls were out of the door and away, the party offer now exposed as unbearably casual, half forgotten already. Malcolm trudged on. Tomorrow night looked like being another long date with Mr D.

Chapter 2

Getting Off

Gray Hall was a three-dimensional matrix of study/bedrooms. It stood on a corner of the campus on the outskirts of a small Northern town. The rumour that it had once won a design award was a simple falsehood, initiated and maintained by the janitor in an effort to forestall complaints. Even so he found it a full-time job diverting the residents' attention away from the whimsical heating, the unfathomable plumbing, the irreparable lift. As a piece of architecture it was perhaps summed up most politely in the college accommodation brochure, as "a prominent feature of the area". As a memorial to its eponymous benefactor it had certainly failed – after so many years, and in the absence of any plaque, portrait or bust in the foyer, the name had come to signify, in the students' perception, no more than the plain, lumpish, concrete anonymity of the place. The rectangular, grid-like layout of rooms provoked all the obvious quips about battery hens and convicts. But for Malcolm, ever attuned to the wonders of science, this grand symmetrical lattice of elements suggested a more natural and romantic model: a giant-sized, inhabitable orthorhombic crystal, with a geometry both elegant and reassuringly regular. Easy to locate from afar. Easy to navigate within.

Well, almost. There were complications, Malcolm recalled, as he lay on his bed in Room 216 and stared up at the ceiling. Those rather widely spaced three-digit numbers, painted boldly on every door, just begged to be decomposed into x, y and z co-ordinates which would specify your location in the whole array. To a budding mathematician this Cartesian interpretation was irresistible. So for his first few days there he'd just assumed that his own ceiling formed the floor of Room 316. Well, you would.

Then late one night, provoked by an extended outbreak of chair-scraping, boot-throwing and what sounded like bed-trampolining from above, he'd fumbled his way along the dimly lit corridors and up to that very room, pounding on the door before swiftly retreating to avoid a confrontation. But Malcolm hadn't reckoned with the mirror-like arrangement of the stairways at either end of the building – the one zigging while the other zagged. This caused a kind of parity flip on alternate levels, and meant that the room numbers ascended clockwise on the even floors only.

The innocent occupant of 316, woken by the complaint, consoled himself with a burst of late-night, Wonderful Radio One, adding his own spirited, foot-tapping accompaniment, and waking 204 below. Sadly for all, the room-numbering misconception was sufficiently widespread to sustain a chain reaction of protest and retaliation, which by dawn had ping-ponged its way through the whole building.

But all was quiet tonight, in Room 216. Or, as Malcolm preferred it, *Study/bedroom* 216. It was such a nifty designation, he felt, somehow giving the illusion of extra space, like a cunningly sited mirror, as well as managing to encapsulate the essential, complementary activities of student life. Of all life, perhaps. If necessary it could be legitimately abbreviated to *study* – for example when trying to entice certain visitors without alarming them. It wasn't, importantly, a *bedroom/study*. The reverse alphabetical order had no doubt deliberately been chosen to emphasise the college's priorities and reassure the tax-payers. The oblique stroke (where, Malcolm had noted, some institutions had a hyphen) suggested a kind of *numerator/denominator* interpretation. And this then raised the question of exactly how you should apportion time between work and sleep. A happy and productive student life depended on getting the ratio right, as tutors never tired of saying. And they were basically right. The results of imbalances were all too clear – swots and delinquents abounded, and were despised, in equal measure.

Malcolm spent a good deal of time pondering, and often lamenting, the particular blend of ingredients in his own term-time life. It wasn't all bad – in spite of some noisy neighbours he did have basic control over study (there was always the library to retreat to) and rest (there were always earplugs and other devices). But that was only half of the story. Or, rather, two thirds. Lurking in the *bedroom* of *study/bedroom* was a third, implicit, recreational component. One unacknowledged, and unsupported, by the college authorities. One which, when in short supply (and even when, more rarely, plentiful) could sabotage both work and sleep.

He padded across the corridor to the unnumbered kitchen opposite. It was bright, with a fluorescent buzz, and a faint but abiding hint of curry. He made himself a sandwich – a modest, single-storey snack, cut along lines of latitude and longitude into the traditional square quarters – and padded back.

Slumped in the easier of his two chairs – a low-down, well-worn, foam-cushioned job with broad, flat, wooden arms you could rest a plate on – he contemplated his little domain. Though he was always ready to bemoan the facilities for the sake of solidarity with fellow residents, he secretly rejoiced in the plain, simple adequacy of the room. It was somehow comfortingly unambiguous – a quality he'd always prized. Yet without being trivially austere – the sort of minimal, schematic environment modelled on computers by the pioneers of artificial-intelligence research: **bed, basin, bookshelf; window, wardrobe, wastebin**. A moderately competent robot would have coped, indeed would have thrived here.

He stared up again at the floor of Room 304, whose ceiling, in turn, formed the floor of 416, and so on, and up, level after level, through the dilapidated penthouse and into the autumn night – whether moonless or moonful was unclear, on account of a thick, drizzling cloud layer. Accommodated vertically above and below him were students of Town Planning, Dentistry, Catering and Architecture, and no fewer than two each of Law and Accountancy. A towering column of budding professionals. A future High Street in the making. Interestingly, a horizontal section at his level would have revealed a more technical fraternity: a psychologist, a biologist and two statisticians, along with several engineers of the electrical, civil and chemical varieties. Plus, of course, one mathematician-philosopher, Malcolm himself, the common element of row and column, occupying a pivotal position at this cross-roads of human knowledge. The remaining rooms housed a further hundred or so souls. All male. But quite a disparate bunch, leading largely unconnected lives, according to the demands of their different studies, separated, albeit inadequately, by common walls yet bound together by common kettles, cookers, fridges, TV sets, landings and stairwells, and by the alternation of day and night – eating, drinking, learning and dreaming in a loose synchrony. Malcolm picked up a sandwich quarter (the north-easterly one) and took a bite.

As midnight approached throughout the length, breadth and height of Gray Hall there was a flurry of washing and flushing. Then the demand on the labyrinthine plumbing system began to fall, causing water pressure to rise until it became slightly too much for the ageing and ill-seated cold-tap washer in Study/bedroom 216. The first few drips were faltering, uncertain in pitch, though not unmusical. Gradually they settled to a steady tone and tempo – persistent, disquieting, unignorable in its mimicking and mocking of the human heartbeat. Life was leaking away. Malcolm draped a dried-out face flannel over the tap, but time ticked on in the silence.

Perhaps he was being unreasonably impatient. After all his life, proverbially at least, had only half begun. Or had some double (or half) life wholly begun? The unimaginable forty was as far in the future as the unrememberable zero was in the past. But though it seemed a wicked wishing away of life he sometimes longed for the calm and contentment that might come with those two-score years. He moved on to the next sandwich, backing westerly.

One score years, and none. So far. And was there much to show for it? Well, it was hard to say, without some reference points. Because this was Malcolm's very first life. He had no preconceptions – about what constituted a reasonable level of accomplishment, about how long a day would last, or how much pleasure to expect from it. How could you gauge such things merely from your own standpoint? For any proper, objective self-appraisal you'd need some kind of running companion, pacemaker, control experiment. A parallel-track, twin Malcolm perhaps? His chewing rate slowed. Parallel universes were handy, and fashionable, things. You could safely speculate about their existence because it could never be refuted. Or verified. Trouble was that meant you couldn't learn anything from them either.

From the basin plug hole there began a steady glug-glugging, echoing the soundless tap drip, with the same periodicity (though out of phase) and a hint of pitch modulation as the water level trembled in the waste-pipe. Malcolm inserted the chainless plug, confident, without bothering to do the arithmetic, that the basin could comfortably accommodate the volume that would have emerged by morning. Little drops of water. Around twenty-thousand of them, in fact. Not a mighty ocean. But enough to wash your face in. There followed a few final, defiant glugs, fainter but more resonant, about an octave higher in the confines. A U-bend swan song.

He took the last two, southern, sandwich quarters from the plate, crossed to the bed, oblivious of tumbling crumbs, and lay looking at the ceiling again. What about *non*-parallel tracks? Somehow divergent lives? Or, even better, the same track but different speeds. Why not? In philosophy, above all in metaphysics, you can postulate anything you want, anytime you like. Especially on a Friday night after a few drinks. Different speeds. Yes, that would do. How revealing and instructive it would be to have the backward perspective of some advanced guard, fast-track observer. Someone who, as you grew older, would grow, well, olderer. A paradoxical twin, triggered by the same little bang from birth's starting pistol, but with the metronome set at, say, twice the tempo – a literal Doppelgänger, playing hare to Malcolm's tortoise, lapping him annually on their common birthday: *Meta*-Malcolm, mega-Malcolm, Malcolm major, Malcolm Mark 2. Or Mach 2. He was out there somewhere. But what would he be doing? Perhaps one could sneak a paradoxical peek, courtesy of Einstein. Or Zeno. Malcolm closed his eyes.

Time warps. If you let it.

Meta-Malcolm 40 sits at a dinner table for eight – a couple of couples and a pair of pairs. Time has furnished him, at least for tonight, with a cosy rectangle of friends. The lights and seats are comfortable, as is the balance of age and gender. The function is well advanced: wine and candle levels are dwindling. A rosy contentment reigns.

A glossy midnight blue-green box of chocolate mints appears; the luxuriously thin squares are dealt clockwise round the company. This triggers shouts for a general-knowledge board game. Battle commences. Unhesitatingly, and without modesty, Meta-Malcolm denies any knowledge of the siege of *Smolgarsbad* (or wherever), let alone its date, suggesting even that the questioner might be making it up. There's an astonished silence, then an astonished chorus of *"FOURTEEN-TWENTY-SEVEN!"* (or whenever) from around the table. M-M shrugs and passes the dice.

In the very next round his unhesitant naming of the composer of *Porgy and Bess* provokes equal astonishment, and suggestions that he's betraying his age. He retaliates with yet more counter-astonishment at this warped sense of time. He even considers asking whether the hostess's recently revealed familiarity with Stonehenge (which allowed her a gleeful advance of several board spaces) makes her, somehow, Neolithic. Chivalrously he lets it pass, conscious of just how much evidence of her own time past is concealed by current candlelight.

She launches a compilation of 'sixties pop, from an expensive and powerful stereo system. Two of the guests have no enthusiasm for this music, which they feel, respectively, is rather before and rather after their times, but are prepared to ignore it for the sake of the others, who are already totally oblivious. Except, that is, for M-M, who takes a long draught of Merlot in pursuit of just such oblivion. It is slow coming. Lacking earlids he drops his eyelids. The hostess interprets his polite but pained expression as musical nostalgia, smiles to herself, and tops up his glass.

Back in Room 216 the silence gave way to a familiar pattern of ticking – metallic, unlocatable, with a gradual *rallentando*, signalling that the heating had either just come on or just gone off. You could never tell which, even by putting a hand on the pipe-work. It seemed to hover permanently around body temperature, so there was never a clear transfer of heat in either direction. Malcolm pulled on a pullover, deciding that on balance, given the hour, it was probably going to get colder. As the pipes reached thermal equilibrium another silence followed, not unlike the earlier one.

Then he heard it. A single, truncated giggle. It was faint but unmistakably female – the unignorable sound of someone somewhere having more fun than you were. He opened a window, letting in the masking murmur of distant traffic, along with the night breeze. What was he doing wrong?

Malcolm often felt he belonged to the awkwardest of species. Sure, he was grateful enough for the binocular vision, the opposable thumbs, the generous folds of cortex, and all that. But he could have lived without the self-consciousness – of time, and death, but, most of all, of courtship (did they still call it that?) that came as part of the human package deal. All other creatures just seemed to get on with it. Why not him? It should have been particularly easy – what with this new Liberation business, so widely and loudly trumpeted. And yet somehow so elusive. Had the papers not reassured him daily he would have been quite unaware of how much fun he was having as a member of the younger generation, in the era of hippies, flower power and protest marches. It was impossible, apparently, *not* to have fun. What with the free love, the music, the fashions.

Prolonged exposure to these swinging times had left Malcolm with a strictly respective love-hate relationship with girls and pop culture. The big problem was they always seemed to come bundled together – the girls gathering only in the noisiest, most fashionable venues. Doubtless *Dingles* would offer just such a triple bill – the price of romantic chances being high-decibel endurance and conformity with some arbitrary dress code. He feared that his old jeans in particular would need repairing, if not replacing, if he was to pass muster. There seemed to be no escape from it. A vicious, infernal triangle. How gladly he would have traded the entire Top Twenty (or Top Two-hundred) and boutiquefuls of trendy clothes, for one, single hour of silent, naked bliss.

Room 216 seemed to be getting warmer in spite of the open window. Or maybe because of it. Autumn could be funny like that. Malcolm opened it wider, and prepared for bed. Then lay staring at the ceiling, with raindrops and footsteps, pipe clicks and tap drips, glugs, giggles and sniggers, real and fancied, ping-ponging round his head.

There was no-one to read him a bedtime story. But even the most rational adult mind has a treasure trove of the fanciful and folkloric, buried in childhood, which will readily resurface to form the stuff of dreams.

Malcolm lets go. Ceiling becomes sky. Walls, woods. He follows the breadcrumb trail, over the rickety-rackety bridge. Trip-trap. Down the winding path. Zig-zag. But to whose house do we go? Well *hers*, of course. Or perhaps *theirs* – these traditional tales often feature heroic threesomes. Student princesses, then? An alluring prospect. Though knowing his luck he'll get the Three Bears, Little Pigs, or Billy Goats Gruff. But wait! Whose dream *is* this? A moment of wishful concentration and, *Hey Presto*, in a sudden clearing, complete with regulation little crooked windows and little crooked chimney, there it is – a humble, thatched, third-floor student flat. Out of reach. With no lengthy dangling golden tresses as an aid to climbing. He huffs and puffs and paces awhile. Then with one bound Big Bad Malcolm is at the door. He sneaks inside.

Nobody home. On the kitchen table (topped with rustic Formica) a fresh pot of herbal tea, cooling, and three waiting breakfasts. BBM begins to salivate (he's really getting the hang of this lycanthropy thing). He samples the dishes in turn: peach yoghurt, high-fibre muesli, ryvitas with low-fat cottage cheese. Surprisingly palatable, given his adopted species. Redolent of young, figure-conscious and sophisticated females. He licks his chops, deep in thought. Red riding hoods. Blue-stockings. It was important to pursue a varied diet.

Footsteps and girlish giggles. The lifting of the latch.

He pads into an adjoining room, slips into the first bed, which is soft. He pulls the quilt (a minty-green Gingham) up to his chin.

Enter Alice (or is it Cinderella?) 'What big eyes you have!' Straight to the point – no reference to the size of chairs or the temperature of porridge.

He is nonplussed. 'Yours ain't so bad either . . . I mean . . . All the better to . . .' But she's gone already.

He tries the next bed (a muted Paisley pattern), which is even softer.

Gretel (or is it Heidi?) puts her head round the door. 'What big ears you have!'

'Who's been eating . . .' he begins, 'I mean, Who is the fairest . . . , Errr, All the bett . . .' But she too has vanished.

Bed three is softer still.

Snow White (or is it Bo Peep?) appears in the doorway.

'This bed's just right,' he offers, pre-emptively, patting the pillow, making room. 'You know, All the better, and all that, eh?'

She backs away, wide-eyed and open mouthed, and summons the others. There is much tut-tutting and wagging of fingers. He apologises for any undue forwardness, tries to placate them with riddles and name-guessing games. Offers of ping pong, chocolate mints. Sandwiches. They demur. Outside there is wild shouting, a crescendo of hunting horns. Exit BBM pursued by axe-wielding woodcutters, shotgun-toting fathers, assorted ogres and crones . . .

Chapter 3

Greens and Yellers

Seasons come and go. It's part of their job. And, with the whole year to cover between them, once come they're officially on duty twenty-four hours a day for a whole quarter (as well as doing permanent, year-round, overtime *a quattro* as labels for everything from pizza to Vivaldi).

In our perceptions, though, they're often more fleeting than extended. Their essence seems to be concentrated in the days that herald them, in those sharp gradients of mood and weather which peak around the boundaries. It's the first cuckoo and the last leaf, the promise and loss, which stir us most.

Autumn is a particularly cuspish affair, spawned at the interface of warmth and cold. Like the mist itself. For Malcolm it had always been the most exciting and the scariest season – potent, pivotal, charged with a kind of criticality. Every year it had sent him back to school with a bump, to struggle with the renewed loss of liberty, the invidious promotion into ever more demanding classes. These feelings were brought into sharp focus by a nauseating double shock on arrival at the school gates: the all-pervasive smell of new paint, and first sight of the monstrous pair of white wooden H's which had resprouted, most unseasonably, on the new-mown sports field.

Several years had passed since, but new hopes and old fears could still be aroused by the faintest whiff of an equinox. In fact the resonant twinges triggered at this chill hinge of the year would last him a lifetime.

It was half light when Malcolm awoke. For hours his brain, though officially off-duty, had been busying itself in some stratum laid down in his early years. He lingered for a while in this era, staring at the patch on the ceiling, till precipitated into the present by the realisation that it wasn't there. As a child his first sight each morning had always been the damp patch of plaster directly over the bed. Such blemishes were common. Indeed most of his classmates admitted to being greeted daily by a similar sight – a reflection of the uniformly ageing housing stock of the small Midlands railway town. But what really bothered Malcolm was that *his* patch had a completely arbitrary shape. Those of his friends were either like gnarled old hags or maps of Australia. He seemed to have been singled out for the arbitrary one. The arbitrariest shape, in fact, that he'd ever seen. Coincidence? It seemed unlikely. Ever since then he'd suspected that life had a hidden purposelessness which would one day be revealed to him. But he was still waiting.

Meanwhile he spent much of his time pursuing girls. Mostly in dreams, but also in reality. Though then with even less success. He fondly remembered a time when pursuit was unnecessary. In primary school there'd been perfect, if almost innocent, integration. Then later, though still sharing classrooms, the sexes had been somehow put asunder. The few officially sanctioned hours per year of immediate and natural contact came around Christmas, with country dancing in the gym. Blissful afternoons of warmth and jollity. But awarded grudgingly, and only when the rugby pitch was frozen so hard that the headmaster would have been sued if one of his charges had broken a limb. So for Malcolm that game became associated with unnatural and painful separation. A feeling reinforced by his mother's own more instinctive aversion.

'A lot of silly men chasing a ball.' That was how she would sum up and dismiss any team game she happened to glimpse on the screen of their tiny, flickering, black-and-white TV set. It was meant to be provocatively simplistic. But the young Malcolm was unprovocable. She was preaching to someone who'd never even needed to be converted. Her contempt for sport only began to impinge on him negatively when he had to change schools and she refused to buy him the regulation kit which she couldn't afford anyway. Hand-me-downs would have to do, and in truth they *looked* smart enough. The immaculate kit he inherited from his older brothers was testimony to a lack of commitment in team games, which rivalled his own. But, sadly, where his school favoured green and yellow, theirs had gone for blue and red. Sadder still, while his feet had already reached size eight, theirs had stopped at seven.

So it was that on the first day of his new school he was still trying to get his left foot into its boot (or more accurately, into his eldest brother's left foot's boot) when his classmates were already on the pitch huddled around Jimbo, who was briefing them on the game. Jimbo (or was it Gymbo, or even Gymbeau? – no-one was ever to see it written down) was the nickname of the short-haired, short-statured, short-tempered sports teacher. He was at that moment pointing out that rugby had *laws* and not *rules*. The absent Malcolm was destined to spend the rest of his life believing it had rules. Even, occasionally, wondering what they might be.

By the time the second boot was almost on, which was as far as it would ever go, the laws had been covered. And by the time he'd hobbled out of the changing rooms and crossed the intervening hockey pitch (admittedly at a snail-like pace on account of its altogether more alluring huddle of girls) the game was well under way.

So, somewhat disadvantaged, Malcolm stood, by default, on the centre spot. Clueless. Motionless. Although he was neither a swot nor a complete weakling the contrast with that morning's physics lesson was striking. At least there the laws had been written out in block capitals on the blackboard. What's more they seemed to have some correspondence with real, sensible life. In the absence of any forces or other compulsions, they said, any body would stay still or proceed with constant speed. Well, so it would! So did he. Rooted to the spot, instructionless, goalless, inactive except for a surreptitious ogling of the now running (and doubtless sweating) group on the hockey field. It couldn't last for long.

It didn't. 'Don't just stand there, boy. RUN!' Jimbo had a taste, though limited talent, for sergeant-major impressions. This simple command, with all its implicit threats, provided the initial impulse which set Malcolm in motion. In the absence of directional information or any further instructions he maintained speed and course, crossed the imperceptible sideline and continued on, all in accordance with Newton's First Law (although sensitive instruments might have detected a little deviation as he succumbed to a gravitational pull from the tight little cluster of hockey players).

He was within drooling distance of that very group when violent whistle blasts arrested his motion and forced him to retrace his steps. Jimbo regarded him with deep suspicion. Malcolm put on a look of supreme innocence (which he only partially needed to fake). This saved him. Jimbo pointed out the freshly painted, whitish line which surrounded them. It was almost rectangular, apart from some wiggly bits on the side closest to the adjacent pitch, where the white-line man (another hockey fan) had had some little lapses of concentration.

'See that line! You DON'T go outside it. RIGHT?'

Jimbo took the silent, exaggerated head nods as promises of wholehearted compliance. In truth Malcolm was humouring him as you might a senile great-uncle illustrating a military campaign on the tablecloth with the aid of the condiments.

So, you had to stay within the rectangle. Not much to go on. But a start. Of sorts. Given time he could arrive at the rules of the game by a process of induction. Maybe. Meanwhile, he couldn't risk provoking Jimbo any further. The game was underway again and he urgently needed a formula for inconspicuousness. Clearly a strict adherence to Newton's Laws was out. What to do?

It came to him in a flash. Like all the best scientific discoveries. All he had to do was regard the white lines as reflecting boundaries, and allow himself to bounce off them. Like a ball on a billiard table. He tried it out. It worked rather well. Total internal reflection! What's more, by carefully choosing his initial angle of incidence he found it possible to follow a particular path repeatedly. A couple of dozen of these rhomboidal romps (with little ogling breaks each time he passed near the hockey huddle) and it was time for 'half time'.

Apparently. Malcolm had often pondered the meaning of time. Without making much progress. It was disturbing to realise he wasn't even sure of the meaning of half time. Was it, for example, a *point* in time, or a *span* of time? An instant, or an interval? He hoped for the latter. But it turned out to be the former, and any fantasies he might have entertained involving orange juice, hot towels or nubile masseuses were quickly dashed.

Jimbo started the second half immediately, by ordering about a dozen players from one part of the pitch to go to another, and vice versa. This seemed a rather arbitrary thing to do and made little difference to the subsequent activity. However, as a sort of acknowledgement of what seemed to be a significant point in the game, Malcolm reversed the sense of his rotation, proceeding now anticlockwise around the pitch. Thus he managed to escape serious notice until the final peep of the whistle. He did however start to get suspicious looks from fellow players. They clearly had doubts about his degree of commitment to victory, and were probably wondering which side would be the one to benefit if he ever decided to play a more active role.

Malcolm set himself sporting homework for the coming week. Something far more challenging than what the French or physics teachers were dishing out. It was to devise a means of avoiding attention for a whole hour while forced to run around in a small area with no natural cover. A major part of the problem was his unique clothing. In the wild to be distinctive is to be vulnerable. He couldn't help thinking about what had once happened to next-door's canary when it had sought companionship among its drabber cousins in their apple tree.

But by the day of the next game he had something of a plan. It had been an easy matter to make a deal with his mother whereby she wouldn't wash his kit if he didn't. Then he augmented last week's dirt with a few rolls in the mud *en route* for the playing field. Only the whites of his eyes now prevented him from being taken for a part of the pitch.

Thus the first half passed uneventfully, and to celebrate he added an experimental variation to the orbiting strategy. By a slight change of the angle at which he hit the boundary his path, formerly a strictly repeating rhombus, became subject to a kind of precession – a progressively shifting pattern which allowed him gradually to cover every square inch of the pitch (as time-lapse, aerial photography would have shown). This was a doubly fortunate move. It not only led to a more even pattern of wear on the grass but also prevented the vague sense of *déjà vu* which had been building in Jimbo's mind from becoming a conscious realisation and demanding some action.

In Jimbo, God had tempered a mild sadistic streak with a dullness of perception which limited the suffering he could inflict on any one soul. Criticisms and punishments he dealt out with an impartiality amounting to randomness, and the bulk of them were avoided if you simply kept your distance, and kept moving. The rare rebukes which found an identifiable target were as well distributed statistically, and therefore as bearable to the victims, as the fleeting pimples of adolescence.

It wasn't easy to learn much from such a man. His coaching was based on a small collection of entreaties with no clear connection to the events on the pitch. His favourite was, *Come on now yellers, mark yer man and let's get that ball through there!* Malcolm just wondered who these yellers were (he certainly wasn't one of them – as part of his anonymity campaign he'd been especially quiet), who, in turn, their man was, why anyone should want to mark him and what with, and where exactly it was that that ball should be got through. Otherwise the instruction was a model of clarity. (And while on the subject of *that* ball, how come there was only the one, between twenty-odd kids – was this some kind of lingering, post-war austerity thing? One ball! And it wasn't even *round*.)

Other directives included *Let's see some decent tackling*, and Malcolm's own favourite, *Pick those feet up Bagley!* These were interspersed with whistle blasts of random amplitude and duration. When feeling especially communicative he would jump up and down with hands on hips. Whether this was in frustration, to combat the cold, or to signal the distance and direction of a source of food to fellow sports teachers, was not clear.

Week after tedious week dragged by. But through unremitting efforts to keep the lowest of profiles Malcolm achieved his goal of becoming the most undistinguished, and indistinguishable, non-player of the season. In attempts to develop a theory to account for the behaviour of the players on the field he experimented with a variety of ground-covering strategies. Some inspired by the early astronomers. He tried circular orbits, and elliptical ones, even flirted with epicycles to throw anyone watching off the scent (and, yes, to indulge his little passion for hockey). There remained, however, a nagging discrepancy. Chance alone dictated that he would only rarely interact with fellow players. They, on the other hand, seemed to be for ever colliding with each other. This theoretical impasse lasted for the better part of the season.

Then one day, in a bold act of conjecture, he tried adding to his conceptual model a mutually attractive force between bodies on the field – shades of Newtonian apples, with a dash of the kinetic theory of gases. Pausing only to allow himself a *sotto-voce* 'Eureka!', he swung into action. The beauty of it was that by regarding the players as point masses he could adopt almost any post-collision course he fancied, without sacrificing mechanical plausibility. It felt wonderful. Malcolm the human pinball!

But his triumph was short lived. An unlucky choice of trajectory brought him within arm's length of Jimbo who, in an uncharacteristically lucid moment, grabbed him by the shirt as he swept past. Malcolm was taken aback. Maybe the man was upset by the new, aggressive style of play, (but wasn't it an essential feature of the game?) or possibly the way he'd been colliding indiscriminately with both green- and yellow-shirted players (but it was unlike Jimbo to notice subtleties of that sort). In truth Malcolm's only indiscretion was in succumbing now and then to a bit of *joie de vivre* and uttering a resounding 'PIIOOIIOOIIOOIINNG!' on impact.

It only needed another display of confusion and innocence and he was released and back below Jimbo's threshold of perception. He remained there for the rest of his rugby career by employing a judicious mixture of previous strategies.

Somehow the seasons passed. To help keep boredom at bay he indulged in silent fantasies. These mostly featured individuals (and sometimes small groups) from the neighbouring pitch. But when provoked by one of Jimbo's particularly loud and incomprehensible orders he would mentally stroll over to the man, grab him by the tracksuit lapels, stare into his eyes till he had his full attention, and then say quietly and simply,

'WHAT?????????????!!!!!!!!!!!!'

A timid and slightly built 12-year-old could only dream. An older, bolder, Meta-Malcolm, on the other hand, just by virtue of being virtual, might intervene with impunity to engineer a just and final resolution.

> There is no bloody revenge, no swift despatch by lightning bolt or landmine. Something altogether lower-key. When he judges the time is ripe M-M signals to an unmarked van which has been cruising the touch-line. Two sturdy men in discreetly plain uniforms emerge, take Jimbo gently but firmly under the arms and lift him into the back. His muffled voice can still be heard through the metal grill as they drive off. 'Come on now greens. Mark your man and get that ball through there!' M-M watches silently as they disappear through the school gates, sighs, then saunters across to the hockey pitch to apply for a transfer.

Chapter 4

The Penultimate Trouser Shop

"MANGLERS MAKETH MAN!" read the sign in the window beneath a model of a frowning youth with an E-type jaw, who was bursting out of a very odd-looking pair of jeans. The pockets were sort of upside-down, and there were what could only be described as "things" attached behind the knees. Malcolm wondered why. And not for the first time in his life. Maybe the British army had ordered twenty-thousand pairs in preparation for a conflict in some extraordinary environment where these oddities would have conferred an advantage over an unsuspecting enemy. Then diplomacy had prevailed, the war was averted, and now they were being offered cheap to unsuspecting civilians. Except they weren't. You could have bought more than two normal pairs of trousers for that price.

Malcolm's desperate trouser hunt had begun hours earlier and now he'd almost run out of High Street. A couple more tries then he could give up, and the agony would be over. From a brief reconnaissance down a seedy side street he'd learned that Dingle insisted on **"SMART CASUALS ONLY"**. The lettering on the sign, hanging so Dantesquely over the entrance to the infernal club, was bold and clear enough. What wasn't clear was what it meant. Did the bouncers – two simian penguins who framed the front door every night – have to exclude the scruffy, the formally dressed, or the dull-witted in any attire? They themselves would seem to be triply disqualified from entry. Lucky devils. But, with his knees showing through the legs of his only jeans, Malcolm (although in fact years ahead of fashion) would be unlikely to get past. And the thought of having to gain entry to such a dump by pleading, bribing or sneaking in, was unthinkable.

So he confronted his penultimate trouser shop, thinking what a good name that would be for a trouser shop, in the unlikely event he ever opened one. Few people would bother to wonder what it meant and those that did might well decide it was one better than 'ultimate'.

Market research had surely shown that arbitrary names no-one understood worked wonders for trade. On the other hand he could call it "Mangles", but then people would think it was a night-club. Or a laundry suppliers. It was getting late, again, and he was prevaricating. Again. Malcolm went in.

Um ching Um ching Um chingum Um ching.

The dull, throbbing music had been lying in wait behind the heavy glass door.

'Yes, sir?' It was very dark inside and the source of the voice was hard to locate. What with the constant umching.

'I need some trousers, please,' said a squinting Malcolm to what in reality was the assistant's image in a large wall mirror.

'Indeed we do, sir!' came a voice from behind.

Malcolm spun round. 'Well, yours aren't quite as worn as mine.' He felt rather pleased with this snappy countersneer, but it was swamped by the umching. 'Could you turn that down a bit?'

'Straights or Manglers?'

'Sorry?' Malcolm frowned as he strained his ears.

'DO YOU WANT STRAIGHTS OR MANGLERS?'

'I wouldn't have thought so. What are they?'

'They're jeans, sir.'

'Ah. Right. And what are "straights", exactly? Or even approximately?' he muttered.

'Well, it's just a sort of style. Really.'

'Really?' Malcolm's frown intensified. 'Is there anything I should know about them? In particular?'

'That depends, sir. Do you have normal feet?'

'Oh yes. No problem.'

'Then you may need to lie down and point your foot to get the heel through the ankle, if you see what I mean. Some people put zips in the legs – but that does invalidate the warranty.'

'I suppose it'd better be Mangles then,' said Malcolm.

'Mang*lers*, sir.'

'Right. Mang*lers*. What are *they* like?'

'There's a pair in the window.'

27

'Oh, yeah. Tell me, what are those things hanging down behind the knees?'

'You can always cut them off, sir. Though that would of course invalidate the warranty.'

'But they've got upside-down pockets. Doesn't your money fall out?'

'No, they're sewn up.'

'So, how do you get things in?'

'You don't sir. They're just decorative.'

'So where do you put your money. If you've got any left?'

'We do have these Mangler shoulder bags.'

'Sorry?' 'COULD YOU TURN THAT *DOWN* A BIT?' Malcolm gestured at the nearest of the battery of loudspeakers, spoilt for choice.

'No, I can't, sir. It's the manager who sets the volume . . .'

'Well how about asking him to set it to *zero*?'

'He's not here.'

'Well, *where* is he?'

'Tenerife.'

Malcolm gritted his teeth. 'Look, I just need some trousers.'

'Indeed we do, sir.'

'Don't start that again. Surely you must have something else.'

'Well, there are some nice hats upstairs.'

Malcolm took a slow, deep breath. 'I just want some trousers, with two legs, one on each side, and pockets the right way up. And flies, or have they gone out of fashion too?'

'You won't get anything like that round here.'

'Why not?'

'Nobody sells them.'

'Why not?'

'There's no demand.'

The door closed behind Malcolm and the umching was replaced by the gentler roar of traffic. He stared back at the dummy with growing sympathy. Anyone parting with his last pound only to find his nether regions painfully constricted by a designer joke could be forgiven a frown. He strode off in the direction of the ultimate trouser shop. Did such a thing exist? Did he care anymore? Maybe one day he would write a treatise on the metaphysics of fashion – its phases and crazes, warps and wefts. Well, warps anyway. For fashion contorts the very fabric of time.

A decade away, on some divergent, shadowy, higher High Street the girlfriend of Meta-Malcolm 30 is asking why he doesn't buy *some of those jeans with the wide legs*. 'Because,' he says, 'in a nutshell, they're really expensive. And look silly.' She sighs and says how inhibited he is. He says everyone's entitled to a few inhibitions, and it's far better they should apply to extravagance and stupidity than to, say, things like, observing speed limits and pulling rip cords. Or breathing. But in the end, for the quiet life, he capitulates, wearing the wretched things a couple of times, after dark, before allowing them to get lost in the wardrobe.

Here, eventually, they're unearthed by the girlfriend of M-M 40, who expresses great surprise that he, or in fact anyone, could have worn *THOSE*. M-M 40 scribbles for her on a scrap of paper the name and address of the girl to placate whom he once bought *THOSE*, expressing the hope that the two might slug it out between themselves at some time and place when he's far far away.

Back on the more immediate and sunnier High Street, stirring a big mug of coffee in a little tea room, Malcolm reflected on the vagaries of time and life and love. The last one most especially. Maybe he'd just picked a difficult decade in which to mature. He certainly felt it would have been easier to get on with (or get off with) the eligible females of almost any other era: the ambushable cave-girl, the turreted damsel, the fan-fluttering, pump-room débutante. Each was confined to some well-defined habitat – a conventional arena with clear-cut rules of engagement. Doubtless there were snares and pitfalls too. But anything would be preferable to these duels with disc jockeys, trials by trousers.

What to do?

Sadly it was about a century too late for copperplate invitations to pony and trap rides. Or parasolled picnics on the river bank. Maybe he could rattle off a birthday sonnet, or something similar. But the briefness of their recent encounter had left him with only very limited poetic material. Dingles . . . tingles? Angela . . . glandular? Hardly bardworthy stuff.

He took a sip of coffee. What about a birthday card bearing a Gray-Hall-basement ping-pong challenge? (". . . **up to two further lady companions may attend, as seconds, substitutes, doubles partners, half-time masseuses** . . ."). No need for new trousers at all. You could play ping-pong in any old jeans. Indeed the well-worn flexibility and *al fresco* knees might give him the edge over unsuspecting opponents.

Yes, a card would be the perfect solution. If only he had an address to send it to.

He drained the coffee mug and felt suddenly weary. It seemed it was Manglers or bust. Back he went. The shop assistant, in a final gesture of triumph, offered to wrap up his old jeans (with the implied bonus of a discreet disposal) thus saving him the trouble of changing back. Malcolm declined, invoking an oily and unreliable motorbike. In truth he was acutely aware that it was still daylight outside.

Chapter 5

Dingles

"PRIVATE FUNCTION" said the sign in little gold letters on a pegboard display. Its proximity to the toilet gave the message a faintly unsavoury ring.

'Can I take your coat,' said the little silver-haired lady, only her head and shoulders showing above the counter. Malcolm got a whole arm out and hesitated. That jacket held his keys and money. Not to mention other things – a pen and pencil set, the notebook containing his unstarted novel, and several pieces of important string. More compelling still, it hid the top half of his recent fashion extravagance.

'Oh, I might as well keep it on, thanks. It's a bit chilly in here.'

His new jeans were not quite pocketless. An exhaustive search had revealed an opening on the right hip large enough to hold a British Railways platform ticket, or several sixpences. The keys might have fitted on his belt, but that still left the wallet which was quite bulky, albeit misleadingly so. He put his arm back in, smiled again at the lady, and pushed through the heavy swing doors.

Umching umching umchingum umching. The record was a bit like one he'd heard earlier in the day, only louder. So was the next one. The lights, though, were quite dark. Mercifully. He wasn't at all sure if the world was ready for a bemanglered Malcolm. He was sure, though, that *he* wasn't. The wretched things were exerting a stranglehold on his vitals which enforced a whole new way of walking.

He recognised no-one as he nursed a half-pint of cider to a spot just beyond the end of the bar and leaned against the wall in his best smart-casual attitude. Bold pink fluorescent letters stuck on to the disco's loudspeakers informed him 'YOUR DJ IS DOUGAL'. Fixing a polite neutral gaze on the glowing, flashing audio stack and the presiding Dougal he wished them, respectively, freak, fuse-blowing voltage surges and painless but chronic lockjaw. In vain.

Malcolm considered the scene. Tastes in music, dress and having fun vary enormously, and maybe we should rejoice in that variety, he thought to himself rather charitably, as the drink began to take effect. We might even allow that the lazy rich, or the especially cautious, should hire a venue like this to avoid all that post-party washing up, and the threat their fun-loving guests might pose to carpets and curtains and neighbourhood peace. But if you had to specify one criterion to separate real parties from mere mockeries, surely it would be that you didn't have to buy your own drinks.

'Same again please.'

'What's that?'

'SAME AGAIN please.'

'No, I mean what did you have before?'

'Oh, right. Sorry. It's half a cider. Please.'

With some concern the barman followed Malcolm's peculiar gait back to his leaning post. It struck him he might have to use his officially sanctioned discretion and refuse to serve him any further. He'd never seen half a pint have such an effect on a man. Interesting trousers though.

From the corner of his eye Malcolm became aware of a willowy Angela alone on the furthest edge of the dance-floor. Her long, fair hair was fetchingly unkempt, and she was swaying, almost to the music. The discrepancy he put down to Babycham and rhythmic licence. She was clad in a party dress the colour and texture of a chocolate toffee wrapper from one of those luxury assortments – a favourite indulgence of his, almost in the same league as draught dry cider. As a child at Christmas he liked to place such treats on his lap, just to see how long he could postpone the consumption. When unable to bear it any longer he would seize the thing and pull firmly on the twisted ends, delivering the succulent kernel with a creaking half spin.

Dougal the DJ, perhaps sensing Malcolm's wandering mind, and clearly concerned at the proportion of guests still managing to communicate with each other, mumbled into his microphone, turned the volume up several notches and switched on a stroboscopic light.

He hadn't come all this way in a mini-van to be ignored by a bunch of wallflowers.

Malcolm ventured a little wave in Angela's direction. To no avail. He increased the amplitude. Almost everyone except Angela waved back. He put down his glass and produced a wave to reckon with – a regular *tsunami*, which did the trick. Angela flickered across the floor towards him in an ultra-violet staccato. The music was rising and falling sickeningly as the now desperate Dougal tried to orchestrate the party.

'HAPPY BIRTHDAY,' mouthed Malcolm, with an exaggeration normally reserved for senile nonagenarians.

'SINCE ABOUT HALF-PAST EIGHT,' smiled Angela.

Although now lacking the carefully prepared pretext he leaned forward to deliver a birthday kiss but succeeded only in pecking the image of where her creamy cheek had been stroboscopically frozen two-hundred milliseconds before.

So near.

'You must be hot. In that coat I mean.' She pointed at it rather unnecessarily.

It was now or never. Again. But what was there to lose, apart from dignity and a wallet, both of doubtful value. With a casual air he shuffled off his mantle of respectability and hung it on the back of a chair.

She stared downwards, frowning. 'What on earth are those things on the back of your jeans?'

'Oh, they're, er, "Dongles", actually,' Malcolm improvised, with an air of knowing sophistication.

'Does he know you've borrowed them?'

'WHAT?'

'HIS JEANS.'

'Whose?'

'DONGLE'S!'

'That's right, do you think I should cut them off? Apparently it does invalidate the warranty.'

'You'd better check with him first.'

'With who?'

'With *WHOM!*' She quickly corrected him with a wagging finger.

'WITH WHOM *WHAT?*'

'Never mind. I just wondered where you got jeans like that?' She was planning to append the name to her list of stores to be avoided.

'Actually, they're not really jeans. They're MANGLERS.'

'What's the difference?'

'About two pound ten.' He grimaced. 'And groin sprain.'

'WHAT?'

'Never mind. Look, do you like ping-pong?'

'SORRY?'

'Do you like PING-PONG?'

'Oh, I've got one already thanks,' said Angela brandishing a glass brimming with fruit and umbrellas. 'Everybody's been treating me!' She made a grand gesture with the drink which encompassed her extensive circle of friends, and left several of them with fragments of pineapple slice in their hairdos. None of them minded, because none of them noticed. When she turned back Malcolm was slightly stooped and appeared to be squinting at her left breast.

'What's the matter?' she demanded, backing away.

'I was just trying to read your badge.'

'Oh that!' She smiled, closing in obligingly.

Encouraged, he risked homing in a fraction more and lingered a little longer than was strictly necessary.

TODAY I'M 20! announced the badge in little red letters.

No self-respecting maths student could let that exclamation mark go without comment. 'You don't look a day over factorial nineteen!' said Malcolm triumphantly, hardly believing his luck.

'SORRY?' 'I CAN'T HEAR YOU WITH ALL THIS . . .'

'I SAID . . . , Oh, never mind . . .' His best joke of the evening, masked by the climax of a moronic guitar solo.

Satisfied, Dougal announced that he'd take a break, allowing the management to turn on some pop music, albeit at a level which was merely irritating. Angela's satiny dress emitted a faint rhythmic creak as her momentum ebbed and her sway decayed imperceptibly to zero. Malcolm was thinking of strawberry fondant.

'Are you doing Maths?' she asked.

He nodded. 'And Philosophy. Are you doing English?'

'Yeah,' she said without much enthusiasm, 'with Psychology. So are the other two. And Mark.'

'Who's Mark?' He was affecting polite, neutral interest again.

'The one I was just dancing with.'

'I thought you were alone,' said Malcolm, convinced there'd been no-one within six feet of her.

'Why don't *you* dance?' She was smiling, but it seemed more of an instruction than an invitation or question.

He paused then cleared his throat. 'Well, actually, for the same reason I don't stand on one leg and recite excerpts from, say, *Madame Bovary*.'

'And why's that?' said Angela, suspecting a trap but unable to resist. This was the most unusual thing anyone had said to her in several days.

Malcolm took a deep breath. 'Don't you think it'd be setting a dangerous precedent, if I justified that? After all, let's say I managed to convince somebody it was an unreasonable thing to do. What's to stop them from saying, "OK, fair enough, but what about *Moby Dick*?"? Where would it end? You see, there's so many more things that we don't do than do, I think we can only be called on to justify what we do do.' He paused and raised his eyebrows. 'So, why do *you* dance?'

'I come from a long line of gypsies,' said Angela, grinning, warming to the game.

'I come from a long line of railwaymen,' said Malcolm, quite truthfully in fact.

'You're weird!'

'And you're tiddly!'

'But I'll be sober in the morning. Almost.'

'And I'll be suffering from auditory threshold shift.'

'What's that?'

'That group they were just playing,' invented Malcolm.

'Well, I'd better get back,' she said mysteriously, 'why don't you mingle. Helen's over there.' Again, it was more of an instruction.

He decided to make the most of the eye of the acoustic hurricane, which threatened to return at any moment in the shape of Dougal. Jacket in hand he hobbled off on a Helen hunt. The cider circulated inside him. And the dongles on his Manglers dangled as he mingled at Dingles.

Chapter 6

Music and Mutiny

They say that melodies linger on. Presumably in the higher reaches of the brain, in some sort of cortical tune cupboard which gets stocked up gradually over the decades. Raw sounds too will leave their mark, albeit at a lower level, through the bruising and fraying of nerve endings and fragile membranes. Malcolm's hearing system was already pretty confused – thanks to the vagaries of the music-education system and the sonic excesses of the swinging 'sixties. The previous evening's assault hadn't helped, forcing him to flee, alone, though the night was still young. He awoke next morning to find his head still reeling with tunes, and ringing with tones, that had long outstayed their welcome.

In his later school years Malcolm had liked to describe himself as 'not unmusical'. True, this was partly just a delight in his recent discovery of the double negative. (At various times in later life he would claim to be 'not unathletic', 'not unartistic' and, in a final burst of gleeful self-reference, 'not unlitotic'). But it was also to forestall any suggestion that his lack of performance skills and his ignorance of Beethoven's birthday (he forgot it almost every year) was due to a lack of natural talent. Luckily what ability he did have was buried deep enough to survive the neglect, and sometimes hostility, that prevailed, and retain the potential to bloom one day in kinder conditions. It would be a long wait. Meanwhile an endless succession of teachers had presided over the gloomy atmosphere of the music room. Their staying power seemed limited to a single school term. They came, they heard, they fled. *Prestissimo*. And each took the easy option, being unwilling to administer more than the occasional drop of theory in a great ocean of hand-clapping and song-singing sessions.

A good proportion of the so-called lessons was given over to practising the so-called School Hymn, though just how the wretched piece had acquired that distinction was a mystery. Was it the least bad from a job lot of remaindered copyrights snapped up by the school founders in some tragic speculative spree? One would hate to hear the rest. It was inexplicable, too, that the weekly practice went on long after it was clear to everybody that the performance quality had already reached its low plateau. But, whatever the reason, No. 666 in the School Hymnal, rendered illegible by countless thumbs, known anyway by all by heart, loathed by ears and brains alike, had somehow become irreversibly associated with the place. Other, more worthy, hymns came and went like dishes of the day, but old 666 seemed to be ineradicably engraved at the top of the hymn board – the staple, chronic speciality of the house, sung at speech days and sports days, the first day of term, the last day of term, alternate Tuesdays (and the ones in between), when there was an 'r' in the month, and when there wasn't. Or maybe just whenever the headmaster sensed that the assembled, corporate morale was in danger of recovering. The devil, it seemed, did not always have the best tunes.

No. 666 reverberated a good while in Malcolm's mental springs after he'd left the school. Though he was quite unaware of its beastly associations that index number proved unforgettable. Possibly because it was the sum of the squares of the first seven prime numbers. Eventually the actual tune was repressed below threshold by some merciful melody-censoring mechanism, leaving him with just a spectre of the harmonic progression which would haunt him for life. It had that irritating premature move to the dominant (daily exposure to which is surely psychologically damaging to a sensitive adolescent) – an act of compositional desperation aimed at salvaging the unsalvageably bland opening line. But Malcolm and his chums, lacking any musical vocabulary or analytical skills, just found it lame and embarrassing. And the words! The words were simply silly – however many times you sang it, "heaven" would not rhyme with "given", nor "word" with "sword", though out of respect for the author they always mispronounced them loudly and confidently as if they did.

Then there was the School Sea Shanty with its bold sailors and merry mermaids, the interminable *Yo Yo Yo*'s and other assorted nautical nonsense. Presumably this had originated as a recruiting ploy, to lure unsuspecting youth to the mast. Why else were there so few references to weevils, rats and scurvy, in spite of the excellent rhyming opportunities they would have provided?

And, finally, there was the School Folk Song. Looking back he was never sure if it really was the only one they ever sang. Did that dimly remembered mish-mash of bold soldiers and merry milk maids in May with their geese and their sheep in the valley-O come from a single song? Or had the passing time distilled from a whole anthology just those features which resonated with the collective folksy unconscious, leaving him with a kind of lingering *Urvolkslied*, burned into the auditory cortex?

But so it went on year by year. Well, almost. Somewhere around the very merry month of May celebrated by that singular song (if such it was) a twinge of professional conscience would lead Teacher to squeeze a theory session into the sequence of song practices. This would have been a welcome, if minimal, concession. Except that the object always seemed to be not to teach the kids anything but rather to test what they were supposed to have somehow learned already.

The reasoning must have gone something like this. After thirty minutes exposure per week for so many months they would surely have absorbed a good deal of musicianship. After all, the music-room cupboards and drawers were laden with gleaming triangles, virgin tambourines and weighty scores by the dozen. There was a big, old upright rosewood piano bearing no fewer than two busts of Beethoven beaming (or rather frowning) musical enlightenment at the tiers of desks in full stereo. At least this was the teachers' favoured orientation – staff arriving later than the pupils were likely to find the maestri turned either narcissistically towards or self-contemptuously away from themselves. And to crown it all, high up on the wall, hiding the unpainted patch where a clock had once hung, was a framed photograph of a bugle. Who would dare to remain unmusical in such an edifying environment?

And so it was that on one such occasion, after finally locating a morsel of chalk (some wag had lodged it in one of the Beethovens' left ears) the teacher wrote the tonic solfa as a vertical list up the blackboard. The class all looked on, mystified and apprehensive. Without a word he played the "Doh" on the piano, and pointed at "Soh" with a conducting baton. He then had the cheek to wince as thirty-five pupils made thirty-five well-intentioned but essentially random guesses as to the musical interval represented by 1 foot 7 inches of blackboard space. They were kept in and each made to write a hundred minims from memory.

Sweet revenge for these indignities came in the anarchic anonymity of morning assembly. Pupils were confined in the square "well" of the hall, cramped in a 20 by 20 matrix of cross-leggyness – a posture which led to numbness in the extreme. And other parts. They were surrounded on three sides by the teachers, who monitored and subdued them with sharp-eyed cross fire, sniping at the slightest sign of misbehaviour.

But they couldn't control the non-visual transgressions. Malcolm's speciality was acoustical. He had the gift (it would have counted as an affliction except he could turn it on and off at will) of being able to sing loudly and consistently a semitone sharper than his neighbours. He'd yet to learn it was called a semitone. But some native musicality told him this was the ideal discrepancy to settle on. Optimally subversive. And lots of fun.

A casual listener might have dismissed him along with those other species of musical incompetents that any sizeable group of schoolkids is bound to harbour, just on statistical grounds. These include the usual wild warblers, wailers and whiners. Plus, of course, that most distinctively deficient group of all: the groaners. We've all heard them, that 5% or so of the population. And winced. Perhaps unfairly – they are, in their way, as remarkable as the perfect pitchers, or mental multipliers of ten-digit numbers. What peculiarity causes them to wander up and down over such a narrow pitch range, responding just enough to the melodic hills and vales to show that they are willing, if unable, participants? Like the pencil in a pantograph their excursions seem to be attenuated by some devilish leverage, raised and lowered by the massive tidal pull of voices around them, but anchored on a short rope, condemned to the smallest scale of compliance. What makes them like that? Some regrettable get-together of recessive genes? A mother frightened by a fog-horn blast, just when critical auditory neurons were forming? Who knows? But they're not to be pitied. On the contrary, since perceptual insensitivity is the root of the problem they're necessarily spared the pain they inflict on fellow singers – just like those whose poor endowment with smell cells leads them to wash infrequently with impunity.

Malcolm would usually wait until around the second line of the second verse, by which time most of the assembled company had grounded their tonal anchors and relaxed. Then, with a look of earnest enthusiasm, like the ones adopted by those caught suddenly on the *Songs of Praise* camera, he'd throw the mental lever, releasing a wobbly wave of chromatic contamination which crept radially outwards through the hall, infecting and supplanting the official key bar by bar, rank by rank and file by file. Eventually it reached the periphery, where it inundated the music teacher, who was forced to bang louder and louder on the piano, unwilling to modulate to what would in any case be a tricky key, for fear of provoking further waves, and finally foundering under a rising tide of rampant tonal inflation. Perched behind the oaken lectern on the stage, begowned and owl-like, the headmaster would look on helplessly, unsure whether incompetence or rebellion were to blame, but resolving that, whatever the cause of this all-too-common catastrophe, tomorrow, he would have every class practising the School Hymn.

Occasional relief from singing came when the hefty, mahogany-sided gramophone was wheeled out from its cubbyhole, dusty and blinking in the unfamiliar light. It was electric, though only just, and looked and sounded as if it had seen better days. But it must have cost the school a lot, because they had only had enough money left over for two records – a diet for the pupils far more meagre even than that dished out by the BBC to its desert-island castaways. So when the teacher pulled the shiny black disc from its plain cardboard cover it was fifty-fifty whether they would get the *Háry* bloody *János Suite* ("put your hand up when you can hear the soldiers marching!") or *Carnival of the* bloody *Animals* ("and which animal do you think *this* is?").

Malcolm never quite picked up the taxonomic conventions. Was it the double basses which were elephants, and the tubas, hippos? Or was it the other way round?

But he did feel sorry for these various brutes – stereotyped, parodied, exploited year after year. Why not pick on another kingdom for once? Why not, in the true, original etymological spirit of carnival, forego altogether the flesh? Some day, he resolved, when he'd mastered this music business, he'd compose a *Carnival of the Vegetables*. It would start with a *crunch crunch crunch squeak squeak* (depicting celery) from the woodwinds, leading to contrasting passages dedicated to various species of legume, and (artistic licence overriding roughshod the botanical classifications) the more exotic fungi. *And*, orchestral resources permitting, why not the algae and herbs? Once, after a daunting day in which a fluke of timetabling had sandwiched a Saint-Saens session between two periods of biology, he'd had a kind of musical nightmare involving an ugly confrontation between phytoplankton and oregano – an irresistible challenge to composer and listeners alike. But all that would have to wait.

Meanwhile, these minimal but puzzling lessons coloured and clouded his musical judgement. For years he remained mystified by the conventions of Music Education. Disappointed too. It wasn't that he expected enjoyment from lessons in general. After all, few adults did Geography or Scripture in their spare time. They hardly seemed to mention them in fact. But Music should have been different. Out of school, listening to music just for the joy of it seemed to be commonplace.

When joy eventually came Malcolm was quite unprepared for it. As a gawky lower-sixth-former he'd once bravely crashed the local college dance, and against all odds gained an invitation to coffee. She was a first-year undergraduate – confident, studious. Did he like music? Yes he did, responding unhesitatingly to those stern but removable spectacles, that pinned but unleashable hair. The evening had begun to show fairy-tale potential – lost sheep and ugly duckling in mutual redemption. Then she'd put on a Mozart quartet.

He was lost in the dreamy *Adagio* when his hostess finally spoke.

'I'm sorry, what?' He leaned forward.

'I said, what do you think?'

He hesitated, not wishing to look a fool. It clearly wasn't a soldier's march, but that still left the whole animal kingdom. He looked around but there were no classmates to whisper suggestions. He'd have to hedge – it was dangerous to be specific. Or even generic. But it might seem unduly evasive to go for a whole phylum. The music did have a certain, well, sort of, swannish serenity. But then there was that intermittent, scratchy pizzicato, which sounded distinctly unwebbed. He closed his eyes and produced a succession of equivocal "hmm"s. The bars slipped by, into a luxuriant, but inanimate, coda.

'Well?' she smiled. It was now or never.

'Is it a reptile of some kind?'

'A *reptile*?'

'Well, maybe amphibian?'

'*Amphibian*?'

'I mean marsupial, I always get them mixed . . .'

'What are you *talking* about . . .?'

'I don't know,' pleaded Malcolm, 'give me a clue! How many legs?'

He never got to hear the *Minuet and Trio*.

Chapter 7

Double Standards

Slowly, almost imperceptibly, Malcolm began to make good his musical deficiencies – tuning in, from time to time, to the old Third Programme, borrowing long-playing records from the local library. Even buying (and reading!) a teach-yourself book. Music, he sensed, with all its supposed charms, might be worth some investment. Could it really soothe a savage breast? Or was it *smooth*? Or a savage *beast* even? There were several possible permutations. None particularly convincing.

Malcolm was generally suspicious of proverbial claims. Especially the more poetic ones. English is a fine language, but in the end the shapes and sounds of its words are largely arbitrary and conventional. What's more the world we have to represent with it is a complex, messy one. So all in all it seems unlikely that the best advice or shrewdest observations would happen to rhyme, alliterate, or sit snugly in some iambic pentameter. What we've done by contriving such features is to render these sayings suboptimal in the very respect they should excel – that of encapsulating wisdom!

Music, music, music. Though seen by many as a great social lubricant, for Malcolm it was more often a source of tribulation. If not positively abrasive. And as for being the food of love? Well, just possibly it was. But served up by fate with scant regard for quality or portion size, leaving him, in the main, starving or glutted, nauseous or heartburnt.

It was no good. Metaphors – musical, amorous and gastronomic – were failing him left, right and centre.

But then literal food too was proving problematic.

Whenever dissatisfied with our dietary lot we should always pause to consider the starving millions. After all, there are few things worse than not knowing where your next meal is coming from. Very few things. But one of them, arguably, is knowing *exactly* where it's coming from. At least if it's the same place day after day, and happens to be the particular college canteen which Malcolm was forced to frequent.

By even the most liberal interpretation the "HOT FOOD" sign over the counter was an exaggeration. Whether or not the "HOT" bit was accurate was a simple, empirical question. You could have resolved it at any time merely by drilling a small bore hole into a sample, inserting a thermometer, and noting that it showed no response whatsoever. If there aren't any therms, you can't meter them.

The "FOOD" claim was more controversial. Doubtless the catering manager would point out in defence of this nomenclature the fact that masses of students regularly paid for the stuff, swallowed largish amounts of it, and went away looking less hungry than they'd arrived. A necessary, but sadly insufficient, criterion. A proper, more rigorous analysis might have disqualified it, on grounds of taste and nutritional value.

The temperature issue had long been a bone of contention between the canteen staff and Malcolm. Although he was taller and slimmer than average his mouth and stomach had normal capacities. Trouble was his throat was relatively narrow – forming what might be called a glottalneck between the two. Hence he was a surprisingly slow eater, and needed his "food" to be served piping hot. Otherwise it would plummet to below body heat by mid course, resulting in the uneasy feeling that his stomach was providing comfort for the shepherd's pie, instead of what nature had intended.

A series of fixed-formula, ritual exchanges had developed over the months. Malcolm would kick things off by asking for the food to be re-heated. There would then be a rolling of eyes and a loud declaration that no-one else had complained. Ever! He would respond by saying how lucky it was for everyone that there was so rarely a problem to be fixed. If necessary he'd add that it was even luckier it only took a couple of minutes to take the chill off the food by sticking it under the grill. Recently they'd been trying to pre-empt him by holding out the plate at arm's length with a heavy asbestos glove. Nothing less than third-degree burns awaited the unwary, it seemed. He would coolly take it with his bare hands, hold it for a few seconds, and then ask for it to be warmed up.

To gain some relief from this wearying daily dialogue Malcolm had started to alternate with the adjacent counter, where "FRESH SANDWICHES" were promised. Such things were acceptable at room temperature. Or even a bit below. The "FRESH" was accurate, at least in the sense that they were prepared while you waited. In fact a sizeable queue normally bore witness to the thoroughness of the two ladies in charge.

But there were problems with the "SANDWICHES". Not with the quality, which was invariably high, but with the quantity, which was, for some mysterious reason, highly variable. Malcolm was regularly presented either with what he considered to be exactly twice or exactly half the number of sandwiches he'd ordered. At first he put this variation down to the context – the time of day, the thickness of the bread, his ordering, or not, of other items in the same breath, the degree of hunger felt and therefore, maybe, shown. However, in a series of carefully controlled trials – arriving at the same time, wearing the same clothes, giving the same order using the same form of words, in a monotone of course – he'd eliminated most factors and established that the identity of the lady serving was of overriding importance. The thin one he'd christened "Hilda", after her habit of halving his order. Her fuller-figured colleague he dubbed "Doris", the doubler. Their own shapes were consistent, perhaps significantly, with their respective frugality and lavishness. Convenient mnemonics as to who or what he was dealing with.

Having thus cracked the system, Malcolm was determined today to circumvent the whole problem. And by the simplest arithmetic. Lengthy lectures on semantics and then number theory had left him with a serious appetite. One which demanded, at least according to his own definition, no fewer than six sandwiches. At the familiar prompt, 'Yes dear?', from a smiling Hilda he made the quick calculation. Allowing for her reckoning in terms of dainty little quarters he ordered a dozen cheese and tomato sandwiches.

'Twelve C&T's!' shouted Hilda through the hatch to an invisible Doris. There were several minutes of pregnant silence in which Malcolm tried not to think the unthinkable. It should have been easy. Even for a philosophy student. But it wasn't. Surely, though, anyone receiving such an order would interpret it according to the known criterion of the person relaying it. Surely. Then Doris burst backwards through the swing doors and turned to reveal a towering platter, a ziggurat of C&T's, its summit adorned with a sprig of parsley.

'I didn't order that,' said Malcolm firmly.

'It's just decorative,' said Doris, with some indignation. She deftly flicked the parsley into the bin with the point of a Kitchen Devil and disappeared once more backstage.

In a mild state of shock Malcolm found himself parting with the better part of a week's lunch money. Hilda wrapped up his windfall in sheets of grease-proof paper, piled the packets into a carrier bag and sent him away with a cheery, 'Enjoy yourselves!'

Deep in thought he trudged off towards the ornamental lake at the centre of the campus. Although unnaturally elevated, and of a colour worryingly far from blue, it was an inspiring little spot – the scene of some of his more successful deliberations. The day was a bit gloomy for a picnic, especially a solo one, but clearly his whole strategy needed an unhurried revision.

His favourite bench was occupied by a solitary, hairy youth, apparently deep in a book but with a twelve-string guitar leaning threateningly against his knees. Malcolm, a great respecter of personal space, passed on, upwind, foregoing the next, empty bench and settling only on the third. Here he had his back to the sun. Or would have, if it came out. Clearly it was going to be one of those thoroughly sub-optimal days.

It really couldn't be that difficult. Could it? A sandwich by any other name would taste as good. What are names, anyway? Simply convenient handles, which allow us to avoid lengthy and tedious descriptions of well-known things. But if the handle becomes loose then it's better to discard it, and revert to the direct approach. Yes, that was it. If the catering world couldn't adopt a consistent naming convention then it was just going to have to accept detailed specifications from customers. They would think him weird, of course. But he could live with that. Manifestly!

Content with this resolution, Malcolm leaned back in the seat and sank his teeth into the first sandwich of the first layer of the first packet of C&T's. The sun broke out pleasantly on the back of his neck. A light breeze ruffled the water. The ducks dabbled and paddled happily to and fro. He was looking forward to his next canteen visit the day after tomorrow. Or at least just as soon as he needed to buy food again.

Then suddenly it all went dark. An *SOS* was duly despatched from his visual cortex. But before it could trigger any fighting or fleeing or screaming response it was overtaken and suppressed by a more calming, fragrant message. Only the best kinds of danger smelled that good. The perfume was cheap, but no less exciting for that. Then came further, verbal reassurance.

'Guess who!'

The fingers over his eyes were delicate and curvy – he could still see bits of the lake through them.

'Guess who what?' Malcolm was in no hurry at all.

'Er, guess who's coming to dinner!' There was a faint rustle and snigger as a cheese-and-tomato sandwich disappeared from the bag. The hand was quickly replaced.

'Guess whose *what* is coming to dinner?'

'I give up,' said the voice, perplexed.

'I'm the one who's supposed to give up,' said Malcolm.

'OK, do you give up?'

'No. Give me a clue.'

'A clue?'

'Yeah. A really devious one.'

'Why?'

'To help me guess who you are.'

'No, I mean why *devious*.'

With a long, slow, audible inhalation he helped himself to another dose of perfume.

'To prolong the ecstasy.'

The hands were quickly removed. Resisting the urge to turn around he savoured the uncertainty a moment longer. Then his assailant clambered over the bench and sat down.

'Hello Malcolm,' said Helen, 'why have you got all those sandwiches?' In the sunshine her hair, a medium brown in his recollection, looked positively golden.

'It's a long story.'

'The day is young!'

He refused to be drawn.

'I know, you had a date with three women, and they stood you up.'

'No, I had a tomato all on my own, and I sat myself down.' It was a bit obscure, but the best he could do at the time.

'You're weird!' She was grinning.

'So I'm told.' He grinned back, not displeased.

'I guess your eyes were bigger than your stomach.'

'No, I just miscalculated.'

'I thought you were a mathematician!'

'Well, it was a communication problem, really. And anyway, it's my lunch break.'

'And how!'

Unprompted, Helen began an assault on the cheese & tomato mountain. Her own morning lecture-mix of rats and Chaucer on an empty stomach had prepared her well for the task. Unprompted too, Malcolm began to outline the sandwich saga, illustrating the dilemmas and ambiguities directly, by shuffling and dividing, folding and unfolding the slices, half-slices and half-half-slices of bread. How easy it was to *show* the problem. How the early Wittgenstein would have approved the wordless depictions! Perhaps he ought to show up at the canteen with a sketch-pad and *draw* his next order for them. But there was weird and there was WEIRD. And anyway he'd already committed himself to the literal approach for next time, to try to reassert the primacy of *words*. Pictures and models would be a last resort. The demonstration over, he ate the apparatus.

As two o'clock came and lectures restarted much of the picnic remained, piled up high between the two on the bench. Neither could manage another mouthful.

Time ticked on. Tardiness turned to truancy, his from Kant, hers from Wordsworth. To ward off the beginnings of guilt Helen walked to the water's edge and brushed the crumbs from her lap. A passing mallard hoovered them up gracefully. She threw him a crust and it disappeared in a flash. They threw more. Word spread quickly across the lake. Reinforcements paddled in. It still took them a whole half-hour to dispose of the remaining food. Then, the principal catalyst gone, they lapsed into a lengthy silence.

It was now or never. Malcolm cleared his throat.

'Do you fancy some coffee? There's a kitchen next to my room. Well, just across, actually, on the second floor. Well it's really the third, if you count the ground as . . .'

She grinned. 'Well, maybe just half a cup!'

Had there been a C&T left he could have pretended to try to put it down the neck of her jumper.

They wandered off watched only by the grateful ducks, who floated, bloated and immobile, their natural buoyancy now dangerously compromised, beak-deep in the muddy water.

Chapter 8

Counting the Ways

Communal kitchens are large, neutral spaces. You can wander round them, happily free from any territorial decision making. And most other sources of anxiety. Coffee, if not literally instant, can be made so quickly it isn't worth sitting down. There's just time for a guest to make a couple of leisurely circuits of the black and white tiles, politely ignore the dust and grease, and, if desperate for distraction, scan the instructions on a fire blanket, or the rules for evacuation. Malcolm savoured the moments of respite in the calm and safety of this no-man's-land, and though still sceptical of proverbial wisdom he found himself watching the kettle intently, hoping to extend the stay of execution. But boil it did, and water was duly poured on to little heaps of Maxwell House powder sitting patiently in the bases of two chipped china mugs.

'Milk?' The less controversial question first.

'Just a splash.'

Malcolm obliged.

'Oh, I want a bigger splash than that, please!'

'D'you mean you want additional, if similar, splashes,' Malcolm gestured with the carton, 'or should I start again, from a greater height? Or . . . '

'*I'll* do it.' She did.

'Sugar?'

Helen hesitated. As did Malcolm – the heaped spoon poised. Eventually grains began to tumble into the mug, though whether intentionally or on account of a nervous hand was unclear.

'No thanks.'

'*I'll* have this one then.' He tipped the rest in.

'Did you want milk though?' She frowned concern.

'Yes. Do *you*, still?'

'Yes.'

'Oh dear,' he smirked.

'What's the matter?'

'I've already not put some in this other one.'

She rolled her eyes, rather fetchingly, and helped herself again.

'Stirred?' He brandished the spoon, eager to re-establish the role of host.

It was her turn to smirk. 'Er . . . yes, please. Eleven and a half turns . . .'

Malcolm began vigorously.

' . . . anticlockwise!'

He just nodded.

'That's *clock*wise.'

'Not if you look from below!' He twisted his head around to illustrate the point, managing in the process to spill more than a splash on the off-white Formica.

That was the easy bit.

Malcolm led the way across the corridor, nursing his steaming drink.

And frantically calculating. How many ways can you place two distinguishable objects in five spaces? Well, there are five ways of placing the first, then, for each of those, four remaining ways for the second. So, twenty in all. And all equivalent. At least in the cold, objective world of a school algebra book.

However, in the fevered confines of a study/bedroom the five sitting places are markedly different in comfort and separation. What's more the two living, breathing objects to be placed aren't just nominally distinguishable – they differ in the most vital, wonderful, terrifying way. Thus each permutation carries a special significance, with its characteristic mix of promise and anxiety. Malcolm prepared himself for a formidable test on the erotic calculus.

Question Zero: who should be first through the door? Conventional chivalry is pretty clear on the point. But that would give her complete freedom of seat choice. And so reveal little about her intentions. Or her likely reaction to his. By contrast, his responding move might seem charged with meaning. And risk. Based on his all-too-limited experience the closer he sat the more rapidly things might proceed. But then, what to? It could so easily go either way. One tiny step can tip you into the longed-for intimacy. Or trigger the dreaded recoil, quickly followed by the polite excuse, the early departure.

So much better then if he took the lead and learned from her response. In any case, windows might need to be opened, urgently; yesterday's socks, or older and worse things, whisked out of sight.

Only then, the even tougher Question One: where exactly to sit? Having barged ahead already it would seem especially rude to take advantage of the lead and grab the larger, softer chair. But to sit at the desk might look affectedly studious, or suggest he was keen to get back to work. He wasn't.

On the other hand if he took the bed she would most likely opt for one of the two chairs. To shun both and join him would be more than one dared hope. And once they were ensconced any repositioning would require blatant quantum leaps; there'd be no chance of a creeping intimacy, through those subliminal shiftings, the old contrived clumsiness.

But maybe it all depended on which bit of the bed he settled on. The middle was saggy and prone to sudden sproinging. More importantly it would leave her with two equally close but highly unlikely options. A shrewd opening in Noughts and Crosses perhaps. But here staking such a claim would be self-defeating. This was about forging alliances, not battling over territory.

In addition to a middle, of course, a bed has no fewer than two ends. But the head end was set some way into a kind of alcove, allowing no proper space for the feet on the floor. Some shoe removal was required. From experience he knew he could get away with discarding just the shoe from the wall-side leg. In fact this was one of his favourite attitudes – half leaning against the pillow with one bent-up knee supporting a good book. But without a book the whole pose would seem unnatural. He could of course take off both shoes. But, quite apart from the hygienic thing, that might be misconstrued.

So, that left the foot end of the bed. This was a much more exposed peninsular and so offered three possible sitting orientations, though one involved mild contortion, and another, facing the wall, was blatantly antisocial . . .

Malcolm's analytic reverie was broken by a loud sproing. Goldilocks had slipped past, and made her choice. He sat down in the comfy chair, six feet away, at an angle of about a hundred and twenty degrees to her. A stable configuration, with no decisions to be made for a while. The turmoil in his head subsided. They were silent for a whole half minute, sipping their coffees.

'You OK there?'

She nodded, triggering a small sproing. 'Perfect.'

With no deficiencies to be remedied what could he do but just nod back? There was a full minute of silence; closely followed by another. Then, in a neighbouring room, a droning mechanical beat began. Malcolm ventured a little grimace, which was returned sympathetically. He leaned over and switched on the radio, fairly confident he'd left it tuned to the new Radio Three. He had.

'What's this?'

'Probably a Mozart quartet.'

It was Haydn actually, but neither of them would ever know that.

'S'nice!' She nodded along to the rather frisky *andante*. This provoked a bed-spring obbligato, albeit off the beat, which Malcolm found peculiarly distracting.

The rival music next door promptly got louder. Things became seriously polyrhythmic.

'Shall I turn it up a bit?'

'If you like.' The tone was neutral – eagerness to please, or total indifference? Was she grateful for the music? If so, in what way? Did it provide a handy substitute for conversation. Or was it a reason for her to stay longer? – there had to be a couple of movements still to go. Unfortunately Malcolm could reach the volume control easily without getting up. They remained glued to their seats.

Under the influence of the stately Haydn strings their exchanges took on a kind of Austenian, Pump-Room propriety. He would periodically enquire about the comfort of her seating arrangements, her need for refreshment, her freedom from draughts. She would graciously express all-round contentment. He sighed inwardly and tried to appear happy that she appeared happy. They sat some more: a stalemate for black and white, he and she, North and South – two poles apart, defining the space between them. It was precisely for such impasses that dancing had been invented – to pluck us from our seats, oblige us to jostle and shuffle, licence the magic contact. But they lacked the space, and indeed the numbers, for a quadrille. Now had they been at a ball in Georgian Bath, or better still, in the returning carriage, curtained and lurching on a bumpy road . . .

Malcolm began to ponder the vagaries of space and time. Then Haydn paused between movements. In the distant concert hall somebody cleared his throat. And back in the study/bedroom they were forced to confront the ringing. The ringing which could have been going on for some time.

'Is that a real alarm?' Helen's own alarm seemed real enough.

'Depends what you mean.' Malcolm, on the other hand, had an interest in remaining calm.

'I mean, is it a real fire?'

'Very unlikely. They test it regularly. The alarm that is. Well, irregularly, actually. Just to keep us on our toes. Quite often though.'

'What if it's not a test?'

'It's probably a hoax then. We have even more of those.'

'But what if it's real? The fire!'

'The fire exit's just across the corridor. If you smell smoke we can be out in, oh, five seconds.'

Her relief was only partial, and short lived. 'What if it's a bomb? I mean a bomb alarm.'

'Oh, we get those as well. They're quite different though. Sort of intermittent.' He pursed his lips and clenched his teeth. 'Like a *beep beep*, then a pause, and then a *beep beep* again. And so on. Don't really know why it's that way round. Just a convention I suppose. But they're always false alarms.' Malcolm grinned, 'now a real bomb would be different again.' Her eyes widened. He took a deep breath, paused, then produced a loud comic-book explosive noise, flailed his arms and finally launched himself out of the chair in her direction. But she was ahead of him, out of the room, through the now open fire door, down several flights of metal stairs.

He caught up with her on the designated square of grass. A handful of students were milling around, looking far from alarmed. 'It normally only lasts a few minutes,' said Malcolm. 'Then I could make us some tea.'

Helen shook her head. 'I've got an essay to finish. Well, to start actually. On *Northanger Abbey*. And it's got to be in by Friday.'

Chapter 9

Brindles Travel

Term time ticked on. Temperatures began to slump. In Gray Hall the heating went off and on more often than before. The cardboard *Out of Order* sign on the lift doors finally came down, and was replaced by a more substantial, wooden one. An asthmatic historian on the top floor moved out and was replaced by an athletic geographer. An overflowing wash basin in Room 304 provided a curiously symmetrical ceiling patch the shape of Vesuvius (or was it the Matterhorn?) for the downstairs neighbour to contemplate on waking. Winter crept closer. But Malcolm heard and felt it coming.

In the grand eternal calendar of things a solstice is no less special than an equinox. But it is less dramatic. Simple calculus tells us that the extreme of the earth's tilt occurs just when its rate of change is zero, bringing a period of repose, a mood more chronic than critical. For Malcolm this season held a particular promise. Water dithered teasingly about its state, before finally fashioning those magic crystals. These are pretty enough in isolation, melting in a trice on the nose-tip and eyelash, but totally engaging when settled in serious numbers. You can do such a lot with a trillion snowflakes, as long as they're tightly compacted and steeply sloping. But to find such a thing you need to go far. And high. And to do that, you need professional help.

For some reason travel agents, like building societies, shoe shops (and indeed trouser shops) have a tendency to flock together when left in high-street environments for long periods. With each cycle of leasing, vacating and re-leasing they seem to side-step and leapfrog other establishments, sometimes getting squeezed out to brief exiles in side streets, but always gravitating, statistically, over the decades, into a cosy cheek-to-cheekiness with one another.

It was just such a mini ghetto which now confronted Malcolm one chilly afternoon in early December, as the long and tiring term was drawing to a close. All that morning he'd fancied he could smell snow, though in fact the nearest flake was nearly two hundred miles away, and melting fast. It may just have been due to an underlying awareness of the approaching season, along with some traces of bergamot from the high-factor sun-cream lingering on the fingertips of the gloves he'd dug out the previous night to help handle a stubborn coffee-jar lid. But throughout a lengthy seminar on the *Dialogues* he could think of nothing else but sunlit slopes, Schwarzwälderkirschtorten, and sleeky ski-suits, containing even sleekier skiers.

Although it isn't known whether Plato actually skied he would not have been offended by Malcolm's distraction. Skiing, surely, is the Ideal sport – substituting God-given gravity for more brutish forces, pruned of redundant competition, purged of mud and aggression, elevated, rarefied, crystalline. And rounded off each night with a sobering spell of more ordinary indulgence in the valley below – the earthly background you tolerate, the better to appreciate the daily dose of the divine.

Malcolm's skiing career had, however, started most unpromisingly, with a sixth-form trip to the Cairngorms in the battered school bus. They spent several nights in a dark and draughty youth hostel living off little more than baked beans on toast. But from the very first brief, wobbly run down the slushy nursery slope he was hooked. Later he'd borrowed, scrimped and scrounged enough to buy an off-peak, last-minute-bargain deal to the Alps. The high levels of frugality he'd endured before, during and after had done nothing to dampen his fervour. When friends demanded to know how he afforded this expensive (and, the implication was, elitist) activity he simply pointed out that it was cheaper and certainly healthier than smoking, say, five Woodbines a day – a common and rarely remarked upon habit of many in his social class.

So, which was it to be? He felt a little wary of "Trafalgar Travel", its windows plastered with banners for Cost Cutters, Sun Seekers and Flight Finders. What *kind* of things were these? What were the relationships between them? And why did it never seem to worry anyone else? Were they subsidiaries? (If so, what of?) Supersidiaries? Classes of client? Or just signs of the owners further indulging a weakness for alliteration? Who knew? The affliction, though, seemed to have penetrated to next door, where "Peregrine Tours" rash of posters for trippers, trekkers, travellers and tropical tourers all but stopped the feeble sunlight from reaching the murky interior. A bad omen, surely! Ignoring "Flyaway", whose staff seemed to have heeded their own advice, that left just one shop. There were no fewer than three signs in the window proclaiming "Brindles Travel". Where to? mused Malcolm. And were they nomadic, migratory or just local commuters? He went in anyway.

The two smartly dressed occupants, seated left and right behind a long desk, suspended their conversation at the sound of the old-fashioned bell, turned and smiled him a stereo smile. With scant regard for good hi-fi listening practice he sat down facing the left channel. The name badge on her left breast pocket announced her as an "ELGA" – the letters were large and legible, perhaps to pre-empt too close a scrutiny, although she was already protected by the wide moat of a desk. In fact, she was a "HELGA" decapitated by a large lapel, as Malcolm might have guessed had he registered the singular "Brindle", similarly truncated, on the opposite side. Helga was flanked by smiling camels, courtesy of an Arabian Airlines poster. This background further boosted Malcolm's diffidence as he steeled himself to ask, 'I know it's a bit late, but do you have any ski packages left?'

But they did! Helga delved into a card index file, riffled through some brochures, then picked up the phone. Her colleague, Doreen, who, courtesy of Air France, had the Eiffel tower sprouting from her head, looked on supportingly, outsmiling the camels. Malcolm just tried to look like someone who could afford a ski holiday without condemning himself to a diet of sandwiches for the next six months – however many sandwiches that might be.

Helga put down the phone.

'We could do you a week in Inglberg from the 27th of December.' She paused. 'But it'd mean flying from Manstead.'

'Is that bad?'

'No, no, it's just, well, rather small. That's all.'

He grinned. 'Well, as long as the runways are long enough!'

'Oh, I'm sure it is,' said Helga of the large lapels, and reached for her adding machine.

By clenching fists, teeth, and what he felt might be his spleen, Malcolm managed to hold back all but the tiniest flinch when the price was finally revealed. He did a quick mental calculation. It showed that he simply couldn't afford it. This was unacceptable. He did an even quicker one which, happily, came out far less clear cut. After all he could cut down on the cinema and cider, and walk everywhere, neatly combining the necessary economy and fitness programmes. The trusty anorak could be patched up. Again. And he could always resurrect the old Balaclava and long johns. (Both items were family heirlooms, and extensively holed – by Crimean snipers, he'd always fancied, though in reality by the dull moths of Blighty. However, neither would be revealed to the world unless he were respectively caught in a blizzard or run over by a piste machine.) A few further austerities would then ensure that by, say, April, he could be off the sandwiches. As long as he didn't put anything in them.

He found himself staring at the camels. Doreen and Helga had tactfully resumed their conversation to allow their client to reflect. He duly reflected, partly out of reciprocal tact, partly on principle – that is, from a belief that a world in which people reflected was better than one in which they didn't. This showed, perhaps, an unreasonable faith in principles since his own decision was already beyond the influence of reflection. The thought of not going skiing had by now become unthinkable. He was merely reflecting on how long to reflect in order to persuade himself, and the others, that he was a reasonable, reflective sort of person.

The beginning of the end came when he suddenly remembered a fifteen-shilling postal order which had remained uncashed in his wallet since his auntie had sent it last birthday. A tiny fraction of the overall cost. But a move in the right direction. It represented a couple of Glühweins, or, more responsibly, a couple of hot meals to alleviate the sandwich penance. The end of the end came when Helga's phone rang. Malcolm was suddenly reminded that there might be competition for last-minute bookings. Helga picked up the receiver and reasserted 'Brindles travel', but before she could elaborate Malcolm leapt in with a decisive 'I'll take it!' She smiled at him and nodded reassuringly, then asked 'Wensleydale or Cheddar?' of her caller and replaced the receiver. Though neither resort was famous for its pistes Malcolm felt a sense of relief at having pre-empted any potential rivals. As his first instructor had told him, skiing is all about commitment.

'Right then, that's Chalet Pengel, from the 27th. You're with Frobisher.'

'Oh! I wanted a single room actually,' said Malcolm with a frown. Alarming visions (or perhaps, rather, auditions and olfactions) were arising, of high-decibel snoring and poor personal hygiene.

'You've got one,' said Helga, 'Frobisher are the operators.'

'They belong to Snowscene,' added Doreen helpfully.

Malcolm maintained his frown.

'It's all part of Panorama, anyway.'

The frown intensified.

'They used to be Overland.'

'Till it went under.'

'Who did, exactly?'

'Frobisher,' said Helga. 'They never should have bought it really.'

'Everybody saw it coming.' Doreen shook her head sadly.

Malcolm decided to simplify matters. 'So, when should I pick up the tickets, and all that?'

'Oh, they'll come direct from Alpine.'

'Alpine? Who exactly is . . .' he began, then thought better of it. 'Of course. So, who shall I make the cheque to?'

'To us, please.'

'Right.' He pulled out his best biro and clicked the button. 'Is it "Brindle" or "Brindles"?'

'It's "Snowscene".'

'Old Mr Brindle died years ago,' whispered Doreen respectfully.

Chapter 10

The Voice

'Manstead please!' said Malcolm breezily. At that time of the morning he had no choice but to take a taxi, although it would add at least another day to the sandwich sentence.

'This *is* Manstead!'

'No, I mean the airport.'

'Which airport?'

'*Manstead* airport.'

'Oh, right!' The driver grinned. '*Chocks away!* eh?'

'Pardon?'

'You know,' the man cupped a hand over his mouth, "bandits at six o'clock", and all that.'

'Oh, yeah,' Malcolm began, ' "Never in the field of human conflict was so much . . ." ' He was aiming for a Churchillian tone but only managed something between Goebbels and Vera Lynne. It was, to be fair, *very* early in the morning.

'We don't often go to the airfield,' interrupted the driver skilfully. 'It was built for the Battle of Britain, you know. Mind you, they've done it up a bit since then. Lights and things . . .'

'I should hope so!'

'Runway's a bit short though. It was designed for Spitfires you see. Now *there* was a plane!' He crouched lower behind the wheel and scanned the dual carriageway for enemy vehicles.

"FLIGHT DEPARTURES" said the sign in large but faded letters. Next to it was a large faded arrow pointing vertically upwards. This all seemed reasonable enough to Malcolm as he lugged his luggage through the huge shed of a terminal, though he had been hoping for a less dramatic take-off.

The ageing tannoy system bing-bonged, then asked someone whose name was unintelligible to go immediately to somewhere unintelligible and do something unintelligible. Malcolm fancied that a number of vague-looking people got up, went a little distance in a randomish direction and did something ill defined. Was everyone except him desperately trying to comply with the message in their different ways? Or was this just the Brownian motion characteristic of any crowd?

He plonked himself down on a bench to check the vital documents once again. Passport, tickets, travellers cheques and wallet had been distributed, respectively, to four pockets, each with buttons and zips enough to satisfy the most neurotic traveller – a title to which Malcolm had a serious claim. The anorak lining, moreover, was reassuringly strong, yet flexible enough to allow you to confirm the presence and identity of each item by touch, thus avoiding the dangers of unzipping. (You could so easily forget to re-zip, or, having in fact re-zipped, forget whether you had, since the act of re-buttoning, by its very nature, concealed this). So in a practised movement of the right hand he swiftly probed the four extremities of the coat and smiled with relief at the satisfactory outcome. A casual observer might have suspected him of harbouring religious feelings. Or fleas.

His suitcase stayed shut. Though not because he didn't care about the contents. Indeed ever since he'd once discovered, when surprised by a snow flurry on top of the Hochwinkl, that his goggles were at home on top of the wardrobe his pre-flight check routines had been worthy of a moonshot. But writing a list, as so many travellers did, was something he'd long ruled out. What real comfort was there in establishing a one-to-one correspondence between items in your baggage and words on a bit of paper? What you really needed was a correspondence between items in your baggage and items needed on a ski trip. Hence, on the night before departure he'd taken to donning his ski gear and mentally rehearsing all conceivable activities in all imaginable weather conditions in an attempt to reveal and remedy any omissions, before undressing into a suitcase which was then locked and strapped, Houdini style, and remained so until it landed on his bed in the resort. This very case he now committed to the safety of the check-in, and celebrated his unburdening with a cup of airport tea.

With well over a hour before take-off he could allow himself a little doze, relying on the intermittent bing-bongs to act like the snooze function of an alarm clock. Soon he was knee-deep in dreamy, creamy, powder snow, in hot pursuit of a nimble figure – tight-waisted, long dark tresses trailing and flailing at every turn. Though handicapped by an absence of skis he was gaining, gaining and, BING BONG. Next he was marooned on an endless chair-lift just behind the same trim figure. She constantly turned and beckoned but they were both joined and separated by ten metres of steel cable. BING BONG. Then he was sailing over a precipice fuelled by a potent, but ultimately inadequate, mixture of Glühwein and adrenaline. A final and most timely BING BONG, and he landed back in the departure lounge. Here there was a new, disturbing presence – the real cause of his awakening.

And it was loathing at first sight.

Or rather, first hearing. The guilty party was invisible to Malcolm but the voice scaled the intervening luggage mountain undiminished and won an effortless victory over a taxiing jet. It was flirting with the woman on the check-in desk, though her contribution couldn't be heard. Hemmed in by weighing machine, conveyor belt and professional duty, she was the ultimate captive audience. And The Voice was exploiting it to the full.

The bing-bongs were coming thick and fast now as Manstead revved up for the day's business. Evidently several departures were imminent, albeit to mostly unintelligible destinations. The chances of having to share a plane with The Voice for two hours were therefore not high, *a priori*. But Malcolm decided a little reconnaissance was in order. By gritting his teeth and clenching his ears he managed to get close enough to steal a glance at the label on its baggage. There were two in fact, both boldly proclaiming "PEREGRINE TOURS" (though it wasn't clear whether he did so with a caravanette, a troupe of acrobats or what). Malcolm allowed himself a less than *sotto voce* 'Phew!' So, it seemed that Peregrine (as Malcolm promptly christened The Voice) was travelling with the competition! But relief had to be postponed when an unusually lucid last-call announcement sent the two of them scuttling off to the same flight.

In the slow shuffle towards Boarding Gate 1 (which had to be so called, apparently, because there was only one) Malcolm kept a good way behind Peregrine. This ensured temporary acoustic relief and also gave him the feeling that he was less likely to end up sitting close by. This was as comforting as it was fallacious. Their immediate destinies were already written in bold seat numbers on their respective boarding passes. However, it would allow him to feel a little consolatory indignation if by chance they ended up close cabin neighbours. Hence, as soon as he saw Peregrine climbing the steps to the plane's front door Malcolm made a dash for the rear.

In the narrow aisle progress was slower still. Malcolm made a mental note of a suggestion for the "Further Comments" section on the return-flight questionnaire. The bulk of aircraft accommodation should be designated "non-shouting", with a special section at the rear, behind the smokers, for those who just couldn't comply. The baggage-weighing machine at the check-in would be augmented by a sound-level meter, with decibel limits set by the Warsaw Convention. As backup, in the seat pockets, there would be heavy absorbing pads which could be placed over the mouths of those who boarded with good intentions but relapsed in flight. Severe cases would be stowed in the cargo hold (with, of course, generous supplies of barley sugar against the extremes of temperature and pressure).

His musing was interrupted by a whack on the shin. The offending object proved to be a piece of hand luggage, poorly padded and stuffed with duty-free liquor. Attached to the strap there was what appeared to be another Peregrine Tours label. But it wasn't. It was evidently one he'd seen before, because attached to the handles was Peregrine himself, who glared at him for impeding his progress down the aisle and then settled in two rows behind where Malcolm had been allocated. This was optimal bad luck, being too close for acoustic comfort but too far away to complain easily, or to take direct retaliatory action. They were all wished a pleasant trip. The estimated flying time was less than two hours. Malcolm would hold them to that.

Captain Pringle eased the ageing DC3 off the runway with yards to spare. It was nothing like as responsive or manoeuvrable as a Spitfire. But then, on the positive side, they were unlikely to be shot at *en route*.

Peregrine distributed nips of duty-free to his immediate neighbours and the adjacent rows, thereby initiating some in-flight bonding and pre-empting complaints. His largesse didn't extend as far as Malcolm, who was thus denied the pleasure of refusing. Peregrine then treated the entire cabin to a loud, unedited and unending account of the piste heroics and drunken camaraderie of last season in Kitzbühl.

For all their size and meganewtons of shiny thrust aeroplane engines are no match for such a voice. And ear plugs aren't much help, because they reduce both the undesired signal and the background noise over which the guilty party is signalling, leaving the message less loud, but no less clear. In desperation Malcolm directed the nozzle of his fresh-air blower down toward the top of his head and turned it to max. But it was too feeble and far away to do much good.

Now maybe if you had a pair of the things, and could stick one in each ear . . .

Our paradoxical, advanced-guard, Meta-Malcolm might be technologically better prepared.

> The partner of M-M 45 has developed one of her persistent, hacking coughs, after a careless, scarfless session on a high and shaded ski piste. He has shown every sympathy – showering her with throat pastilles, soothing syrups, cheap but drinkable local brandy, even administering Vick Vapour Rub to back and chest. To little effect. In the small hours in the small hotel he's resorted to direct defensive action. After tossing and turning for some time she flicks on the bedside light to find him, eyes closed and smiling, wearing little earpieces.
>
> 'What are you listening to?'
>
> He smiles on.
>
> 'I SAID, WHAT ARE YOU LISTENING TO?'
>
> He opens his eyes. 'Oh, it's just some . . . background . . . sound. Effects, like.'

She plucks the plastic bud from his left ear, plugs it in her right and is startled by an alien sound: a constant rumbling, rushing and hissing. 'Don't they use that to brainwash people?'

'Use what?'

'White noise, or whatever it is.'

'Who?'

'I don't know. Fiendish foreign governments. And the like. Isn't it outlawed by the Geneva Convention?'

'Well, maybe . . . it can have beneficial effects too.'

'Like drowning *me* out?'

M-M, a veteran of the disturbed night and something of an audio buff, has indeed prepared the cassette tape from an electronic noise source, spectrally sculptured with a graphic equaliser to mask only the relevant, coughing region of the frequency range. He turns the volume down. 'I'm just trying to put myself into a deep meditative state.' He attempts a beatific smile 'They say it facilitates alpha waves.'

She brightens. 'Really?'

'Yeah, and releases endorphins, and stuff.'

'But it sounds so . . . soulless. What is it? Where's it from?'

'It's random. So it might as well've come from anywhere.' He gestures expansively with his hands. 'And it can be . . . anything you want it to be.'

'Well what do *you* think it is?'

He closes his eyes, gradually restores the volume. 'It's . . . Victoria Falls . . .'

Her eyes widen.

'. . . recorded one Spring dawn . . .'

She presses the bud more firmly into her ear, entranced.

' . . . with the Zambezi in full spate. They say if you listen carefully you can hear monkeys in the background.'

She closes her eyes, starts to nod. 'Elephants too,' she murmurs. 'Or are they hippos?'

They slide their pillows close together and, united by the flimsy white cable, are soon sound asleep in blissful stereogamy.

For the real Malcolm, captive at twenty-thousand feet, sleep was out of the question. He reclined his seat, shut his eyes and began to conjure up little dramas in which Peregrine might play a starring role.

The one-man chairlift is stalled over an abyss, swivelling and lurching in the mounting blizzard; the tortured cable strands part one by one in an irregular series of unnerving (but not-unmusical) twangs . . .

The bold, vociferous one strays a little too far from the piste and is engulfed in an unseasonal avalanche – nature's own humane, fluffy-white, ten-thousand-ton sound muffler . . .

. . . or is abducted by a group of yetis who, quickly learning the true nature of abomination, abandon him on a remote peak and flee . . .

In front of the Arrivals building the transfer coaches were lined up with Germanic precision. Malcolm's luggage label was spotted by eagle-eyed Olga the courier, who directed him to the frontmost one. A familiar sound greeted him as he joined the queue to board. The Voice was telling tales of long-distance vomiting feats in the Pyrenees. Malcolm sighed a sigh which could have triggered avalanches, causing everyone except Peregrine to turn round. This time, though, there would not be the constraints of seat reservations, so even in the worst case, where the source of irritation sat dead centre, one could still choose to be half a bus away.

Malcolm lingered at the back of the queue, engaging in a little applied maths, counting passengers, considering the seating capacity (conveniently written in bold figures on the coach side), invoking the laws of permutations and combinations. How many ways could you arrange thirty-nine people in fifty-four seats? Reassuringly many! So many you didn't need to bother calculating. On finally mounting the steps, however, he was presented with a scene to make a statistician pinch himself. The remaining sixteen vacant seats formed a contiguous group. And at the centre of it sat Peregrine, momentarily mute. Perhaps at the seeming improbability of it all.

Olga clambered aboard, counted the heads, shook her own and then counted again. She seemed dissatisfied, as if it didn't correspond to the number of bodies. Malcolm stood agonising, but since he couldn't drive, and was forbidden by no fewer than three signs in four languages to stand, he finally forced himself into a seat less than two metres from the epicentre of the disturbance to be. He'd survived two hours. There remained another three at most. With any luck Peregrine Tours would alight before Brindles anyway.

Noting that none of his new neighbours had been near him on the plane Peregrine took the opportunity to re-re-live his skiing memoirs. Now though he upped the volume further to ensure better projection across the vacant seats, and set a pace and level of detail to suit the longer and slower journey. From time to time he would selflessly interrupt himself to point out obvious features of the landscape.

Malcolm ground his teeth while silently adding to the catalogue of accidents that might befall his tormentor. These involved the services of many agencies, from careless lumberjacks to short-sighted wild-boar hunters, thin-ice to freak winter lightning, ravenous wolf packs to runaway piste-preparation machines – sometimes acting separately, sometimes in amusing combinations. When his imagination finally began to tire he rounded off the operation with a single, gigantic, cartoon-style granite block. From a great height. Just to be sure.

Within a couple of hours they had run out of Autobahn, and as the coach began to grind its way up the winding Ingltal there was the first glimpse of snow on distant peaks. Peregrine celebrated with another round of duty-free and a demonstration of yodelling, to widespread groans of dismay. To make it clear he was a man who took criticism seriously he practised diligently for the next fifteen kilometres.

Once above the snow line the coach made regular stops. At each village Olga sent sub-groups slithering off to their chalets. Then on they went. Unteringl. Hinteringl. Pingel-an-der-Ingl. At the latter,

Malcolm was able to move to a seat which had become available near the back.

His new neighbour was a rather large, furry woman who made more room for him on the seat than seemed strictly necessary. A quick glance at her luggage revealed that she too was bound for Chalet Pengel. Malcolm gestured back at Peregrine, now engaged in solo community singing.

'It's all right, he's not with us!'

Any relief the woman might have had that he wasn't was tempered by the realisation that Malcolm was. For a start she was concerned at the state of his jeans – the holier and less fashionable of his two and only pairs. Perhaps confusing economics with politics she saw them as an assertion of student power. But it was their grubbiness and proximity that most alarmed her. In death, as in life, the ocelot is a delicate creature – highly susceptible to corrupting influences and most unresponsive to dry-cleaning. It saddened her to think that the improperly dressed were even admitted to the Alps. Alas, there were no doormen at the Brenner Pass.

'Old Pengel looks quite cosy from the brochure!' said Malcolm, cheerily. She edged a little further towards the window and stared out. In her formative skiing years one arrived by train in St Moritz and took a sleigh to the hotel, neck-deep in woolly blankets. It was hard to come to terms with the new democracy which, thanks to the package tour, had settled on the region and been irreversibly compacted by a million proletarian ski boots.

He tried again. 'Have you been to the Ingltal before?'

'No, we haven't.'

He looked around but saw no obvious sign of the rest of the "we". 'Where d'you normally go then?'

She sighed. 'Well, we often take a chal*et* in Zermatt, actually.' She gave a quite undue emphasis to the second syllable, perhaps to avoid confusion with the Butlin's variety he might be more familiar with.

'Sounds nice!'

'It's *magnificent*!' she exclaimed, finally provoked by the sheer inadequacy of this assessment, 'We overlook the Matterhorn!'

Malcolm nodded sympathetically. 'Easily done. What with all those mountains about.' Straight faces were his speciality.

She gathered the fur more tightly around her and stared even harder out of the window.

The coach ground its way ever higher and slower. Snow banks deepened at the side of the winding road. Bored Malcolm played at not swallowing between one bend and the next, relishing the consequent ear-popping which signalled the escalating altitude. At Oberingl, with the journey telling and the air thinning, he began to doze. In no time at all he was back in a dreamy white landscape, this time being pursued off-piste by a pack of large furry creatures, baying for blood. A succession of tumbles reduced him to one ski, then no skis, then just one bent ski stick; yellowing fangs began to snap at his already ragged jeans. He was rescued just in time by a rather fierce application of brakes and cries of *'Inglberg!'* and *'Pengel!'*

'Come along Gemma!' his neighbour called over the back of the seat.

A dainty, rather fetching figure, who seemed to have been asleep, rose up yawning and stretching, then disappeared into a bulky, luxurious hooded anorak before Malcolm could make any fuller appraisal.

As he descended the coach steps Malcolm received a whack on the calves from a duty-free bag. It was noticeably lighter than before but the wielder had compensated by increasing the velocity.

'This is Chalet *Pengel*, actually,' said Malcolm firmly, turning to his assailant. 'Brindles Travel here, but Peregrine Tours elsewhere, I think you'll find!' He was beginning to enjoy himself.

'They're all part of Panorama!' smiled Peregrine. Then, barging past, doubtless in a quest for the best room, he delivered a whack to Malcolm's remaining shin.

Chapter 11

Rise and Fall

Paradise is the last run of the first day. Over and done with are all the little traumas of arrival and initiation: accommodating that familiar unfamiliarity of borrowed boots, then sussing out the connection between the reality of the local pistes and lift layout, and its representation in the jokey, snakes-and-ladders, artist's impression which passes for a ski map. Blissfully remote still is the day of departure, held at bay by the mountain ranges of Monday through Friday – sun and funpacked peaks of pleasure, groynes against the sands of time. Paradise.

For this first final fling Malcolm would always try to be the last person on the very last lift to the highest skiable point of the region. That way he could wring every last Joule of potential energy from that potent but extortionate ski pass. His timing today was bordering on the perfect, but from the more cautious side. He'd learned a lesson that time in Grindeldorf where, having been delayed, and then accelerated, by an irresponsibly large and late mug of Jagertee, he'd sighted the chair-lift just closed but still running. An irresistible challenge. He'd dropped down into his best approximation to the classic *schuss* position then finished the run in a high-speed limbo dance under the roped-off entrance and slipped aboard. This earned him a sharp, if unintelligible, rebuke from the lift man. He'd been lucky to lose only the bobble from his woolly hat.

This time just one more got through behind him. Looking back he saw the lift man arrest the barrier in mid descent and let her slip under, unbeating Malcolm by several chairs. She must have resorted to hip wiggling – a gesture that would be enhanced by the sleek and snaky ski suit – for even the most exaggerated eyelash flutters would not have been visible behind those large, dark, cool and trendy goggles.

Up out of the valley rode the last convoy. Six chairs ahead of Malcolm two enormous Germans sat in silence, comfortably oblivious of the fact that when they reached the mid point between pylons they divided the cable into two straight sections with an alarming discontinuity of gradient; or that a fall from such a height could kill each of them several times over. Or that someone somewhere in a distant valley power station was shovelling a little harder on their account. They were unaware too of being watched and faintly resented by the more modest-sized Malcolm, 70 kg with skis attached, who'd paid just as much for the ride. He in turn was being watched by the scarlet-clad sylph floating along behind, the cable's gently curving catenary unperturbed by her presence. The less-unperturbable lift man dutifully watched her till she disappeared behind the first ridge, sighed, and got ready to ski home.

Paradise.

Well, almost. The deficiency was a tiny one, taking the form of a slight but sharp pressure on Malcolm's left hip bone, disturbing really only because its cause was mysterious. It had taken all day to creep into his consciousness. A brief investigation yielded a lone half peanut from the folds of his trouser-pocket. Lacking the energy to agonise about its history or future he threw the thing in the air, caught it in his mouth, crunched once, swallowed it, and immediately felt hungry. Paradise receded a little further.

But not irredeemably. Distributed about his person were the remains of yesterday's in-flight meal: two and a half cream crackers, a 60-degree Kraft cheese sector, an allegedly "refreshing towelette", two barley sugars and a wafer-thin mint. This was augmented by a now wafer-thin bread roll in his back pocket. Wholesome and rounded when sneaked from the breakfast table, it had been an early morning casualty in an emergency braking manoeuvre on a steep descent. So, there were certainly the ingredients, but was there the time, for tea?

The top station was invisible. Probably a good way off. On the other hand Malcolm was in new territory and there was no guaranteeing it wasn't lurking in the trees over the next ridge. He'd already passed a good many lift pylons. These were numbered with big, bold painted digits in ascending order, numerically and altitudinally, in a rare and refreshingly straightforward fashion.

Trouble was, there was no way of knowing how many there were. And anyway their spacing was far from regular, being dictated by the capricious geology of the Inglberg. The chairs, however, were always numbered cyclically in a wrap-around fashion. There were several strung out between every adjacent pair of pylons, and they would have been passing him, valley bound, at twice his own ground speed. There, surely, lay the key to his ETA at the top.

Malcolm had always had a more than passing interest in numbers, whether they were floating in Platonic abstraction or bolted to railway engines and ski-lift chairs. He once boarded, quite by chance, No. 1 of a no-less-than 383-chair lift system, and rode to the top beaming regally, affording salutes and sneers to the descending parties according to their numerical significance. He sniffed dismissively at the more undistinguished primes, nodded knowingly at the higher perfect squares (it takes one to know one) and all but blew a kiss at the two raven-haired nymphs in No. 223 (the sum of three adjacent powers of two. Well, almost). Strangely, he'd failed to notice what was arguably the most significant number of all. Though he might have deduced its whereabouts. He was, of course, being directly pursued by No. 0 – the skeletal aluminium frame, replacing the normal chair, which he'd spotted on previous occasions laden with crates of beer and catering packs of noodles bound for the summit restaurant. Later in that same week he'd discovered its more sinister function when it went by bearing one of the non-walking wounded of the piste, making what was clearly his last descent of the season, strapped to a stretcher in a mercilessly horizontal attitude and grimacing in synchrony with every jolt from the pylon pulleys.

Today, if there was a No. 0 on this particular wheel of fortune it was far away, pursuing, like an angel of death, some other poor devil. Malcolm could just make out a No. 27 on the back of the chair in front. The descending chair passing on the left just then turned out to be No. 187. That meant a whole 160 chairs between them, and therefore 80 between him and the top. He timed the inter-chair interval from the intermittent rattle over the pulleys. 8 seconds. This suggested a good ten minutes to go. Tea time!

He began the delicate and cautious manoeuvres that were needed. A major problem was gaining access to the various food packets, which were quite ununwrappable without removing the oh-so-droppable gloves. And so it was that he had the left glove by its middle finger in his front teeth, the right under the left armpit, anorak unzipped and scarf flapping, ski poles between clenched knees and fast-freezing fingers fumbling with the red paper fuse of the cheese sector, when disaster struck. Glancing round to check on the progress of his scarlet pursuer he read the back of a passing chair. No. 206! How could that be? He held breath, gloves and ski poles till the next chair came past, praying that No. 206 was an anomaly, misprint or hallucination. But, sure enough, No. 207 swung by, triggering a revolutionary reversal in his mental model. Though the merry-go-round itself was turning anticlockwise, the chairs, it seemed, were numbered clockwise, with the beginning and end of the sequence therefore above and in front of him.

Momentarily confused and judging that any sudden movement could cost him vital equipment he stayed hunched and motionless, expecting the top to be just over the next ridge. And the next. And the next. His frozen pose was fast becoming permanent when, almost exactly ten minutes later, he arrived at the summit station.

With some concern the lift man helped Malcolm out of his seat and with a gentle shove sent him off down the snow ramp which led to the piste. Arthritics seemed to be getting younger. In the interests of professional impartiality he then repeated this charitable gesture for his very last, and manifestly able-bodied, customer of the day.

Poised on the brink at the top, ready for launching, hunger forgotten, Malcolm ran through the well-practised ritual. Buttons were buttoned, zips were zipped and then unzipped and re-zipped just to be really sure, the state of sureness arising more from the *process* of zipping than the *state* of zippedness. Lift pass was tucked snugly between pullover and shirt, the former being tucked anyway into trousers so that the precious piece of plastic would be retained even if both of the elastic loops around his neck were to break. He estimated a far less than 1 in 10 chance of breakage per loop per holiday and had adjusted the second loop (he told them at the ski-pass office it was for a friend) to a very different length, feeling that any breakings would then be independent of one another, thus making the chance of the two failing simultaneously far far less than 1 in 100 and also ensuring that a change of tension would trigger a kind of amber alert if the first, presumably shorter one, were to go.

He felt the last, low sun thawing his limbs. She'd be somewhere behind, making her own preparations. He didn't look round. He would race her down. Down, down into the valley of hot showers and soft beds. Of Schnitzel and Schnapps and Schwarzwälderkirschtorten, and who knows what, or whom?

Left and right they set off, respectively, each on a whim, they felt, though each in fact obeying some unconscious bias arising from little muscular asymmetries. Malcolm accelerated through a foresty bit, gaining a little confidence at every turn. When the piste widened he pulled out the stops, fancying himself the bat out of hell, but only managing to look like a Brit out of practice. Luckily his fancied audience had yet to emerge from the trees.

A branch of the piste wound precipitously off to the left. Malcolm followed it, precipitating an instant sunset behind the Inglstein, looming across the valley. In the sudden shade the snow squeaked characteristically at every turn. An experienced Eskimo could have told you the temperature just by listening. But the nearest one would be a couple of thousand miles away. And quite likely fast asleep.

After a short while he rejoined the main piste stream, now divided by a long, thin island of boulders and trees with mogul rapids on either side. He stumbled his way down through these, grateful just to remain upright and out of sight. The trees dwindled, the boulders petered out, the two streams converged.

They collided along a contour, sharing their momenta (and, according to ski law, any blame) quite equitably. Loosely entangled they slid gently on to a small horizontal patch of snow, finishing in attitudes more ignominious than painful. Something in the physical and legal symmetry of the situation triggered an uncharacteristic confidence in Malcolm.

'Alles OK?' He had a sizeable first-aid kit of foreign phrases.

'Ja, Ich glaube.' She thought so, though seemed a little shaken in spite of her reassurances. 'Und Sie?'

'Ja, Ich glaube.' If in doubt, mimic.

She was dusting off snow, having got her left ski back on. He began fiddling with the bindings of his right one, anxious to regain his own skiworthiness, aware of how far she was from a captive audience. It was now or never again.

'Wohin fahren Sie?' They both knew it was stupid to ask where was she going. Gravity alone guaranteed them a common immediate destiny.

'Nach Inglberg!'

'Ich auch!' Me too! He regained a bit of credibility through the undisguisedly affected surprise. 'Und dann?'

She thought a moment. 'Dann, eine Dusche, etwas zu essen, ein Schläfchen.' Shower, snack, snooze – an enticing sequence. He didn't have the linguistic skills to ask if anyone might join in.

'Und *dann*?' He didn't really mean to push his luck – he was just loath to abandon a simple formula which yielded so much (and such engaging) information so easily.

'Und dann, vielleicht, zum *Schpindlhof*.'

His heart sank a little at the name, even before he realised why he recognised it. The bus had passed the place yesterday on the way through the village. The brochure had dedicated a whole half page to supporting its claim that this was one of "the liveliest discos in the Alps". There was one such in every resort, opposite the main lift station, to which young, rich, beautiful Europe flocked to preen and pose. The visual aspects might be delightful, but acoustically it would be the blackest of runs. *Dingles* with Lederhosen.

Malcolm could see she was ready to slip away. All he really needed was a few minutes of her undivided attention, to lay some groundwork. But how could such a thing ever come about? A technical hitch on a two-person gondola lift? A brief ensconcement in a benign and downy avalanche? Yes, that was it. They would huddle like heroes, awaiting the St Bernard, sharing the mini banquet, now handily concentrated in his left pocket. He looked up hopefully at the snow banks above, but Spring was months away. A high-powered, well-focused burst of yodelling might just do it, but would be very hard to explain.

'Auf Wiedersehen!' The merest glance over her shoulder.

'Auf Wiedersehen!' he echoed, hoping it carried a modicum of literal meaning.

Chapter 12

A Room with a View

'I have a room with a view!'

Malcolm sat on his narrow bed, toying with opening lines. What kind of response might that one get? Was it too obvious? Well, it all depended on the audience. A sophisticated English Lit. student might dismiss him with a 'Read it. Years ago. *Boring!*' Or might just play along, with a 'With a view to *what?*'

What he was actually hoping to provoke was 'With a view *of* what?'

'Of the *Inglstein*, of course,' he'd say – bait taken, trap (verbal at least) closing. It was unlikely any guest would have a sense of direction robust enough to survive the two and three-quarter cycles of winding stairs and then breath enough, given the altitude, to point out the reality. Which was that even if it were displaced 10 km southwards by some overnight seismic event which miraculously left everything else intact, from Malcolm's room that famous peak would still be comfortably eclipsed by Frau Finkel's less than famous cow shed across the road.

Inevitably, though, at some stage he'd be challenged to reveal the promised spectacle. He would then triumphantly indicate the colour photo of the snow-capped Inglstein he'd ripped from the Panorama brochure (left by a previous tenant under one leg of the bedside table to make good its length) and drawing-pinned to the wardrobe door. Would this revelation of word play prove amusing enough to offset the disappointment and suspicion? It all depended on the audience.

After-dinner music wafted up the stairwell from the ground-floor Stube area, where the roaring log fire, according to the brochure, formed the "cosy focus of chalet life", the pride of Herr und Frau Pengel. The melody was jolly and unpretentious enough, which left the lyrics exposed to scrutiny. And though mellowed by food and wine Malcolm felt himself challenged. What good indeed *was* sitting alone? In one's room?

Well, since you're asking, he thought (and ignoring for the moment the rather patronising insinuations of social and other inadequacies), for a start it's warm and cheap. And fairly peaceful. More than you could say for a good many environments.

'*Come hear* (or was it *Come here!?*) *that music play!*'

Shan't! It's amply clear from up here, thanks!

'*Life is a cabaret . . .*'

Whoa, hold it right there! Rhetorical questions and coaxing imperatives are one thing (well, all right, *two*, *classes*, of thing), and might be dismissed with a flippant retort. But unsupported assertions, especially ones with metaphysical overtones, deserve rigorous analysis from any would-be philosopher. Even if he's on holiday.

Malcolm kicked off his shoes and lay down, hands behind head. Life might be many things – a four-letter word, a monosyllable, "continuous animate existence" (just one among a whole list in the OED) etc. etc. But it was manifestly NOT a cabaret, in much the same way, really, that it wasn't (in spite of the claims of other songs) a circus or a merry-go-round. Assuming, that is, that there were different ways for things not to be other things. Neither was it a bowl of cherries, box of chocolates, or, for that matter, barrel of Chihuahuas. What's more, in spite of claims by generations of Sunday-school preachers and the like, it wasn't a rusty tin-opener, a beehive, a pair of nutcrackers, ball of string, set of dominoes or garden fork with one bent prong.

Where on earth do people get these ideas from? To be fair, in the school assembly Malcolm's headmaster had been more cautious – opting for the form of tentative, qualified simile – 'You know, life's a *bit like* a . . .' But then he'd go and spoil it all by choosing the most implausible things: uncut wholemeal loaves (with, of course, incipient mould), wire coat hangers, revolving doors, hula hoops or inflatable mattresses. Malcolm had sat through scores of these sermonettes with mounting irritation but, sadly, never quite summoned the courage to stand up and scream out, "NO IT ISN'T!"

As indeed it wasn't. Life, like most things, isn't most things. Or even a bit like them. And, what's more, we've no obligation to say why *not.* The onus is firmly on the songwriters, teachers, preachers and all those other pedlars of arbitrary and irresponsible metaphors to justify their own, positive assertions. So there!

The song had come full circle during this musing. The question was re-posed, the command reiterated, the assertion reasserted in a crescendo of conviction.

'*LIFE IS A CABARET . . .*'

Malcolm remained unconvinced. And as for "*old chum*" – was that supposed to be a term of endearment? It sounded more like something you scraped out of the bottom of the dog's bowl.

It wasn't really such a bad song. In itself. He'd heard far worse. It rhymed and scanned, had finite duration, a beginning, middle and end, recognisable cadences and warm intentions. He just rather resented its underlying message: that anyone who passed up the chance of paying to watch overweight transvestites in black suspenders play raucous saxophones must be some kind of deviant.

Nevertheless it was a spur to some sort of action. On the bill of the grand cabaret which life so clearly wasn't were featured also more mellifluous sounds. And, come to think of it, supple sylphs in ski-suits. Hmmm! It had been easy enough to persuade himself of the joys of solitude. But maybe, in the interests of scientific objectivity, he should invite a witness.

But where from? The Stube was now effectively out of bounds to him. Although it had turned out to be even gemütlicher than the brochure had boasted, he had to avoid it for tactical reasons.

It had happened like this.

Peregrine had presided over dinner, generously tasting and approving the soup unbidden; passing the vegetables and making jokes about their vaguely suggestive shapes; pouring the wine and making jokes about grape-trampling peasants. He was momentarily disappointed by the appearance of brandy sauce with the dessert because he'd prepared what he felt was a really good joke about custard. He made a mental note to request it for the last night, and consoled himself with attempts to ignite the now highly alcoholic Strudel with his new lighter – his only duty-free purchase still unconsumed. In the event the proof of this particular pudding was below the critical threshold for combustion and he managed only to singe his purple-spotted cravat. The damage he accepted philosophically, refusing several quite genuine offers of extinguishment by water jug from around the table and reflecting how lucky it was he hadn't worn his special bow-tie on the first night. Its revolving capability might have been seriously impaired by the heat.

Throughout this performance Malcolm had sat in stony silence, hemmed in from both sides by fellow Penglers. It had already been a long evening. In spite of the handicap of two and three-quarter flights of stairs to descend he'd been first at the table, clutching a spoon and salivating before the last of Frau Pengel's mighty strokes on the cow-bell dinner gong had ceased to resonate through the chalet.

Next had come his neighbour from the coach, relaxed and glowing from the day's exertions, her frigid furriness having mellowed into more of a sort of Tyrolean tweediness. She sat down right next to Malcolm, possibly because to do otherwise might have seemed rude, or to make up for her previous stand-offishness. Or perhaps she was shielding him from the elusive Gemma, who shortly after slipped in through the door and then promptly disappeared, remaining effectively chaperoned throughout the meal by total maternal eclipse. From time to time her voice, sweet but soft, rose above the background, but never enough for him to know what she was saying. His other neighbour was engrossed in her own companion, allowing Malcolm himself to concentrate all his efforts on trying to ignore the self-appointed master of ceremonies.

Between courses Peregrine entertained them all by playing percussion solos with his cutlery on the huge and resonant pinewood dining table. As the meal progressed and the musical resources diminished he felt the attention of the company slipping from his grasp. With his last remaining teaspoon he rapped on the table for silence and said, 'Right! Who's for *Jingles*?'

Nobody responded, largely because nobody knew even what *kind* of question that was.

'You mean you've never had *Jingles*?' cried Peregrine, affecting great astonishment.

'I think my auntie did once,' volunteered Malcolm. 'Came out in this awful rash.' He gestured vaguely at his midriff.

'No, no, it's this fantastic cocktail for après-ski. Two parts gin, two of rum and two of wine, or maybe it's the other way round. Anyway then you add hot lemons and a sprig of holly. Oh, and some fresh snow. We always drink it standing on your head, you know, but it's really good anyway. I'll make it if you just get me a bucket. Oh yeah, and you've *got* to down it in one. It'll be great! Then,' he added beaming, 'we're ALL going to play charades.'

Opportunity chimed in Malcolm's mental belfry. He put on an instant and concerned frown, looked intently at the four corners of the room in succession as if in some frantic calculation, crossed to the window and stared out, and finally said with a mixture of casualness and diffidence, 'Bet you a pound we're not.'

Having followed Malcolm's little display Peregrine was now frowning too. But, unable to imagine what architectural inadequacy, local by-law or other factor could possibly thwart his proposal, could only say grimly, 'You're on!'

With an extravagant gesture Malcolm had consulted his left wrist (which was bare because it was Monday and on alternate days he wore his watch on the right to even out any suntan), made a *good-heavens-is-that-the-time?* face and headed off to his room. Pengel was looking up.

But where to go now? Well, *out*, would be a start, he supposed. So it was back down the stairs, this time at a creeping pace. The door to the Stube was ajar. Voices came from within.

'Er . . . Vesuvius?'

'Etna?'

'Popocatepetl?'

There was a brief silence.

'*Sounds like* Popocatepetl!'

He tiptoed on out into the night.

He crossed the flat wooden bridge which joined and separated Pengel and the road. An invisible torrent was thundering underneath. Later in the season such a sound would be unsettling, being a direct indicator of the rate of dwindling of the skiers' basic resource. But Spring was still months away. And a quick calculation showed that any depletion was being more than made up for by the large, sticky snowflakes which were dropping everywhere. Tonight the rushing water would just lull him to sleep, masking words and music.

And now where to? Well, valley lift stations, and all the associated facilities they attract, need to be accessible to unpowered skiers. So it follows that they get built in just those positions to which otherwise aimless folk will naturally gravitate. Malcolm's tough, sensible town shoes, though adhesive enough for the High-Street habitat they'd been reared in, seemed to have little choice but to carry him slithering irreversibly into the local minimum which was Inglberg village centre.

Um ching um ching um chingum um pah – the invisible disco's acoustic signature was unmistakable, despite the token Teutonic accent. He followed its siren call, round the corner, across the road, round another corner, until he stood under the flashing neon sign. Drifting snow had clung prettily to the windows of the Schpindlhof, in patterns more Dickensian than Alpine. Malcolm scrambled up on to a window ledge, cleared himself a porthole and peered in.

Under the pulsating strobe-light fashionably furry-booted, partnerless après-skiers jiggled in ionic isolation. He frowned and pressed his nose hard against the glass. Couldn't the famous Schpindlhof social chemistry engender any closer bonding? (One or two of the daintier figures triggered thoughts of something altogether more molecular). Couldn't the homeland of the Strausses whip up a simple waltz to foster a bit of familiarity among its visitors? Less rhetorically, and more pragmatically, how might the local DJ react to a request for a military two-step, or progressive valeta?

' 'Ello, 'ello, 'ello!' The voice from behind was vaguely familiar, rather refined and distinctly soprano. Coupled with the location this made it unlikely in the extreme that Malcolm was about to be apprehended by an English village constable. All the same he started sufficiently to hit his head on the solid pine lintel and stumbled backwards off the ledge, landing with both feet on something soft.

Having cost her mother several guineas, Gemma's new Christmas boots were *especially* furry. But, sadly, their design was optimised for toe cosiness and afforded no protection against Blakey-clad clodhoppers from a height of several feet. As the two stood rubbing their respective extremities and exchanging apologetic looks the music underwent a step-change increase in loudness. Malcolm glowered back up at the window.

'Why don't you go in?' she asked.

'I suffer from normal hearing. Why don't *you* go in?'

'Because I've just come out.'

There would have been a long silence, were it not for the incessant noise. Continuing to rub his head to retain, and divert, her attention, Malcolm was able to make the first close-up survey of the object of his recent interest, albeit half lit and half buried in a luxurious, expensive-looking jacket. From the voluminous furry outline he deduced the probable shape of the body beneath – a tricky but pleasurable exercise. He was guided by the delicate face, the rather balletic stance and the sheer power of imagination. He liked both what he could and couldn't see.

'Where're you going now then?'

'Back to the chal*et*.'

He made sure he exaggerated his already considerable disappointment, to allow for the poor lighting.

'But I might have a night-cap, *en route*.' Her French pronunciation was impressive, if a little dissonant in the Tyrolean ambience – the legacy of a finishing school, perhaps.

'Can I join you? I could do with one myself. Purely for medicinal purposes,' he added, affecting the slur of a stage drunk. He rubbed his head again to remind her of their bond of discomfort, for which she was partly responsible.

'Well, if you promise to keep your feet to yourself!'

The walls of the Jodlerstube were bedecked with Alpine paraphernalia. In faded photos sepia-bearded heroes clambered over crevasses on flimsy ladders or clung implausibly to vertical ice. Unlucky mountain fauna peered out from alcoves and dusty ledges, the fatal moment of surprise frozen on their faces. And scaling the huge, sloping chimney breast were pitons, hanks of rope and wooden-handled implements, worn shiny by some mysterious use, sprouting straps and spikes, looking more inquisitorial than sporting. All in all, sights to inspire awe and vertigo. Even in the stone-cold sober.

'Zwei Glühwein, bitte.' Malcolm proudly emphasised the umlaut, anxious to distance himself from the majority of skiing Brits who (he'd heard the locals snigger) tend to say "glue", as in "sticky". Practice had made perfect. But who was he trying to impress? There was, of course, his fragile-looking companion – de-coated now she was in the warm. And de-booted – the better to give her toes a prolonged massage after their recent trauma and before the demands of the next morning. But then the waitress had come to complicate the equation – a dark, slender, dirndled figure with a creamy, high-altitude complexion, whose departure barwards left a longish silence. Otherwise the place was empty. Apart, that is, from two enormous Germans, sitting in their own silence a few tables away, each contemplating a foaming Stein. Each oblivious of the contribution they were making to the ethnic stereotype.

'So, on your own tonight then?' He winced inwardly as he said it. As an ice-breaker it was little better than, Did you have a good day on the slopes?, or even, Read any good books lately?

'Yes, Mother's turned in early. She didn't sleep well last night.'

'Neither did I,' said Malcolm.

'Neither did *I*, come to that. Every time I was dropping off someone started yodelling.'

'Probably a lonely goatherd. They're indigenous you know.'

'Did you hear it too?'

'No, thank goodness. My room's quite quiet,' said Malcolm, setting a scene on which one might build.

The Glühwein arrived in steaming mugs.

'So what kept you awake, then?'

He sighed. 'Words. As usual.'

'*Words*?'

'Yeah, words.' He leaned towards her. 'Don't get me wrong, though. I really love words. Use 'em all the time in fact.' He chuckled, 'There I go again, see! But sometimes they just, well, get to me, somehow. Can't stop thinking about them.'

'What about them? Exactly?' She took a sip from her drink.

'Well, I suppose it's that I find words more ambiguous than most people.' He checked himself. 'Than most people *do*, that is. So I spend a lot of time thinking about the exact meaning of them. Trying to sort 'em out. Pin 'em down. But in the end they just start going round and round in my head, getting more and more ambiguous. Keeps me awake. Hour after hour, sometimes.'

'Have you thought about counting sheep?' She wagged a school-marmish finger at him.

'Depends what you mean.'

'It does?'

'Yeah, I mean, I've often thought about sheep, and I reckon they probably can count, at least, you know, *zero, one, two, many,* sort of thing. For keeping track of lambs. But I've never thought about them actually counting, so I don't think that counts as thinking about counting sheep.' He frowned. 'But, if you mean *counting sheep*, like, putting sheep into one-to-one correspondence with the set of positive integers – for its putatively soporific effect – well, yeah, I have thought about that.'

'And does it work?'

'Oh, I've never actually got round to *trying* it.'

Her woolly-socked toes connected temporarily with his shin. A promising little engagement, if still several notches above the level of a caress.

They succumbed to a second round of drinks, which went down a little quicker than the first, triggering an exchange of yawns and thoughts of departure and sleep. Tomorrow, though a short day relatively speaking, as they were only just past the solstice, would still be a couple of minutes longer than today. And that was clearly long enough at that altitude to make one wonderfully tired.

The snow had stopped and the sky was moonless and starry. Several inches of powder lay in greeting for them, affording much-needed traction for their ascent to Pengel. As well as promising a feast of piste hi jinks for everyone in the morning. Gladdened by Glühwein and the glistening landscape they broke into a two-step. It was much more civilian than military – their residual discipline having dissolved in the alcohol – and only marginally progressive – the two steps forward being followed by at least one back. All in all it was a good while before they crossed the bridge to Pengel.

The Stube door was still ajar. Weary voices came from within.

'Jelly?'

'Trifle?'

'Blancmange?'

There was a brief silence.

'*Sounds like* blancmange!'

They tiptoed on past and up the stairs.

Gemma stopped and gestured at the first door on the first-floor landing, with a finger to her lips. There would have been a long silence were it not for the snoring.

'Well, looks like we're in for a perfect day tomorrow,' he whispered.

'Hmm, if my knee holds out.'

'Your *knee?*'

'Yes, some idiot ran into me on the slopes this afternoon. Gute Nacht.'

'Gute Nacht,' he echoed.

As she disappeared into the room, finger still on lips, Malcolm fancied he caught the glimmer of a smile. And the tiddliest of winks.

Chapter 13

Ups and Downs

Alcohol and altitude, even separately, take their toll. Malcolm was grateful for the banister rail as he clambered up the final one-and-three-quarter flights of stairs. Shoes removed, he lay on the bed and stared up at the rough-hewn pine rafters.

It would, of course, have been premature to ask her up. The room was cramped, with very few seating permutations. And he had no real pretext for an invitation. No etchings or stamp collection, chocolate biscuits or bottle of schnapps (though he was fairly sure that somewhere in his luggage was the nub end of a tube of fruit gums). In any case they'd had a night-cap already. Arguably two. Or even four.

He yawned. What exactly *was* a night-cap? Did it refer to each individual, countable beverage? Or embrace all the drinks, and even drinkers, that make up the cosy event? It was she who'd used the term. Had it been meant to encourage, or to pre-empt, any ideas he might have? The 'night' bit was enticing. Unquestionably. But the 'cap' bit was more open ended; was it the climactic icing on some cake? Or, rather, did it draw a kind of line under things? Or over them? Night-cap. Long, tall milky, malty soporific? He yawned again. Or short, sharp, fiery prelude to passion? Night-cap. Chaste, straightlaced headwear? Yes, it was that too. And wasn't there a deadly night-cap – some femme fatale of fungi? Night-cap. He repeated it several more times. All in all, a tease of a word.

Malcolm gave an extra-long, unstifled yawn, and thought back to the several, shorter, discreeter ones she had given earlier. What did they represent? Natural, neutral, healthy tiredness? Positive boredom? Or hints of something else? He wriggled his left toes where the ski boot had pinched.

Had it really been her he'd run into on that last slope? Too late to ask now. Maybe it didn't matter – whoever it was was worth running into again. Tomorrow he could ski that same piste repeatedly, affording numerous opportunities to fate. *She* would recognise *him*. Surely. Apart from at meal times he had been, and would be, wearing his anorak, which was a startling greeny-yellow. And tatty to the point of unmistakeability. Probably unique in the whole of the Alps. Being broke had its up side.

They could play snakes and ladders on a grand scale. That chair lift was a long one, he remembered with a shiver. And more dog's leg than ladder. But the piste was particularly serpentine, crossing under it repeatedly. How many times? He shut his eyes. If he spotted her riding up while he was skiing down he could wait at the bottom. On the other hand, if she was going down and he up, he could shout out a greeting. Even propose a rendezvous. She might, though, just carry on to a lower piste.

More impressive would be to catch and overtake her on the descent. He gently massaged his left big toe, through the sock. But what if they naturally looped around the system at almost the same rate? Being speed-compatible – a basic requirement of at least a skiing relationship – could be the very cause of them never meeting. Out of phase, out of sight, out of mind. A clock that loses or gains a second a day is right only once every couple of centuries or so. Better, famously, is a clock that doesn't go at all, and so is right twice a day. In fact, if it hadn't involved defying gravity he could have gone around in reverse – a clock running backwards is right *four* times a day! The problem is you don't know when. Unless you have a clock.

Alternatively he could stay on the lift, claiming aerial reconnaissance for, say, a lost glove, to the man at the top. But if she boarded some way ahead and out of sight he might just be doomed to go round and round all day long. Or for ever – like that flying Dutchman. Or was it Scotsman?

No, it was best to wait at the bottom, playing the role of the stopped clock. The most he could lose would be half an hour's skiing. Simple. As long as she wasn't on any of the other thirty-seven runs the area boasted.

He could of course follow her from Chalet Pengel, at a discreet distance, and try to contrive a meeting. Except that seemed a bit creepy. He began to massage his right toes, which were feeling a little left out. OK, why not simply ask her at breakfast where she was going, and try to tag along? Well, simply, because a whole week in a small chalet, after a possibly public rejection would be too much to bear. In any case, did she ski alone? Or did her mother come too? They'd be an easy pair to spot – the starkly contrasting profiles on a background of brilliant white, the tell-tale tilt of the ski-lift's double-chair. Did he want to play an apex in what would be a far-from-equilateral skiing triangle? Not really. An accidental meeting was the best way.

He opened his eyes. The rafters seemed closer than before. He became aware of the rushing of the stream far below. Then somewhere in the village a church clock chimed. Sweet and resonant. With just a dash of cowbell. Malcolm took the hint and turned in.

With the light out the tiny room shrank further. Quite unnecessarily he closed his eyes. The darkness collapsed to a point, and sleep was instantaneous. Something just seemed to turn inside out, and there was light. Whiter-than-white light. He was moving through a cold but benign landscape, propelled relentlessly onwards. Though not by the usual alternation of powered lift and gravity. Some other kind of force was at work. Onwards, upwards and downwards. Upwards, downwards, until climbing and descent lost their distinction; he sensed only some mild impulse at the transition between them. Snow and sky met seamlessly, wrapped around, swapped around. Time and space stretched and interleaved. His dreamy domain began to broaden, slowing to a rest as it did so, until it was spread across the ages, across all the mountains of the world. And there he remained, cosily frozen in the great downy duvet of time, until far beyond the dawn.

Almost too far. Frau Pengel's view of time was strictly down to earth, and he was lucky to catch the tail end of breakfast. Of Gemma and her mother there was not a sign. But off he went into the day, rested, fed, relaxed, and not unrelieved. He was on holiday after all. No hurry – even a short week is a long time in sporting pursuits.

And that short week bounced, skidded and ploughed along, from piste to piste, from lift to lift. He rode them all: the vertiginous Finkelspitze cable car, whose tightly packed occupants shrieked in concert, with not-altogether-mock alarm, as it lurched over each set of pylon pulleys; the slower and more stately Dingelwald gondola, which glided silently along through a fairytale forest; and, not least, that short, humble, nameless drag lift – the only way out of the dip he kept somehow straying into. A hundred times he was spirited uphill – a total height gain, if his arithmetic was right, equivalent to two-and-three-quarter Everests (reckoned from sea level). That was half a dozen Matterhorns. More or less. A hundred times he launched himself from the top, to end up where he started. More or less.

Many times, too, he lost control, becoming, through the extensive practice, quite a virtuoso of the fall – from the slow-motion, almost graceful, Bambi-on-ice impression before an appreciative audience lunching on a sunny terrace, to his most spectacular, high-speed, wipe-out of the week. Though could a fall be spectacular if there was nobody there to see it? Had there been a spectator it would have looked far worse than it actually was. Happily, no trees in the forest were involved. The prime cause was his forgetting that it was not one of those alternate days when he wore his watch on the opposite side, and glancing down at the wrong wrist, that is, the right one. All would have been well had he chosen the right wrist, that is, the left one. But by the time he'd thought it through he'd wrong-footed his own right leg and was flat out in the middle of the piste on firm, but forgiving, snow. On his way to the ground he managed to squeeze in a vigorous pirouette and a half. Only the fact that they were firmly attached to his body prevented his limbs from being centrifugally scattered, as skis and sticks were, to the four winds – leaving a kind of exploded view of a skier, from a How-Not-To manual. In two minutes he was up and underway again, having appended the incident to his burgeoning mental logbook of experience.

It was with some pride that Malcolm totted up his mounting score of minor bruises in the shower every night. On Thursday, noting that they'd begun to blend uncountably into one another, he awarded himself a long, hot soak in the bath. There are, of course, few things more conducive to leisurely reflection – for anybody, at any time, let alone a budding philosopher, on holiday. He leaned back against the warm enamel and felt the last little stresses of the day dissolve. His coarse-knit socks had left a mesh pattern, like livid graph paper, along the length of each shin. With his forefinger he idly traced a soapy sine wave across the left one, then erased it by submerging his knee. He watched the circular ripples radiate and die away.

Ups and downs. He'd had quite a few in his time. Of more than one kind. There were ups and downs, and ups and downs: the alpine, and the amorous, for an alphabetical kick-off. And for a young wintersporter the parallels between them were inescapable. Slippery though, too. Are we, for example, talking about states, or processes? Skiing is all about process. *Being* up, or down, might afford you, respectively, a nice view or a hot bath, but getting there is what really counts. So maybe we should talk about up*ward* and down*ward*. Which is more important? It's tempting to say that the downward part is everything. That first lift on the first morning seems to take for ever, as you struggle to contain a year of pent-up energy for a few minutes more. You just have to endure it, as a means to an end. But the balance shifts as the day, and the week, progress, and you begin to tolerate, then appreciate, then positively relish that preparatory, mounting phase. Time to get the breath back, check a map. Sneak a snack. While still on the lift you are safe, unpressured, immune to falls or stylistic criticism. You can affect frustration at the enforced immobility, sighing at the sight of others whizzing on down, even criticise their styles with impunity. Meanwhile your oh-so-grateful legs try desperately to recover for the next run.

He let out an inch or so of the now tepid water and topped up with hot. And what of the ups and downs of love – the other leg of this, oscillating, even plodding, metaphor? Well, metaphorically, Malcolm had so far spent most of his time on the lift. A creaking, creeping, single-chair lift, it often felt. True, he'd been down a few nursery slopes, and the occasional gentle, 'blue run'. But he yearned for more precipitous descents, voluptuous moguls, waist-deep powdery romps.

So what was stopping him? Was his natural alpine wariness somehow carrying over on to the slopes of romance? After all, those had their own corresponding set of hazards: the analogues of rocks and ice, avalanches and crevasses. What's more, there was no piste map, and you entered with minimal padding and insulation. A man could get vertigo and anoxia. Not to mention fractures and frostbite. You just couldn't prepare too carefully for such an environment. Hence the hours of lingering on the upward lift, plotting, agonising, flexing muscles and polishing the goggles in anticipation.

But in Inglberg he had been keeping himself open to possibilities – casually announcing his next day's route at the dinner table. And on the slopes he'd kept his eyes peeled, waving and smiling effusively at a dozen girls skiing alone in sleeky red suits, and, more cautiously, at several more trailing matronly partners. All to no avail.

Some possibilities came and went fast. After some agonising he'd boycotted the Schpindlhof's New Year Disco to which, Peregrine had informed everybody, everybody was going. He'd even gone to bed early and woken up only briefly at the sound of distant fireworks around the magic midnight hour and then some trampling on the stairs a while later.

There was always tomorrow. At least for several days there had been. And of course the last day was the best day to let go, to risk all. To get hurt, if it came to that. If it should come to nothing then it would be a lesser loss. And if he did manage to forge some provisional links with her – or whoever – so late in the day, they could always be maintained and strengthened back home. Back home there were no winding pistes for high-speed hide and seek, but there were telephones, and postal services. Then walks in the park, ducks to feed, mugs, or dainty cups, of tea. Sandwiches to share.

Malcolm pulled out the plug. The metaphorical lift was close to the top station. Tomorrow was crunch time.

Mind you there was always the summit restaurant in which to finally fortify yourself for the off.

Chapter 14

A Room without a View

Lunchtime already, and not a single book written! Outside it was still snowing hard, though this was not known to Malcolm, because for several long minutes he'd been resisting the urge to check. A watched pot never boils, as his old granny never stopped saying. And he had resolved to stifle his curiosity until he'd written at least another word. Every little bit counts, as his other old granny used to say. (Mercifully all his younger grannies were less proverbose.)

In frustration he wrote a word. It was monosyllabic, four-lettered, and didn't fit the context at all well. He paused, and then scrubbed it out for fear of sharp-eyed waitresses, totally failing to appreciate that he'd just generated and destroyed what could be seen as the world's shortest story.

He turned to take his dubiously earned look out and saw the snow was still falling. Only just though – the wind was carrying it at a grazing angle to the horizontal. That didn't help, of course, because all of that being blown out of view to the right was being made up for by that being blown in from the left. And God, or somebody, was sending the stuff with an alarming density and speed. Malcolm wondered just how many such flakes were held fleetingly within the area of the window. He closed his eyes fast and hard to freeze-burn a sample image on the retinas, which he then introspected at relative leisure. He reckoned around a thousand swarmed in each frame. And every one different, so they said. (Well, all except one, anyway – there'd have to be a designated standard for comparison, a reference flake.)

Why did *they* always say that? He'd heard one of *them* make that very claim just two hours before in the lift queue, with the same confidence (springing from who knows where) with which *they* assert the equality of all men, the insensitivity of fish to pain, and the likeness of peas in a pod. It seemed there was no part of nature that was spared their pronouncements. What made them so sure? It was hard to say. But probably the same thing that compelled all those teachers and preachers to relentlessly compare life itself to common fruits and kitchen utensils. What a nerve! It would serve them all right if they were greeted at the gates of hell by an indignant and bloodthirsty audience of scotched myths and proverbial counter-examples from the natural world, anxious to set the record straight. Malcolm pictured a Noah's-ark-style queue, with snowflake twins (who through their identity and their solid refusal to melt cocked a double snook at conventional wisdom), recalcitrant lemmings with a lust for life, and parched and weary camels jostling with amnesiac elephants for ringside seats in the arena. All of them eager to test the legendary intransigence of Homo sapiens.

He opened his eyes. It was still snowing. The visibility was poor enough to reduce even good skiers to a snail's pace. He said the word he'd just written, unerasably, but *sotto voce* – well aware of its Germanic origins. Waitresses, as well as walls, had ears, as well as eyes. It fitted the context perfectly. Purgatory is the lasting blizzard on the last day.

But Malcolm was skilled in the art of self deception. Unconsciously he knew that by staring out until some kind of accommodation set in (the kind which, taken to an extreme, would lead to snow blindness) you could begin to believe that the average snowflake area was decreasing. And if you switched your gaze suddenly outwards from the relative gloom of a cafe interior it was easy to think that the sky was lightening. And by moving the eyes in a rapid scanning diagonal you could track and freeze the flaky trails, eventually persuading yourself of an increase in the mean inter-flake distance. So why hadn't it stopped snowing?

Paradoxical stuff, snow.

Of all the things which might fall out of the sky on you – radioactive isotopes, albatross droppings, fragments of glowing Boeing – snow was surely the least offensive. But responses to it varied enormously. The sprinkling which had settled in the night back home just before Malcolm's departure was to him a titillating aperitif. But not to everybody.

'Isn't it awful!' a passing neighbour had hissed. She was middle-aged but perfectly able-bodied.

'What's that?' said Malcolm, affecting grave concern, 'I didn't hear the news this morning.'

'No no, I mean *this*.' She pointed an accusing finger at the 5 millimetres of glistening powder clinging to the trees.

'Oh. I thought it was rather pretty.'

She'd given him a look normally reserved for the irretrievably dense, and shuffled off to panic-buy bread and candles.

Snow on snow.

He had carefully planted his skis a little way outside the window of the Schpindlhütte (Altitude 1948 m) where he could watch over them. Though he'd had to move tables to maintain a clear view when a large party of large Germans arrived and promptly fenced them off with lankier palings of their own. Parked out there, red on white, signalling his determination not to give in to the weather, they functioned, too, as a crude snow gauge. Since his arrival the level had crept up beyond the rear bindings, but in spite of this extra support the skis had tilted apart to form a capital V-sign, copiously adorned *avec serifs* of stick straps and safety bindings, waving in the wind. Would they carry him on one final fling – the season's swan-song descent – before their return to the hire shop? Or would he have to ride down ignominiously? Like that time in Grindledorf when an irreparable goggle defect forced him to squander a day's food's worth of potential energy in heating up the bearings and brake drums of the Grindleberg Gondelbahn.

He'd had three drinks so far – each accompanied by a totally unrequited flirtation with a different literary form. Perhaps, after all, he should have persevered with the postcards, however painful the struggle and pathetic the results usually were. Only a small fraction of the cards he'd ever bought abroad had landed on anyone's doormat, and these all bore the signs of protracted and painful generation, usually starting 'Dear Auntie', continuing only very briefly in a different coloured pen, and carrying an embarrassingly legible UK postmark.

Earlier he'd got just as far as filling in, in his best writing, the addresses and salutations on the backs of six views of the Inglberg glacier. Six identical views. He'd long ago given up scouring the shops for different cards to suit the imagined tastes of individual recipients. Variety was quite unnecessary. Relations were cordial amongst his parents and the various aunties, but their meetings were confined to weddings and funerals, where the only coincidences likely to be noted were of hats, hairdos and digestive disorders. Then Malcolm had sat frozen for half an hour, pen hovering, dismissing one opening line after another. "Having a nice time" seemed a rather feeble response to the Christmas tie or postal order (though there'd been one particular pair of socks which deserved no better). Then in desperation he'd ordered a Glühwein and switched to an essay on Hegelian Idealism, breaking at a stroke his two most recent resolutions, outlawing homework on holiday and booze before lunch. In the event, though, neither infringement was to last more than five minutes.

Snow on snow on snow.

Funny stuff, snow. They claimed (that is, those narrow-minded but widely cited myth makers again) that Eskimos had forty-seven different words for it. They (the Eskimos, that is) would probably deny this, even if it were true (and there were plenty of myth *breakers* who said it wasn't), just as we'd deny having twelve different words for "month". Funny stuff.

Snow on snow on snow.

He found himself talking to himself, realised that was silly, and gave himself a good telling off. He would never have admitted, except perhaps to himself, just how often he had to do this or just *how* silly was the content of these conversations. If that's what they were. According to a popular psychology book he'd recently read we all thought that no one else's mental goings-on could possibly be as ridiculous as our own. But, let's face it, he told himself, excluding the possibility of a dead heat, one of us is right. So just in case it's you, I'd better keep quiet.

This all led to an ingenious attempt to bootstrap himself out of literary infertility by starting on a story about someone trying to write a story about someone who was trying to write . . . and so on, in a long and convoluted spiral, triggered by his own all-too-real and problematic case, and leading to a purely fictional central core of terminal writer's block. It would be a singular, if circular, saga, replete with Russellian self-reference yet logically coherent and compelling, in a house-that-Jack-built kind of way, but avoiding any need for that most elusive commodity, substance. He'd filled the better part of a table napkin in this way, skirting around the Schpindlhütte Cafe logo (bopping chamois sporting bobble hat and furry boots) in spindly biro, folding in the nested layers of complexity, along with some flaky Strudel fragments, as he progressed.

But he returned from the briefest of visits to the gents to find it gone. Had it become over-burdened with its own recursiveness and imploded in a puff of Gödelian paradox, taking with it the coffee cup, saucer, spoon, dregs and dribbles, but not, for some reason, the cruet of "Maggi" Kraut or the quiver of toothpicks? Or had it fallen victim to a swooping waitress? Whatever, he had neither the nerve nor the German to pursue it further. So, maybe it was going to have to be a novel.

Over an abstemious Apfelsaft he considered just how many books it was he'd so far failed to write. It all depended on how you counted. An infinite number, in a sense. Though perhaps to say so was to be a bit hard on himself – no writer, or indeed non-writer, could fail to fail to write that many, even on a good day. His first truly authentic failure, though, had been at the just-less-than-innocent age of ten, sparked off by the least uninspiring Christmas present he'd had from the very Auntie to whom he had only just now not written. It was a one-off, anomalous Enid Blyton, sandwiched between the long series of annual sweeties and socks, stretching back to the year he was born in and forward to the one she would die in. As much as anything he was stimulated by the title – formulaic, banally alliterative, yet full of an unknown promise. All he needed to do, he reckoned, was modify the successful recipe enough to avoid any copyright wrangles.

Thus the Secret Seven were exposed, assonanced and inflated to become a Blatant Eight – namely, Amanda, Lucinda, Angela,

Deborah, Melissa, Priscilla, Malcolm, and Bob (as her friends teasingly dubbed Roberta, the shortness of whose hair – it was merely halfway down her back – made her the only possible candidate for token tomboy). And we mustn't forget the uncounted Rex, the multifunctional, token dog – sniffer-out of vital clues, catalyst in the long-grass rough-and-tumble, faithful shepherder of the nymphs. Until, that is, his brief, incapacitating encounter (planned for Chapter 2) with a pantechnicon, the very vehicle suspected by the youthful sleuths of being used to smuggle gold bullion.

But Malcolm's first fantasy never got beyond the Society's inaugural meeting in the large and airy attic of Amanda's house (there was to be an alphabetic rotation of hostess to ensure variety in the catering and a democratic distribution of joist fatigue). There they pledged loyalty and laid plans, braving cobwebs and spiders in the candle-lit sanctuary. On hand was a bountiful mother who, by unspoken agreement, never ventured further up the ladder than was necessary to pass a tray of lemonade and fairy cakes through the hatchway, swiftly retreating with an indulgent smile and drawing altogether spurious comfort from the proverbial safety of numbers.

Snow on snow on snow on snow.

It was hard to know where the snow stopped and the snow began. It really did seem less heavy now but the light was fading fast. His skis beckoned rudely, as did the short pedestrian path from the cafe to the top lift station. He agonised a moment longer, then gave in. Better safe and sorry.

The descent seemed unusually slow. Maybe the high winds had forced the lift operators into low gear. Yes, he'd done the sensible thing. Damn it. The gondola cabin sank below the tree-line. Malcolm pressed his nose against the cool of the window, but had to keep moving it every few seconds to avoid the resulting local fog patches. Each exhalation wrote a translucent pair of inverted commas on the perspex. A memorable nasal quotation to greet any occupants of ascending cabins.

Ears popped at the increasing pressure, spirits sank with the dwindling altitude. His senses were in disarray. Let-downs didn't come any more literal than this. He would have been extra mad if he'd known that in returning his unspent potential energy he was helping to raise two enormous Germans who would find, between snow-stop and true dusk, a tiny window for one last ski run.

Chapter 15

Those Boots

It was getting dark when Malcolm arrived back down in the village centre. In another hour his hired boots would be walking on doubly borrowed time. This he couldn't risk – notices in the ski shop in three languages boldly declared that a whole extra day's rental was the penalty for any tardy skiing Cinderellas. But there was time for a quick après-non-ski loiter over a consoling drink.

On the threshold of the Schpindlhof Cafe he executed a brief but spirited snow-removing dance. Then he pushed open the heavy glass door and clumped in. The familiar, alien voice that greeted him was impossible to locate with any precision, being distributed through a dozen separate loudspeakers. These had been wedged in wall recesses, slung inaccessibly from roof beams, or secreted behind ceiling panels. It was an ingeniously robust set-up, the speaker cabinets sturdy, boot-proof, bomb-proof affairs – a direct hit on the place by an artillery shell would probably have left several still working. The voice poured out its usual gleeful lamentation of the world's predicament. In self defence Malcolm sprayed a volley of hateful glances back up at the many sources of sound. To no effect. Looking on the bright side, though, he reckoned he must have missed at least nine verses of this particular song, because Mr Dylan was already up to that bit where he breathed in and out through a harmonica for eight bars.

Most of the inhabitants of Chalet Pengel were gathered around a large pine table, in the middle of which was a mountain range of steaming anoraks, gloves and goggles. He squeezed in between Peregrine and Gemma – his apologies to them for the intimacy respectively totally heartfelt and totally specious – and ordered what would be his very last Glühwein of the trip. Although an inner compartment of his wallet still held a thin cushion of Schillings, these were strictly for emergencies. Or possibly presents. He was depending on being able to change them back into sterling to help him survive the Spring Term.

Meanwhile, in the foreground, the universal soldier of song trooped on, his message of doom unheeded by the cafe's many suppers of grog and gorgers of Apfelstrudel. Most people seemed to be able to talk, read and even sleep through this kind of stuff. Lucky devils. Poor Malcolm simply didn't have the option, having been born with two deep, cylindrical holes, one on either side of his head, which led to fancy transduction mechanisms, with connecting nerve paths all the way up to the auditory cortex. Quite a handicap. If you lived on Earth.

'Have a good last day?' Malcolm turned to Gemma and raised his glass.

'I'll try. They say the weather's going to clear.'

He gave her a puzzled look. 'Aren't you going home tomorrow?'

'No! Sunday. Are *you*?'

He was about to say 'of course.' But there was no *of course* about it. True, Brindles had said one week, and weeks have seven days. But weeks also have ends. And weren't weekends for travelling? He took a slurp from his glass. Then, how many ends does a week have? *Two*, arguably. But if so they must be regarded as only one day long each. Surely. He took a second slurp, or was it the third? In principle that could mean he had six, seven or even eight days, depending on how you counted. Not to mention one more or one fewer nights. Malcolm felt his simple-arithmetic grip slipping. The innocent, everyday week held little surprises packed away in its folds. It was beginning to seem more like one of those club sandwiches in which the multiple, varied layers conspire together to tease the would-be consumer – defying the eye to distinguish boundary from content, end from middle from other end, the identity and function of each element being lost in the anonymity of the crowd.

But in the middle of all this confusion were some crumbs of comfort. Here, perhaps, was a brief reprieve from homegoing. Time for another drink then? Maybe. Then again, maybe not. Any extra day he might have been awarded would need funding. Abstinence, not celebration, was in order here.

Checks around the table seemed to show Sunday as the favoured day of departure, and led to a very public discussion over when Malcolm should leave Ingleberg. Unsure how to interpret this sudden solicitude he found himself fielding a volley of enquiries.

'Who did you come with?'

'I'm on my own.'

'No, I mean which tour company?'

'Frobisher, I think.'

'They're just the operators.'

'Are they?'

'Yeah, who did you actually *book* with?'

'Brindles.'

'Oh, that's just Alpine.'

'It is?'

'Yes. Who's the actual, like, company?'

'I'm not sure. Flyaway?'

'Flyaway's a flight company.'

'Oh, right. I seem to remember there was a mention of Snowscene.'

'They only do tickets. Sure it wasn't Sun Seekers?'

'No.'

'Or, Overland, they *are* part of Panorama . . .?'

'*Were*! Till it went bankrupt.' There were knowing snorts of agreement from around the table.

'They never should have bought it really.'

'Everybody saw it coming.'

'. . . and they use the same handling agents.'

He tried to look grateful for all this information.

'Maybe you should phone them.'

'Who? Exactly?' said Malcolm.

'You!'

'But, *they*'ll have gone home by now. Surely,' said Malcolm, with an almost convincing tone of disappointment. Hope was still stirring.

'Well, you could always wait outside the Schpindlhof tomorrow. With your luggage. They do *ad hoc* pick-ups around 6.30 am.'

'*Who* does?'

'All of 'em do. I think.'

'You might as well stay on and go with the rest of us. There's always spare seats on the plane anyway.'

'Very few. This time of year.'

'Well there's nearly always one next to me' said Peregrine triumphantly, putting an end to the discussion.

Malcolm knew that his fate would be written unambiguously on the return portion of the flight ticket, and, if there were still any doubt (and even if there weren't), faintly but still legibly repeated on the attached carbon. All this was safely tucked away in his passport, hidden in a pocket of a combination-locked suitcase, camouflaged by a week's washing (a not inconsiderable deterrent and diversion) in the bottom of a wardrobe in a locked room up the road at Chalet Pengel. Such manifold security was part of his routine. He would check the departure date before dinner. Maybe. You could be forgiven for not doing so. For assuming, by default, that you were meant to depart along with those you'd arrived with. If that turned out to be a mistake it would be an easy one to have made.

But, then, possibly a very pricey one. How understanding might Brindles, or Flyaway, or whoever it was, turn out to be? But they wouldn't leave him on the tarmac. Would they? He looked to his right and caught a smile from Gemma. Maybe the vagaries of time designation and travel-company interrelations had their uses after all. Damn it. He would *not* look at his ticket. He'd let a cast die lie. Probably.

The decision almost made, he could now risk a rational analysis of the situation. Could he afford to accept this windfall of a post-ultimate day? Physically, yes. Financially, no. His planning in these two respects had been geared to a Saturday-morning departure. This meant that on account of today's weather he was bodily underexerted and facially underexposed to UV photons – deficiencies that could be neatly remedied tomorrow. Weather permitting. But extending equipment hire and lift pass would more than totally exhaust his Schilling reserves.

But then again, there would be still several extra mealtimes to go, each affording the chance to slightly overeat and to squirrel away supplies for the return journey, and beyond. He could hitchhike home from the airport. Or even walk. That would further heighten the soothing sense of penitence. With luck the almost inevitable flight delay would mean he'd miss the last bus. In which case he'd be saving a taxi fare and not just a bus fare!

And come to think of it, wasn't there a half-crown wedged under a leg of his study desk, as an anti-tilt measure? This could easily be swapped for a threepenny bit, or even three halfpennies. It was weeks, too, since he'd probed down the back of the armchair in his room for coins. With a few such little acts of enterprise and austerity he'd survive the term. He downed the rest of his drink.

One residual worry was that he'd completely run out of clean socks. He'd have to wash a pair and dry them overnight. This risked a repeat of that time in Finkelwald when, after an exceptional temperature plummet, he'd snapped the left one in removing it from the balcony rail. Luckily the fracture was not longitudinal, but rather in the plane parallel to the top hem of the open end. As a result he was simply able to wear both bits, re-uniting them properly on his return home with sturdy, if ill-matching, darning wool.

The call of the hire shop having faded and his precise degree of destitution now less clear he ordered a second Glühwein. There had arisen an additional reason for lingering. It came in the form of a mild, unresisted pressure on his right ski boot. And it was coming from Gemma's left. But who had been the initiator, he wondered? Who was pressing whom? Well, that was an almost meaningless question – mechanically speaking. Newton's Third Law tells us that force is a mutual kind of thing. *If body A exerts a force on body B then body B exerts an equal and opposite force on body A.* A simple appeal to physics confers a symmetry of guilt and innocence on the alleged presser and pressee. He resisted the temptation to turn towards Body *B*, positively savouring the uncertainty.

Funny things, ski boots. Their great mass and rigidity came from the need for firm linkage between legs and skis, to cope with the rigours of braking and tight turns. But when off duty they would seem to present serious barriers to intimacy. However, liberties of approach could be taken under the cover of their very clumsiness. And at the end of the day they could be undone and removed! Yes, there was promise in this brutish encounter.

Malcolm sipped at the new drink. What a pity though, he thought, that Newton III doesn't automatically extend to the affections. For he, Body A, was very *interested* in Body B, and reciprocation was devoutly to be wished. The situation called for serious lingering. But then tea time was the perfect setting for pre-seduction manoeuvres. While the leisurely, vicarage overtones put both parties nicely off guard, could the night be any younger?

To complete the picture of innocence Malcolm had been turned attentively to the left, listening with a fixed smile and gritted teeth to Peregrine's tale of recent battle with the elements on the Inglstein. To help maintain the smile Body A pictured Body P exploring a deep crevasse C with acceleration g. Meanwhile, beneath the table, the pressure hadn't diminished. Emboldened, he allowed a subtle increase in the inter-boot force. The response was optimally encouraging – yielding, with just a hint of token resistance; compliant, but no pushover. He could afford another day. Surely.

Confident of ground gained on the tactile front, he turned to consolidate his position through the more usual verbal and visual channels, only to see the supposed occupant of the boots toddling back woolly-socked from the bar, both hands clutched around a cocktail glass brimming with fruit and umbrellas. Then the music got louder.

Malcolm sighed and re-buckled his own boots lightly for the climb to Chalet Pengel. There, after some minutes of indecision, he dug out the return half of his plane ticket. Printed on it in bold, black, unmisreadable figures was tomorrow's date. His week had ended. He skied back down the road to the hire shop, return-trip town shoes laced around his neck. It was his first and last run of the day, and with almost a foot of newly fallen snow, one of the bluest he'd ever done.

Chapter 16

Living Standards

Days and nights. Weeks and ends. Vacations and terms.

The term *term*, originally, indicated an end, limit or boundary. That is, a point in space, rather than a space between points. Or a point in time, rather than a period stretching between such points. It still has a lingering feeling of something more instantaneous than intervallic. You could be forgiven for thinking that the Easter Term, for example, marked the end, or possibly the start, or even the middle, of Easter – instead of, in reality, being some period just leading up *to*, and finishing a bit *before* it. What's more, while the Autumn Term starts in Autumn, the Summer Term starts, arguably, in Spring. Winter doesn't seem to get a mention. Confusion reigns. Then there's Michaelmas, Epiphany, Hilary, Lent and Trinity, beloved of some older and posher universities. Perhaps this proliferation was a vain attempt to avoid those other, simpler-sounding, but most uncertain, terms.

Slippery stuff. No wonder we go wrong. If we're going to count we must be sure what it is we're counting, and where to start. And end. Often dismissed as academic, these distinctions are far from trivial. Ignore them and you may even risk life and limb . . .

'Ready?' says Teacher, 'after three; one, *two, three . . .*'

On the word *three*, two of the enlisted pupils, at the treble end of the hefty upright Bechstein, start to lift and shove. Obedient Meta-Malcolm 15, at the bass end, along with Teacher himself, is preparing to lift on the unspoken *four*. M-M receives a whack on the left shin, several stubbed right toes, and a priceless lesson on the importance of synchrony in cooperative ventures.

Decades later the wiser M-M 65 lies supine at the bottom of a gully, awaiting the critical transfer to a stretcher by the four mountain-rescue volunteers, just arrived on the scene. His walking holiday in the Cairngorms is not going to plan. He feels little pain, which means either he's not badly hurt, or some neural pathway is critically damaged. The team take hold of a limb apiece.

'Right', says the leader, 'after three.'

'Wait!' shouts M-M. The team freezes. 'I'd be much happier if you all lifted me *on* three.'

'We're going as fast as we can!' says left-arm.

'The helicopter's on its way!' says right-leg.

M-M has no time for analytical discussions. 'Just humour me,' he groans, 'it's kind of a superstition.'

They finally comply with much eye rolling and head shaking.

The lift is a model of coordination. Within a week the patient has made a full recovery.

Thus can a moment of seeming pedantry prevent permanent paralysis.

But the Easter Term really is an interval. And even by the standards of school and college life it's a pretty drab one. Somehow featureless, unsure of its own status. Perhaps because of being sandwiched in, and partially eclipsed by, its more celebrated celestial boundaries: the winter solstice and spring equinox. Or, more mundanely, by the corresponding vacations.

Malcolm was not looking forward to it. He'd be even broker than usual, on account of the ski trip. Busier too, probably. And lonely? Possibly. Luckily, just before it began, he managed to squeeze in a week or so of home cooking. He was much heartened by the familiar faces, of parents, brothers, even the odd aunty, along with the plentiful, and free, kilocalorie absorption which would give him a head start on the funding front.

But after that it was back to a familiar diet.

'Yes dear?'

'I'd like a cheese and tomato sandwich, please.'

'How many?'

Malcolm frowned. 'Just one. Please.'

'You mean, like, just one sandwich?' Hilda waved her hands back and forth above the counter by way of clarification.

'Yes.'

'Like, two rounds?'

He raised his eyebrows. 'Is that the same as one sandwich?'

'Well, it depends how many you want.'

'No, it depends on how *you* define a sandwich.'

'Sorry?'

He cleared his throat. 'I said, it depends on how *you* define a sandwich.'

'What does, dear?'

He sighed. 'Whether two rounds is the same as one sandwich.'

Hilda adjusted her apron. 'What would you like, exactly?'

'I'd like to know how you define a sandwich!'

The words rang out over one of those spontaneous little lulls in the general hubbub. There was a further one second of silence, then a loud collective groan from behind. Malcolm turned to find himself facing a ragged queue of a dozen weary, hungry souls, shifting their weight, rolling their eyes as their lunch half-hour ebbed away. It seemed this wasn't the best time to start a discussion on sandwich nomenclature. He left hurriedly with a packet of plain crisps and a small, unambiguous pork pie.

They say (yes, those blighters are still at it) that tomorrow is another day. It follows, by induction, that the day after tomorrow, when his next sandwich-buying attempt was scheduled, would be another, other day.

They say too (yes, they're *still* still at it) that if you know what question to ask then you're already halfway there. They usually fail to say, though, whether that's on a logarithmic or a linear scale, and sometimes seem unclear as to where *there* is. A cynic might add that if you hadn't bothered to dream up a question in the first place then you wouldn't have a there to have to get to. On whatever scale. But

Malcolm did have a goal – to be able to communicate clearly his simple, modest lunch-time requirements. He now had a specific question to ask:

How do you define a sandwich?

The problem seemed to be never ending. Insoluble. He'd no clear idea of why this was so, but a tedious succession of experimental trials, leading in the main to lunch-time famines or feasts, had established it as a plain, empirical fact. He was evidently long overdue for some theoretical work, some unhurried reflection. But the days of the new Easter Term were packed with lectures and tutorials, and his evenings and weekends with essays and exercises.

And then suddenly he got a break. The respective Professors of Statistics and Epistemology, whose successive turns made up his Friday-afternoon lecture schedule, obliged with synchronised attacks of 'flu. This was a conjunction as improbable as it seemed, since an old feud had ensured that for years the two had never come within spitting distance of one another, in spite of many temptations.

So Malcolm suddenly found himself with a whole half-day off to spend as he pleased. Sandwich-theory time! Those voluminous stacks of the College library beckoned more enticingly than usual. And as a bonus he'd got an excuse to cruise Home Economics – a section whose bays were as famous for harbouring delectable cooks-to-be, as cookery books.

He arrived comprehensively prepared, his top pocket a stockade of sharpened pencils, his shoes shined with a rough paper towel in the gents adjoining Politics & Economics, his hair combed cursorily, as an afterthought, as he hurried through History.

But disappointment was in store. The weekend promised to be unseasonably warm, and that had led to uncharacteristic forward planning among the student body. So, in his area of special interest, far from there being too many cooks (if that were imaginable in this context) there wasn't a single one. Mingling and ogling were out.

Malcolm had no option but to revert to the more serious purpose of his visit.

The better part of one wall was dedicated to mass catering, and no less than a whole shelf to books on snacks and light refreshments. But a flip through the indexes revealed something amazing. Almost all of them passed straight from 'salmonella' to 'sanitation' (and in one case, to 'sausages' – an adjacency that surely violated the most basic hygiene regs).

He replaced the last book with a curse. Only a mild one though. The afternoon was still young. Maybe his search was just too specific. Yes, a broader and more lateral approach was in order.

He crossed to an adjacent bay – a general reference section with a splendid, four-by-four, mahogany-drawered matrix of card-index files. The sixteen curvy, shiny-brass hook handles on the front beckoned the fingers to enquire within. The first drawer slid open on smooth and silent runners, releasing an beguiling mustiness of knowledge. He began to riffle.

His heart skipped a beat at the *Handbook of the Association for Sandwich Education*. But the slim volume that the entry led to contained only lists of schemes for integrating periods of industrial work and college-based study. Likewise, the promising *Catering for Students* proved to be no more than recommendations on residential and classroom accommodation, library facilities and welfare provision. Its location among the journals on nutrition could only have been an oversight, or an act of waggishness on someone's part.

It took only a few further dead-ends and non-starters to persuade him that the domestic-scientific front was simply not going to deliver the goods. Maybe a less culinary and more technical, quantitative domain would be more fruitful. It could hardly be less sandwichful. Yes, it was time to get formal.

So, it was back through History, left at Political Science, right into Engineering Design, and then straight to that wellspring of wisdom and authority, the catalogue of the British Standards Institute. In these trusty, weighty volumes the particulars of every conceivable structure, material and device had been considered and quantified. He found himself a cosy corner and began to browse.

A whole half-hour later he'd waded through scores of pages with not a mention of bread, or butter, or anything that might be built out of them. The emphasis here was heavily on the mechanical. The altogether harder wares. He pressed on with dwindling optimism.

But mounting awe! There was a humble magnificence in this parade of cast-iron spigots, socket soil pipes, watertight glands and high-voltage bus bars; of shackles and shafts, funnels, nozzles and orifices. Not to mention sprockets and gudgeon pins, buffers and manifolds, galvanised studs, suction strainers, snap-head rivets and internally illuminated traffic bollards. Beacons all to British ingenuity and rigour. As well as potential themes for all those inveterate inventors of metaphors and similes for life itself. Any lay preacher scratching his head on a Saturday night for ideas for Sunday morning could surely do worse than browse through (or for a real challenge, stick a pin in) the BSI catalogue. Any congregation, once its appetite had been whetted, would just have to stay awake to find out *why* life was (or even was a bit like) a chlorosulphanated polyethylene rubber-coated-nylon wind sock, a bronze oil-retaining thrust washer, or spiral-wound gasket flange. Wouldn't you?

He read on, enthralled. What cosy assertions of trustworthiness were to be found here! How hopefully you might travel, when such meticulous attention has been paid to the robustness of pneumatic brakes and lift cables; how optimistically embark, knowing some far-sighted soul has already charted the vagaries of bilge, pulp and slurry; with what confidence commit full weight to pitons, paving slabs and manhole covers; and how soundly sleep thanks to strict limits on the ignitability of duvets. All material and mechanical life was here, tabulated and appraised, from the accuracy of carpet-tuft withdrawal-force determination methods, to tests of toxicity to zebra fish.

Other students trickled in, thumbed through a volume, and trickled out again, query resolved. Malcolm watched them a little jealously, feeling further and further from his own goal, half wanting to tear himself away. But each time he was drawn back by the lure of ladder rungs, wood-holding chucks, fishplates, hoists and knotted netting.

He looked up to rest his eyes from the demanding 8-point typeface. Surely this was a bit on the small side, even in a document designed for reference rather than cover-to-cover reading. Weren't there regulations about this sort of thing? There surely were! Indeed somewhere within this very work there'd be a short paragraph in that very font and point size whose purpose was, in effect, to declare its own legibility. He resolved to seek it out on his next visit. Just for the sheer joy of gazing at its self-celebrating self-reference – as you might loiter between pairs of parallel mirrors, or contemplate the word "word" or "dictionary" in a dictionary.

Meanwhile it was back to the conformity of slag and clinker, and stipulations for the fungus proofing of Hessian sandbags.

With the passing pages came a growing awareness of his own glorious heritage. Of Whitworth and Napier, Kelvin and Watt. This was stuff to bring lumps to the throat; every entry a little gnomic hymn – to the consistency of activated sludge, the intricacies of crimp and creep, of warp and rupture.

The journey was a long one. The room warm and quiet. Malcolm rested his head on his hands, pushing the book aside in case he dribbled on it during the doze he felt coming on.

Soon his brain was reverberating with the gentle jingle of toggles and spindle assemblies. Ferrules, cleats and eccentric faceplates danced entwined on the insides of his eyelid screens. Serrated slats, gimbals and trunnions swelled the ranks of grommets, nibblers, winches and wrenches, striding forward, line abreast, to an Elgarian march. And lining the route, cheering hordes of their fellows in prescribed functionality: the bevelled pinions, rasps and ramps, clamps and cladding, knurled nuts and self-splining ratchets.

And that was only Volume 1.

zzzzzzzzzzzzzzzzzzzzzzzzzzzzzzzzzzzzzzzzzzzzzz

Funny things, dreams. Mental tea-breaks. Holidays for the mind, free from all the tyrannies of conventional, blinkered thinking. Cauldrons of creative activity, where fresh ideas bubble up and hitherto intractable problems dissolve. Or so *they* say. It was a dream, allegedly, that revealed to Kekulé the ring structure of benzene, and gave one Elias Howe the idea for the lock-stitch sewing machine.

And what's more, allegedly, these weren't simply chance results which happened to work, filtered out from an astronomical number of meaningless cases which were conveniently forgotten. No. The claim was, rather, that underneath the brain's random surface ripples there are intelligent, guiding currents at work. The pool of monkey typists in your sleepy head harbours some experienced, disciplined members with high wpm counts and an eye for the interests of the boss. So they say. But in the long run, if we're to determine the balance between fluke and design in these dreamt-up ideas, we have a duty to report any and all counterexamples. Tedious as that might be.

So, it would be nice to think that Malcolm awoke with the definitive answer to the sandwich problem. Along with a foolproof formula for dispelling ambiguities of all kinds. But in reality the fruits of his slumber were no more than the usual neck stiffness and mouth staleness, plus a wrist-watch-shaped indentation on his forehead which lasted till tea time.

His book was gone. The now missing gap in the row of volumes above told him the re-shelving fairy had been at work. (Had she watched over his little sleep, smiling? Had she kissed him Good-day?) He carried out the standard combined yawn-stretch-scratch manoeuvre, and realised it was getting late. Half past four. But there was time still for a final investigative fling before closing. Systematic searches had failed. Maybe a less disciplined, *ad hoc* approach was called for. He wandered off with a kind of calculated aimlessness, to see what might turn up.

The complete Oxford English Dictionary may well have two-hundred and fifty thousand main entries and forty-four million words of text in all, but on the subject of sandwiches it's almost as pitifully vague as its lesser shelfmates. The entry contained only a brief mention of the eponymous 18th-Century earl who started it all off, and a structural specification of a vertical section through the item, amounting to

bread, {butter}, beef, {butter}, bread,

in Malcolm's own notation, devised specially for this study. The curly brackets were meant to reflect the claim that the buttery bits might be omitted entirely. This was an option which Malcolm thought unthinkable. In his own experience, though, the two pairs of brackets were much more likely to contain margarine, and in times of particular austerity had blended beeflessly together. But more importantly the OED, final authority on so many things, simply makes no reference to the crucial *area* and *shape* of a slice in plan view.

The only quantitative information he could find anywhere was in Mrs Beeton, who said that to qualify as 'dainty' (and so presumably be suitable as tea-time treats for vicars and their guests, or for the ageing, refined, dentally handicapped) the bread thickness must be less than or equal to three-eighths of an inch. Beyond this it seemed we progressed rapidly to the so-called doorstep (or was it door*stop*?) beloved of blacksmiths and navvies. Was this widely known? he wondered. What insecurity might arise among genteel folk if they discovered that the class distinctions they'd been so confident of might now need to be verified with Vernier callipers?

The Britannica Micropaedia was just as unhelpful. And, amazingly, its Macro brother, which boasted "knowledge in depth" on every one of its thirty-seven gilt-lettered spines, not only had no reference to sandwiches, but by chance acknowledged this very omission, implicitly anyway, on those very spines. In the heat of the chase Malcolm failed to pinpoint his quarry with enough alphabetical precision and to properly inspect the word-index ranges (just legible although the books were on a highish shelf). Otherwise he could have avoided the scaling of the flimsy ladder, and the yet more perilous and wobbly backwards descent with an unwieldy volume under each arm. Because calmer scrutiny at the big mahogany table revealed that Volume 26 finished at *Sacred* and Volume 27 started again at *San Francisco*. So the homely sandwich was banished (along with, more xenophobically, the samba, samovar and sampan) to the wrong side of the covers.

Malcolm, hardly believing such a defect, and suspecting he was being denied occult knowledge, prepared to march indignantly on the enquiry desk. But he was deterred by more sober reflection (augmented, it was true, by the prospect of the formidable Miss Angle, with her implausibly pointed glasses and uncompromising little date stamper). Another day. Maybe.

The ten-minute bell, although designedly discreet, was still shocking in the prevailing silence. It triggered in him a half-conscious, Pavlovian hunger and called him to the exit. On the way he made a last, rapid, and rather hopeless scan of the *Handbook of Chemistry and Physics* and *Pears Cyclopaedia*. Neither of them seemed to have a single reference to anything edible.

Chapter 17

Sounds of Silence

So, the chase had been fun, but it was an empty-handed hunter who returned to his room, eyes bleary, pencils unblunted. Ahead of him loomed an evening of homework – line integrals and Schopenhauer, will-power permitting. Or maybe matrices and Locke. He sighed and flopped into a chair. Or even probability and Spinoza. Though not just any old permutation of these things. Malcolm would always try to choose a pairing which was endurable and digestible, as you might mix equally dull but complementary ingredients in a peasant diet. But which should come first? The easier, as a warm-up? Or the harder, as an anaesthetic?

Joint-degree studies abound with these little dilemmas: Scyllas & Charybdises, sticks and carrots. Frying pans and fires. Still, he could always flip a coin (and then of course do the opposite of what was indicated – there was nothing more annoying than being dictated to by a dumb piece of metal). But an hour or so of each subject would ease his conscience, and justify a small alcoholic reward in the Union Bar. A hard bargain, perhaps, for a Friday evening.

And the prospects for the rest of Easter term were equally bleak. What with upcoming tests and other assessments. The title of his 2nd-year dissertation had to be submitted and approved within a fortnight. Not to mention the 10000-word thing itself by the end of the term. The countdown was well underway. Months earlier he'd marked the deadline in bold red capitals, and noted with relief the good few millimetres of diary pages that could be pinched between finger and thumb, between now and then. At that stage it was more comforting to think of the intervening period in mass-noun terms – look how *much* time is left! But in order to keep up the self deception as that time ticked on he'd had to switch to a count noun – look how *many* days there are still to go! More than fifty. More than enough. If only he could concentrate.

Part of the reason the sandwich problem had been dominating his thoughts was that it made such an attractive distraction from essays and maths-problems. Whenever the academic pressure was high he found a new fascination in routine things – precision trimming of toenails and pencil points, marshalling rubber bands and paper clips, flossing teeth, rounding up different coloured biro caps and re-uniting them with their matching biro bodies. His little study/bedroom offered an inexhaustible supply of engaging hygienic and administrative tasks to call on whenever any serious work beckoned.

But the problem did have content. Real, meaty content. On the purely practical side there was the regularly recurring famine or glut whenever communications with the canteen staff went awry. More importantly though, there was a principle at stake. Things ought to be properly defined. Or at least capable of being defined. Or at the very least, if they aren't, then people should acknowledge that they aren't, and be willing to talk about the matter. The world's a busy place. Sometimes a vague and complex one. But it's one thing to fail to be specific, through inability, laziness, carelessness, tiredness, or just lack of interest. It's quite another to perpetrate that failure and then implicitly defend it by treating confused seekers after clarification as trouble-makers and deviants. That's adding logical insult to contingent injury.

Ping! Malcolm flicked on the switch of his Anglepoise lamp, provoking faint, resonant twangs of its several springs – quite discordant *en masse*, but surprisingly scalic when sounded separately. After a bit of practice he'd learned to play the opening of *Teddy Bears' Picnic* on them with a biro. In fact only the previous Saturday night he'd confided this curiosity to a first-year zoologist in a conversation shoehorned between records at the Hall disco. But even with the promise of this musical bonus she'd still declined the offer of a cup of coffee *chez* Malcolm. He was currently working on something altogether more virtuosic.

Someone somewhere in the block turned on a record player, and a voice, unmistakable despite the low-pass filtering effect of concrete and carpet, grated into gear. In fact the source was three rooms north of, two east of and one below his own. But once any sound got into the structure it carried through the whole building unattenuated, re-radiating from every wall and window. In this hellish haven of acoustic democracy all residents were equally favoured and tormented.

The perpetrator, now seated again at his study-desk, elbows firmly planted, eyes rapidly glazing over, was about to become the only party in Gray Hall not sharing the musical experience, by falling fast asleep. (To be fair it was a *very* boring book he was reading.) While the stack of LPs on his *Dansette* autochanger held out, and indeed for ever after, he would remain immune to complaint or retaliation by virtue of being unlocatable. In any case he would have been amazed to learn he was intruding on anyone as remote as Malcolm. But, acoustic flukes apart, was there any conceivable distance, short of astronomical, which would have lent the much-needed enchantment to such a singer, to such a lengthy compilation of dirges?

Insults and injuries. There was a lot more to this sandwich business. Something altogether deeper. The lunchtime confusion was just the tip of a logical iceberg lurking in murky waters. Waters which begged to be plumbed. And what were philosophers if not intellectual plumbers? Something deeper. Deep enough for ten thousand words, he wondered? Deep enough to satisfy an exam board? Maybe. It would have to be very carefully handled. Malcolm picked up a pencil – an HB Staedtler – and stuck it between his teeth.

Even if he managed to get his tutor's approval for the general idea, any mention of sandwiches, snacks or packaged food in the title might draw premature disapproval from the more conservative examiners. What's more references to such things would have to be minimal in the text itself. Although it was the inspiration for the whole study he'd have to smuggle in the familiar sandwich as a particular, *ad hoc*, light-hearted example. As if an afterthought. Other philosophical writers (at least a certain eminent, older subset of them) were allowed to do this. Why not him? His specific obsession would be camouflaged by generality. And while he was about it he could rope in all those other confusions associated with beginnings and ends, posts and spaces, intervals and instants. He removed the pencil and tried to balance it on its end.

In fact the whole business of ambiguity was ripe for a working over. Properly peppered with references, garnished with a few fancy phrases and well wrapped up in rigorous analysis the discussion might well fulfil the stated criteria (relevance, timeliness, originality, and all that) for a passable dissertation. And, who knows, later he might even persuade the publishers of Britannica to accept parts of it as a pamphlet – to be slipped into the Encyclopaedia as Volume 26a, the Sandwich Supplement (or at the very least an addendum pasted into the beginning of Volume 27, or the end of Volume 26). Or, should it turn out to offer the ultimate (or even penultimate) solution to the posts-and-spaces problem, it could become Volume 0. Then his life's mission would be to travel the world, Gideon style, leaving a complimentary copy in every roadside cafe and catering-college library.

The distant *Dansette* autochanger pickup politely stepped aside to allow another disc to drop. It then planted itself back in the outer groove. Two seconds of hiss. Then a song a lot like the one that had just finished. Only longer.

Malcolm began to nibble the pencil. It was always a bit of a gamble to submit work on an original topic. But there were high-grade pay-offs for those who dared and won. The alternative was to play safe and choose from the official list of suggested titles. A list which had been unchanged for decades. And that so often led to submissions which were waffly and formulaic. He'd seen enough of these in the work of his predecessors.

'. . . *Kant, of course, claimed that* {Blah blah blah}, *whereas Hegel felt rather that* {Blah di blah di blah}. *But then one may question whether these viewpoints are really incompatible, for after all, as Schopenhauer put it,* {Blah di di blah blah} . . .' and so on.

Once pre-fabricated these structures could be padded out, re-ordered and recycled, with only the names of the combatants changed to fit the given title. With such a *Philosophisches Würfelspiel* you could generate a whole series of 3000-word essays from a pool of 300 words.

All it required of the "author" was the disposition, courage and integrity of a wrestling promoter.

Such servility was unthinkable to Malcolm. He was happier to expend a lot of midnight oil and ingest many a pencil end in the quest for originality. His own use of quotation was sparing. So much so that by forgetting to close inverted commas in the *Introduction* of a first-year project report, he had effectively attributed the bulk of the work to Thomas Aquinas, including an Appendix with the spec. of the 741 Operational Amplifier, and several dozen lines of FORTRAN code. This peculiar case of inverted plagiarism went unnoticed by candidate and examiners alike, and the slim, spiral-bound volume was duly consigned to his tutor's bookshelves, where it sat undusted and unread alongside dozens of its fellows.

He aimed the desklamp at the notepad in front of him, wrote AMBIGUITY at the top, and underlined it. Then he underlined the underlining, and broke for coffee.

Under the brief but merciful masking of water hammer from the cold tap Dylan gave way to Leonard Cohen. Then, by coincidence, or maybe some kind of musical contagion, another inmate (three rooms south, two west and one above) put on the same record, rather fainter and half a song behind, giving the impression that Mr C. was performing in some dismal and unimaginably vast canyon.

There's a limit to how long even a large mug of coffee can be made to last. Especially if you like it hot, as some do and Malcolm most certainly did. It helped if you used the notepad as a heat-retaining cover – though that did tend to produce odd-looking water marks, which weirdly came and went over the following weeks. It also meant that writing had to be suspended. And it drew attention to that yawning, accusing, waiting white space.

So, 'what *is* ambiguity?' he began again boldly, pausing a whole half minute before adding 'It depends what we *mean* by ambiguity' and then wisely declining to pursue the realisation that much also depended on what we meant by *what*. Not to mention *is*. But this was to be the first draft. The very first, no less. If not the zeroth. The most preliminary of sketches.

It certainly was a funny thing, though. Ambiguity. Was it even a single thing? No less a figure than Empson distinguished no fewer than seven types. And took a book to do so. Malcolm would have to be more restrained, limiting himself to the vaguenesses of wholes and halves, boundaries and interfaces. All those things which snared the unwary consumers and vendors who, mistaking commonness for simplicity, underestimated the subtleties of sandwich structure, the slipperiness of starts, middles and ends. He scribbled a few keywords, then passed on to a rather more concrete and much more familiar question. *What is a sandwich?*

There were by now seven channels of music competing for Malcolm's attention. Worst of all, it was more or less a dead heat. Taken together they formed a fair representation of the strident yet essentially pessimistic spirit of the 'sixties – 3 Bob Dylans, 2 Leonard Cohens, one Joan Baez and a Radio One program which played all three, albeit in rotation. As each sound source had entered the fray its turner-on set the volume high enough to mask out all the others. Mercifully the fabric of the building had just enough absorption to stop the escalation short of acoustic meltdown.

The means of sound distribution were the usual much-loved but modest and battered, lo-fi student models: two *Dansettes*, two *Bushes*, two *Grundigs* and a *Pye*. All had a fair share of worn idler wheels, perished rubber bands, jaded speaker cones, and blunt and wobbly styluses. The resultant smearing of pitches and tempi was the last straw, daubing the already dense musical wattle into a suffocating, impenetrable, jungly wall of sound. Driving one to distraction.

Malcolm sighed and plugged in his trump card – a magnificently unportable valve radio he'd rescued from the family loft, as a going-away present to himself. He twirled the big, brown bakelite tuning knob, surfing the Medium Wave in silence, until a polyglottal crescendo signalled that the cathodes had reached full glow. Then onwards, past the voices of Hilversum, Leipzig, Vienna and Budapest, to that realm beyond the border where the magic static reigned.

Useful stuff, static. Wide-band vanquisher of lesser sounds. Omnipotent. Omnipresent. The very ether made audible. With a tweak of the tone control, and a bit of imagination, it could be whatever you wanted – distant surf, a summer rainstorm. Even a waterfall. Malcolm adjusted the volume till the balmy, off-white noise (each loudspeaker and cabinet added a little spectral tinge of its own) bathed the whole room with its shimmering, eclipsing infinity. Political causes, protest singers, DJs and radio stations all are destined to fade in and out. In the end it is the random noise, that pre-echo of the heat death of the universe, which shall overcome. Malcolm sat back in his chair and began to think again. Radio Nought (as he'd dubbed this oasis at the dial's end) was wonderful!

Chapter 18

WANTED !

The handwritten poster on the big cork board just inside the Students' Union had been designed in an eye-catching, Wild-West style, with a frame of dollar signs, and a scrawny, token cactus. Malcolm approached with caution. The Department of Psychology were seeking volunteers for experiments. You had to be between twenty and thirty, with normal hearing and vision. The reward sounded reasonable enough – fifteen shillings per session; but then how long was a session? Was it worth it? There was no mention of sleep deprivation, fasting or electric shocks. On the other hand neither was there of any bonuses, like food pellets or post-trial tea and biscuits. Malcolm stood a while, pondering the sign. He didn't know much about psychologists – the only ones he'd ever met were students. But then he remembered that those had all been female. He went straight to the porters' lodge, as directed, and signed up for the following Wednesday afternoon.

What's in a name? The *Weiss* Building, home of Psychology, was conspicuously black and grey; and the Austrian professor in whose honour it was named had in fact been a pioneer of colour-vision theory. What's more, from the beaming, benevolent portrait in the foyer, he appeared to have been a paragon of virtue. The poor man himself had largely been forgotten, his true legacy a fund of paradoxes and puns to keep staff and students entertained.

Malcolm was sitting waiting under this very picture when there came a familiar voice.

'Aha!' said Angela, looking him up and down, 'the man with the funny trousers.' Her hair was up. She was wearing glasses and a smart skirt. And carrying a clipboard. In the transition from tipsy disco-party girl to earnest undergraduate she'd lost none of her allure.

'Not today!' He stood and did a little twirl to show off his respectably old and untrendy jeans. She seemed less than impressed. 'I've come to be a guinea pig.'

'Yes, I know.' She ticked off his name on a short list. 'I'm conducting the tests.'

'Oh. *Right*,' said Malcolm, outbeaming even the good Professor Weiss, 'I was expecting someone . . .'

'Older?' she offered. 'Male?'

'Well, no . . .'

'With a bow-tie? Beard? Viennese accent?'

'Not exactly. I hadn't really thought about it . . .'

'We students do some of the preliminary screening. It's part of our lab work.' She smiled and beckoned him to follow, down a long corridor and into a small room. It had low lighting and was warm and quiet, apart from a steady hum from somewhere.

'Have a seat.'

'Can't I lie on a couch?'

'I think you're confusing psychology with *psychiatry*.'

'Oh no I'm not!' He put on his most devilish grin.

'OK, we start with Stage One.'

'Isn't there a Stage Zero?'

She sighed. 'Let's assume that's been done, shall we. You are between twenty and thirty, aren't you?'

'Well, it all depends what's meant by *between*. I'm actually twenty, so . . .'

'That's good enough,' she said swiftly. 'With normal vision and hearing?'

'Yep!'

'Sound mind?' she added.

'You tell me!'

'So, Stage One.' She handed him a thin, stapled sheaf of printed pages.

'What *is* Stage One, exactly?'

'Well,' she began, 'it's kind of a personality test . . .'

'Personality test?' Malcolm pretended some alarm. 'What happens if you fail?'

She grinned. 'Well, there is rumoured to be a euthanasia chamber. In the basement. I think that's mainly for rats though.'

'I'd better do my best then.' He took out a brand-new black biro and removed the cap. 'Ahh, the hard ones first, eh?' he muttered, as he began to fill out the top sheet with name, address and date of birth.

She left him to it.

Being asked to reduce your world view to a few dozen responses on a five-point scale is quite a challenge. An affront, some might say. But it appealed to Malcolm's sense of economy and order. It did, though, take him a while to decide whether he should put ticks in the little boxes, or crosses. Or were you allowed to do both? Or neither – leaving some questions blank? He settled on ticks, as conveying the clearer, more positive message. A cross would seem to introduce an extra layer of uncertainty – it might be taken to mean either you did, or didn't, for example, strongly disagree that others sometimes thought you were unselfish. And who'd want to give that impression?

After that he breezed through the set, happily agreeing and disagreeing, both strongly and mildly, just occasionally feeling neutral, and only once not really knowing, or caring.

Glancing back through the answers he hoped he'd given at least an interesting picture. He wasn't at all sure what they were looking for. If anything. And whoever *they* were. But surely they'd want to know more about someone who could be both shy and sociable, reflective and spontaneous, deep and frivolous, intellectual and modest? A plain, straightforward oxymoron of a man.

Ten minutes later Angela reappeared and relieved him of the questionnaire, slipping it into a large brown envelope.

'Do you get to see my answers?'

'Well, yes. But we don't want that to influence you.'

'Right, then.' He nodded and frowned at the same time. 'I'll try not to have let that influence me.'

'It's a bit late now!'

'I only said I'd try.'

She gave him another, thicker sheaf. He flicked through the pages. They were crammed with diagrams, numbers and word lists.

'I guess this must be Stage Two.'

'No, we're still on Stage One.'

'Part Two?'

'If you like.'

'Is this an IQ test?'

'Well, it's more of an evaluation. Of, let's say, cognitive function.' She waggled the clipboard in a vague gesture. 'But what's in a name?'

He filled out the front page. Just name and date of birth this time – it seemed they were confident his address was unlikely to have changed in the interim.

The next thirty minutes were a mix of frowns and satisfied smiles, along with exclamations of Errrr, Ahaaah! and What? as Malcolm tried hard to show his cognitive functions to advantage. He supplied missing words and numbers, spotted differences, circled odd men out. He rearranged crosses, stars and stripes, wrestled with blobs, black, white and grey, big and small, circular and elliptical. He juggled polygons and pyramids, poured over lines thick and thin, dotted and dashed, straight, curved and wiggly, crossing his eyes to bring shapes closer for comparison, and once resorting to turning the paper upside down. If they were monitoring him would they deduct marks for cheating? Or add them for ingenuity? *Were* they monitoring him? And, if so, who were they?

They, mused Malcolm. A mysterious and much-cited group. Dogmatic too, some of them – the they who boldly state, among other things, that love is blind, ignorance bliss and history bunk. Then there are the more guarded they, who claim merely that east is east and west, west; a rose a rose, a deal a deal. There were a lot of them about, it seemed. And that's not to mention the they who, so they say anyway, are all out to get you. They had a lot to answer for.

He looked around. The wall to his right had a mirror which seemed unnecessarily large. If not unnecessary altogether. He pulled a series of silly faces in it. Nothing happened. But then it wouldn't, would it?

He was sitting back trying to look casual when Angela returned. 'Do I get tea and biscuits?'

'Well, they're always available in the canteen,' she said. 'Sandwiches too.'

He stood up. 'Care to join me?'

'I've got to enter your data.' She frowned. 'And other things.'

'I could keep a seat for you.'

'I think it might compromise experimental objectivity.' She made to take the paper from him. He held on. 'We're supposed to stick to a strict procedure. You know, everything has to be double-blind.'

'I could keep both eyes closed!'

'They'll be in touch,' she said enigmatically, tugged the paper from his grasp and strode off down the corridor.

Chapter 19

Powers of Two

Malcolm pressed the switch on the base of his Anglepoise. Ping-twang. The ring of light it cast on the foolscap pad showed it to be empty save for a dozen or so scattered words and phrases. The seeds of a dissertation? Yes, why not? He would nurture them through the vital stages of growth: tutor-pleasing title; clinching, one-page outline; ten-thousand-word, world-changing, philosophical treatise.

A long, uphill task. But conditions were right for making a start at least – a surprisingly quiet room, for a Friday night, a mug of tea gently steaming on the desk. He removed a red cap from what turned out to be a blue biro. He parked it firmly on the blunt end. It struck him there was probably a similarly, but reversed, clashing combination lurking in some pocket or drawer, but resisted the urge to go searching. He would savour the resolution at some later date. Bigger issues were afoot.

So. Ambiguity. Where do we begin?

Malcolm himself had begun, in a sense, on a wet Wednesday in mid September, some twenty years earlier. He even had a certificate somewhere testifying to the achievement. The first, and in a way most impressive, of quite a few.

He found out, much later, that he'd in fact been born eight days prematurely. And felt rather pleased. Being early for your birth seemed like simple good manners – as noteworthy in its way as being late for your funeral, but without the overtones of incompetence. An adult perspective no doubt. What would the man of the moment have made of it all?

If Meta-Malcolm 0 has any concept of language or number he may well be puzzling already over the origins problem, and how easily he's thwarted the auguries. Funny thing, astrology.

Though apparently intended for the Libras it seems he's balked at the zodiacal boundary and landed in the Virgos. Only just though. Hence from day one he's a borderline case. *On the cusp*, as the astrologentsia have it. We can predict for him lifelong confusion over ideas of abutment and adjacency. Not to mention days when he's torn between surrendering to a romantic impulse and avoiding confrontation with senior colleagues. Virgins and librarians. Just how distinct should they be? Long-term he was destined to meet a few. Stereotypes notwithstanding, he found the overlap to be quite a small one.

The period by which M-M 0 has jumped the gun seems no handicap at all. He's as intact and functional as any full-termer. A week is not a long time in obstetrics. In fact it will give him a sense of being somehow permanently ahead of the game – of having a lifelong edge on things. In his later years he'll be quite content to read three-day-old newspapers, and when the two-tier postal system arrives, gleefully put second-class stamps on his letters, safe in the knowledge they will still get there days before they would have done had he been born on time.

Well, where *do* we begin? What a little gem of ambiguity that was for a start! It could serve as an enquiry into the origins of mankind, or to provoke a discussion of whether we should count up from one, or from zero. Or even as a rhetorical cry of desperation at the enormity of either of these first two tasks. Luckily we haven't yet managed to start at all, otherwise it would be tempting to start again, and then where, or when, would we be?

Talking of origins, perhaps there was a time when ambiguity was impossible. In the primordial soup, before differentiation of any kind had set in. Then again, you might argue that amorphousness was the ultimate ambiguity. If sandwiches are poorly defined, soup is positively vague! However in that earliest soup, or slime, there couldn't have been any form of life to experience confusion. Nor even any distinct thing to confuse with any other. So, a dull time it may have been, but hardly confusing. No, ambiguities, like philosophical problems generally, can't exist if there's nothing there to perceive them. Probably.

Ambiguity as a *problem* seems to start when we have two things. And not so much *at least* two, as, rather, *exactly* two. In the real beginning was the *bit* – the binary digit. We cope easily with memorising 'phone numbers – taming the unruly, arbitrary strings of symbols that we are dealt by imposing stress patterns, conjuring up vague, Bingo-style mnemonic images, parsing and coercing them into digestible schemes of rhyme or rhythm which seem, somehow or other, to make special cases of them all (in defiance, surely, of some overarching necessity of information theory).

Really big numbers are even less of a problem. We just break them up and spend longer learning. Or write them down. No, it's individual *bits* that defeat us every time. The zero or one, yes or no, left or right, up or down.

And while we really should revere these little information atoms, for their very fundamentalness, we're often quite dismissive of them. At our peril. How many millions of outings and occasions have been haunted, and ruined, by the nagging one-bit question: did I take the tablet, lock the door, flush the toilet, put the cat out? It should be easy. For all their banality these acts are rich collections of countless elementary sense data – each one a little hook to help hold the event in memory. Together they would seem to add up to an infallible panel of mnemonic Velcro.

The trouble is our brains are clogged up already with so many memories of having done, and having forgotten to do, these very things in the past. The multiple images blend and cancel, the resulting smear tells us nothing. In the end we can only be sure when faced with the manifest result of the event itself: Schrödinger notwithstanding, when you come home the cat either is or isn't on the mat. And when you return from the bathroom in the small hours you can tell directly from a thousand dulled nerve endings which side, left or right, you've just been sleeping on. This extravagant use of a whole body as a one-bit store takes us right back to analogue representation. Maybe we should never have strayed from it in the first place.

A dull, repetitive beat started up in the room above. Malcolm sighed, wriggled his toes a while to combat creeping pins and needles, then popped across to the kitchen to see if he'd left the kettle on. Stimulated by the many square metres of empty white formica he engineered himself a snack. An unambiguous, optimal snack. And effortlessly matched to his exact state of hunger, because it was unmediated by words.

What is a sandwich? Well, among other things a sandwich is a strikingly dualistic affair. A squaring up of opposing layers – bread versus butter, butter versus beef, and so on. There is already ample opportunity for bedazzlement in that manifold sequence of interfaces. The act of cutting the thing up only adds exponential complications. Each division is a further surrender to the mysterious power of two.

Malcolm took a bite from his and contemplated the exposed cross-section as he chewed. Upstairs, the beat went on.

Food thoughts. Food words. Food phrases.

It's a reflection of the fundamental role of food in survival that our language is so liberally garnished with related proverbs, similes and metaphors. There ought to be some clues here, among the familiar spilt milk, red herrings and warm toast; the jam of yesterday and tomorrow, the apple carts, cool cucumbers and turkey talk. Perhaps even in the more enigmatic known onions, and sky pies. Clues to the ever-present duplicities of measurement. Quantitative considerations get a mention too – the big cheese, the baker's dozen, the relative merits of half a loaf. And, most promisingly, there's one allusion to the deceptive potential of food.

But it's not so much that the eyes are *bigger* than the stomach (except maybe for someone with an unlucky combination of anorexia and thyroid trouble). It's rather that they're more *accommodating*. Our eyes (and indeed noses and other sensory bits) may perceive logarithmically, but our stomachs, in spite of the elasticity of their walls and their essential three-Dness, seem to respond roughly linearly to input. And to be tolerant only to ten percent or so. Deviations by a factor of, say, two, either way from the desired amount, while only just noticeable by other senses, would soon lead to starvation or bursting.

In principle it wouldn't be hard to achieve the required degree of precision. If sandwiches were a more durable, storable, transportable, negotiable sort of commodity then we'd probably quantify them by volume or weight, as with milk and honey. But their freshness is of the essence. So they get treated as hand-to-mouth items, produced and consumed *ad hoc* on a small scale. And since the elements of fabrication are still visible in the finished article, like unrendered brickwork, the makers tend to reckon partly in terms of the number of items used in construction. That cuts will be made during the proceedings is a complication often over- or under-allowed for. Each step in the cutting and stacking halves the horizontal area and doubles the depth, moving us towards the cubic shape. This increases the volume–to–surface-area ratio and so makes it easier to keep the things cool and fresh. A spherical sandwich would be the ideal in this respect.

A rather different, and even more slippery, kettle of fish are the so-called *club* sandwiches. These trendy, imported, rondo forms seem specially designed to be unholdably and inedibly thick. This is probably to allow for the fact that most of the contents will cascade from lip to table to lap to floor during the eating. They are monstrous constructions, better eaten with a knife and fork. Maybe a spoon and bib as well. The inventor of the sandwich must have turned in his grave at this perverse subversion of his original idea. For the story goes that the good Earl wanted to eat conveniently without leaving the gaming table (fearing, perhaps, a loss of concentration, or the chicanery of fellow players). And it seems only fair to assume that those who would keep their cards close to the chest should eat with one hand. Indeed the assertion has a kind of Confucian authority to it.

Whenever *he* had any say in the manufacturing process Malcolm would make sure of this single-handed integrity by means of long, slow, firm, palm pressure, applied to the top slice before the final cuts, blending the cheese, tomato, bread and margarine into a thick, nutritious amalgam. Iron rations. Hero fodder. In this act of compaction you consciously turned light and fluffy mother-made luxury into dense, serious, Arctic-crossing fuel.

But the club sandwich seems to delight in its own lack of integration. And it connects us directly with the other major manifestation of ambiguity. When confronted with a lengthy, stainless-steel-platterful of the things, propped vertically against one another, it's hard to know where one sandwich stops and another starts. Especially if the whole array has been trimmed with fuzzy borders of parsley or watercress, so that matters can't be resolved simply by counting inwards from an end. You can so easily be attracted by a slice of corned beef around the middle of the stretch and unthinkingly associate with it the two pieces of bread which lie immediately on either side. On removal, however, what was taken as a conventional sandwich unit turns out to be buttered on the outside and have lettuce-leaf accessories. *Faux pas* don't come more literal than this.

There are similar confusions for guests seated somewhere around the middle of a lengthy banqueting table. Unable to see the end points of the array of place settings, they may, quite innocently, violate the local bread-roll-placement parity convention.

Trickier still here is the round table. In spite of its democratic intentions this can easily lead to a kind of dining anarchy. Flouters of protocol have been known to deliberately claim a neighbour's roll, thus precipitating a rippling phase-shift around the table. This returns full circle, forcing the other neighbour, unaware of the originator of the dislocation, into apologetic complicity. (It was even more fun, Malcolm had once discovered, to create a distraction, claim the rolls on *both* sides, and then watch the twin rarefactions propagate clockwise and anticlockwise till they met, leaving the person diametrically opposite floundering in a deep dark, breadless minimum).

Food thoughts. Food games.

Music began in the room below. In isolation it might have been quite pleasant, but coupled with the on-going rhythm from above it was hard to make much sense of. Malcolm put his pen down, rubbed his eyes, looked up at the clock, and found it had allowed almost three hours to slip by. Unwatched clocks did that kind of thing of course. Especially if, like this one, they had a second hand which swept rather than ticked its way round. Ticks are harder to ignore, even if they are inaudible, (and even if that's a contradiction). Probably because they are so close to heartbeats. Uncomfortably close. Though not coincidentally so – our one-second time unit is derived from our roughly one-Hertz hearts. Ticks provide a chronic and unsettling reminder of the limits of life. To be fair, tocks are just as bad. Strangely, in the traditional alternation the two can seem harmless. Even comforting.

Three hours for just half a page of notes. Half a *side* even. But of course that would expand considerably, when written up. To, maybe, a thousand words. A fair chunk. A whole picture's worth even, at the proverbial exchange rate. Things were underway.

Malcolm recapped the biro, almost oblivious of the colour clash, and pressed the switch on the Anglepoise. Twang-ping. He took a short stroll around the campus, then turned in, earplugs firmly in place.

Chapter 20

Fun and Games

Saturday morning was chill and grey. Malcolm pinged the lamp back on, then made tea and toast, and sat at his desk. With heavy rain forecast there was no excuse for not pressing on with the outline. All day, why not? Even through Sunday. There was little to interrupt him. Except perhaps another fire alarm (in all likelihood brief, and false, again). Or a spot check by the Lord's Day Observance Society.

For today he'd planned only a trip to the barber's. There was likely to be a lengthy queue, but he could always take along his notes and scribble while waiting. Even if it wasn't the done thing. His heart still sank slightly at the prospect. Though physically painless, haircuts did have their irksome side. Especially on Saturdays, when all males over the age of three were expected to take part in the tedious trading of sporting observations. Or if not, at least to sit and listen with a look of resignation which said, 'I should of course be on the terraces, or even on the field. Only this urgent haircut keeps me here.'

Malcolm had no particular reason to be ungrateful to his hair. It grew largely in the conventional places and, though eventually it would lose its colour on account of genetic and other factors, it was destined to remain faithful to him for decades. Funny thing though, hair. It was subject to the same peculiar cyclic changes as toe- and finger-nails – waxing naturally and subliminally before being forcibly waned in a single drastic step. So its length was a sawtooth function of time, with a period of around six weeks (or eight to ten in times of extra austerity or laziness). The cutting was always a mild shock to the system – on emergence from the barber's traffic noise had regained its keenest edge, and for a week or two Malcolm would remain acutely aware of his ears. Especially in winter. Others would too, he felt, on purely visual grounds. And irrespective of season.

Then the hair would enter a comfortably unremarkable, manageable stage – a week-or-so's window of acceptability. The fourth week was marked by a creeping unruliness, the shape becoming very dependent on the conditions of drying. Relying on the ninety-second blast you got for a penny from the multi-kilowatt 'Sirocco' machine at the swimming baths left him looking like a multi-megavolt coconut. A vigorous towelling led to a similar, if slightly more impressively Einsteinian, profile. And allowing it to dry naturally was not without risk. Nature could be capricious, and sometimes cruel, producing wild sculptured effects reminiscent of ancient cedar branches, tilted geological strata or towering, threatening cumulonimbus, depending on the atmospheric conditions prevailing at the altitude of his head.

These odd shapes weren't uncomfortable or hazardous, and were rarely commented on. He sometimes worried though that others were too polite to ask after his motives. The late 'sixties were a time when dozens of well-known people, and millions of their unknown mimics, were adopting peculiar hair shapes and colours as gestures of protest or self-expression. Malcolm considered implanting a little 'keep-off-the-grass' style sign, stating that, while he wasn't actually ashamed of the form of his hair, it wasn't intended as any sort of fashion or political statement. In fact it wasn't intended at all.

He stared at his head in the wardrobe mirror. He was clearly ripe for a trip to the High Street salon. The image seemed to wobble in a dreamlike fashion, and suddenly he was back in that big swivel chair, cowering slightly under the stripey sheet.

In the corner, tethered on a frayed and knotty flex, the obligatory radio burbles the obligatory commentary. Largely incomprehensible. Largely ignored. Its only function is to establish sport as the default subject for all discussion. It's Saturday, and there's no place for the unenthusiastic or uninitiated.

The barber executes a decent number of snips before the customary overture. 'I see they've dropped Tunnicliffe then!'

Malcolm lets another few snips go by while he studies the man's ill-groomed head in the mirror for any signs of mischief.

He then produces his classic, non-committal 'hmm' – an utterance honed over the years to a perfect neutrality. In this context it doesn't do to nod assent. Quite apart from the danger of losing an earlobe, he fears this might be a trap – a test of his right to membership of the Saturday fraternity. If he should give the slightest acknowledgement of the existence of this unlucky Mr T. the barber might start to smirk, at which prompt the whole circle of waiting customers, forgetting for a moment the rivalries of the queue, would toss aside their tabloids and chortle in unison, 'He fell for the old *Tunnicliffe* trick!'

Whether Terry Tunnicliffe (he would surely have to be a *Terry*) is in reality the very tangible, lumbering Northern full-back the name suggests (complete with debilitating, Friday-night, brown-ale habit – the cause of his downfall), or a simple fabrication of the barber, Malcolm will never know.

Nor will he ever understand how half-a-dozen blokes sitting in the barber's on a Saturday afternoon can conjure up a sporting atmosphere so potent it spills out of the shop as he leaves and follows him down the High Street, infiltrating the other, more innocent and neutral premises.

His next call is the supermarket cheese counter. You might hope that such a place would be as free as anywhere from sporting presumption, with verbal exchanges, without being unduly restricted, centring on the cutting, weighing and selling of cheese.

How many reasonable responses are there to *'Half of English Cheddar, please.'*?

Quite a few. There's the simple repeat of the order for confirmation before the irreversible wire cut; the even simpler *'Certainly sir!'*; the enterprising *'Wouldn't you prefer the Cheshire, it's on special offer?'* (better value, maybe, but more costly in absolute terms). And then there's the suspiciously frequent *'It's a bit over, shall I cut some off?'* spoken loudly, and addressed more to the impatient queue behind. Variations abound, of course, and we expect a sprinkling of coughs, sneezes and meteorological pleasantries, according to season. But what Malcolm gets is not on this list.

'They're ahead!' is what the cheeseman says.

'Sorry?'

'They're three-one up!' he adds by way of clarification, wrapping the slab in greaseproof paper and writing *1/3d* on it.

'Yes, of course they are,' says Malcolm, grabbing the packet and backing away.

An odd but isolated response, perhaps; the result of a long-inhibited part of the man's brain finally firing off in creative frustration – it must get pretty dull working with cheese all day long. But no, the syndrome has spread through the whole store.

'How are they doing?' says the woman at the checkout.

Malcolm frowns, 'Sorry?'

'HOW ARE THEY DOING?' The accompanying mouth movements are of an amplitude normally reserved for the over-nineties.

All eyes turn to Malcolm expectantly.

'Er, they're three-one up.'

'Good, keep your fingers crossed!' She does a little demonstration on each hand.

Three? One? Up? What could it mean? There are times when Malcolm feels he's been mistaken for a secret agent and is being used to convey the location of a safe house. Or a missile base. In the interests of national security he sometimes adds or subtracts a small number from each of the co-ordinates before passing them on. Or simply reverses the order. That's a more plausible mistake to make.

Malcolm appeared at any rate to be a marked man. Somehow. Had it always been so? And are some of us *born* with a dislike of ball games? It seemed unlikely. He remembered, dimly but fondly, a beach-ball with bold, jolly, primary-coloured segments – oversized, underinflated, and short-lived, the victim of an ebbing tide. Then the soggy, balding tennis ball he'd shared, rather unequally, with next-

141

door's spaniel. But there would have been some first encounter, on the local park perhaps, with a real football. And it would have been decisive:

> Meta-Malcolm 5 has fed the ducks, collected a fistful of lollipop sticks, climbed an easy tree, and now lies against a grassy bank watching the clouds go by. He's distracted by the shouts of another boy – older and bigger, though not threatening. The boy grins, looks straight at Meta-Malcolm and moves the ball between toe and toe in a manner which is clearly meant to provoke a response, though of what kind M-M is unsure.
>
> 'Come on!', says the big boy with good-natured enthusiasm. M-M's frown intensifies. 'You've got to try and get the ball off me!'
>
> No I haven't, thinks M-M, and wanders off towards the swings.
>
> With swings you get one each. Swinging is essentially non-competitive. He takes his place on the shiny wooden seat, grasps the cool metal chains, dangles in uncontested luxury.
>
> Sailing clouds. Sighing trees. Distant contented quacks.

How much more relaxed and less tedious the world would be if there were simply twenty-two times as many footballs.

Malcolm's deliberations continued over a snack lunch – peanuts, soup and a banana. The notes had hardly grown, though bits had been circled, boxed and multiply underlined. He felt that was progress. It wasn't all about writing text – there were links to be made, background considerations, peripheral matters that had to be ruminated on, seemingly irrelevant ideas to be exercised. Or exorcised. Yes, these were distractions. But not *mere* distractions. Ambiguity was tied up with the whole business of miscommunication and misunderstanding. All was grist.

And games had their part to play. It had often seemed to Malcolm that the whole sporting business might just as well be a fabrication.

Like God or Santa Claus. Part of some global psychological experiment to monitor or exploit the credulity of the population. Or maybe a purely philanthropic act dreamt up by the authorities – a benign conspiracy. If the pleasure sought by the masses could be given to them at minimal cost then so much the better.

Events would be particularly easy to fake if they were meant to be geographically remote. Ever since watching fragments of the last Olympics on the family's tiny, flickering, black and white TV, Malcolm had been flirting with a theory.

It went like this: the political and financial difficulties, so effectively played down by the organisers, had, in reality, led to a complete cancellation of the games, forcing them to cobble together the broadcasts entirely from old footage. Doubtless all seemed well enough to the typical viewer, blinded by athletic and chauvinistic passion. But a cool, objective observer couldn't fail to notice the haste, and occasional panic, behind some of the cutting and pasting.

For example, in one clumsy attempt to disguise both men, which showed scant regard for ethnic sensitivities (not to mention physiognomical plausibility) the notorious moustache of Herr you-know-who had been transposed to none other than the legendary Jesse Owens – the mounting suspicion that it was an optical artefact coming to a head when it failed to keep pace with him on the spurt round the last bend of the 400 metres.

In an activity where huge excitement for millions could be generated by tiny differences in times and distances the opportunities to falsify were surely irresistible. Even when the jumper or the object thrown is kept in shot throughout, a simple process of re-scaling the image could be used to counterfeit record-breaking performances in field events. And a frame or two removed here and there would clip vital tenths of seconds off sprint times.

But again there was a lapse in vigilance by the continuity department, resulting in an apparent loss of height by one competitor which was unusual even in long-distance runners. And were we to believe that a one-man luger could apply an Elastoplast to his own nose during the descent and still come away with bronze?

Malcolm checked himself again in the wardrobe mirror. The hair now seemed less than urgent. Another millimetre wouldn't matter much. And there was still cheese in the fridge. The High Street could wait till Monday.

By evening the predicted rain had materialised. He closed the curtains and continued to muse and scribble, taking nourishment in dribs and drabs while remaining at his desk. Even the many, clashing strands of music that came and went from all sides failed to distract him completely. A whole new page of the notepad was filled – in places there were almost complete sentences. The boxes began to sport coloured boundaries. Solid, dashed and dotted lines joined and separated them. Some with little arrows on. From time to time he sat back and smiled – at what was starting to look just a bit like a masterplan. Then on he went, oblivious of the worsening weather and the non-ticking clock.

Suddenly it was midnight. 12 pm. Or would that be *am*? Either way, Saturday was becoming Sunday. Malcolm executed a dutiful yawn to acknowledge the moment. The music had stopped. It would no doubt start up again in the late morning. Till then the Hall would enjoy some 20000 bars of well-deserved rest. He would have liked more of course. But then an eternal one would come soon enough. Meanwhile this was a welcome window of silence. RIP.

He teetered a good while on the borderlines of sleep, savouring the instability of this extended instant. He shut his eyes. Half sleep. Just sleep. Fragments of dubious melodies he'd somehow managed earlier to banish from consciousness whirled and recombined in a kind of Musikalisches Würfelspiel. Trills, tremolos and rampant glissandi echoed around, then burst through into the visual domain, sprouting and branching in a dancing forest of notation. Bough-beams bent, stalk-stems withered, deciduous note heads fell and were caught in the stave netting. Clefs, slurs and leger lines fused and folded into piste maps, snakes and ladders, bus routes and benzene rings – beguiling forms teasing ears and eyes, inviting and defying classification. Bars of rests and rests of bars, repeating *da capo al fine*. But *where* do they begin, and end? What are they? *Essentially?*

Malcolm opened his eyes. The rest, of course, was silence. But what, exactly, was a bar? Presumably, given its name, it started life as a post and then, with a dangerous disregard for class distinctions, we somehow promoted it to a space, between posts. Hence we now have to say bar-*lines*, with that annoying trace of redundancy. We've given in once again to the duplicities of time.

And the same thoughtless convention has been applied in the domain of pitch. A musical interval is, in essence, a *space* between pitches, a number of steps. To arrive at its name by counting the note *posts* between which these steps are sandwiched is just asking for trouble. It means that, for example, a *second* plus a *third* amounts to a *fourth*. You could be forgiven for thinking it was more. So, if we're not to trip up when adding intervals we have to rely on our hearing and not our arithmetic sense. But better keep the light on too!

Malcolm finally switched his off, succumbing immediately to the magic modes and rhythms of sleep, which carried him through the darkness on a nocturne soothing and serene, extending well beyond the dawn.

Then it was violently interrupted by a medley of tuneless singing and water hammer from the shower next-door. Awakenings didn't come much ruder.

Though having strictly only a one-eighth share in the bathroom facilities Malcolm had developed that disproportionately proprietorial sense that comes with proximity. Provoked by the double intrusion he set off up the stairs clutching soap, towel and a bundle of cleanish clothes.

To find a shower that was both unoccupied and working he had to go up several flights. Here the water pressure was always much lower, making you extra vulnerable to the vagaries of the elderly plumbing. A turning on or off of a single tap anywhere in the block could send freezing or scalding temperature step changes coursing down the pipework in your direction.

This only added to a more basic uncertainty built into the temperature controls of the showers themselves. The rim of the stainless-steel knob was divided into two semicircular arcs, boldly coloured red and blue, and immediately suggesting the ideas of hotness and coldness. From months of investigation Malcolm had found that in about half of the showers turning the knob clockwise made the water hotter, and in the rest, the opposite.

He'd quizzed the janitor, who explained that it was all very simple – if you wanted it hotter, you had to 'turn *it towards* the red' and if you wanted it colder you had to 'turn *it towards* the blue'. Sadly though he was quite unable to say what 'it' was. Or how on earth you could turn whatever 'it' might be towards the red, when the red was painted on the thing you were turning. Eventually the man went off down the corridor chuntering about colour blindness and modern educational standards.

This morning Malcolm established, by trial and bone-numbing error, that clockwise was colder at the west end of the fifth floor. He made a mental note. Back in his room, conscious of the frailty of memory, and of naked skin, he made a physical one in the back of his diary, in bold blue biro. Underlined in red.

Sunday. Sweet Sunday. A second lecture-free twenty-four hours in which to sit and ponder his current obsession, to read and write anything that took his fancy. He opened the curtains on bright sunshine. It was still early. Things looked more promising. He took the day off.

Chapter 21

The A5 pro-forma in Malcolm's Gray-Hall pigeon hole was short on detail. In a smudgy type it simply invited him back to Psychology for the following Wednesday afternoon. The cheque for fifteen shillings paper-clipped to the back he removed to his wallet. There was no reference to his previous assessment, or any reason given for the continued interest. He re-read, then refolded and pocketed the note. Were his results perhaps exceptionally promising? Or grossly anomalous? "Recalled for testing" could signal a star performance. Or a suspect crankshaft. Whichever, he assumed another payment was on offer. Not to mention the possibility of beguiling company. Business was business.

Wednesday found him pacing the foyer of the Weiss Building. He felt better prepared for this visit. Both physically and mentally – in the intervening week he'd done some brisk walking and eaten several portions of fish. Visually too – that morning he'd put on an almost clean pullover. Even combed his hair.

This time the voice that greeted him was not familiar. Though the face was. Vaguely. Pale and roundish, with a full mouth. The third of the trio from the Union Bar.

'Aha!' said Jenny, 'the man who doesn't like jukeboxes.'

'It's only the noise they make,' said Malcolm, 'they *look* just fine.'

She conducted him to a small lab off a narrow corridor, off a wider one.

'Angela not on duty today then?' He was in no way complaining – with her long, dark, glossy hair and big brown eyes she was an admirable substitute.

'She does Stage One – personal and cognitive. I'm Stage *Two*,' said Jenny, with mock pride, 'auditory and visual perception.' She gestured at a small rack of electronic equipment.

'You should wear a white coat,' said Malcolm.

'Why?' She scanned the room for anything hazardous or vulnerable to contamination.

'I think it would suit you!'

She got him to sit at a table, which had a frame with a chin rest, facing a small white screen, and gave him a form to fill in. This time they wanted his name, height and weight. What next?

'OK, I'll need you to place your chin on the pad and shut your left eye . . .' she briefly shut her own in a quite unnecessary demonstration. Malcolm winked back, just to show he understood. ' . . . then look at the green cross on the screen, with your right, and tell me how many red dots you can see.'

'Zero,' said Malcolm.

'We haven't started yet.'

'That's a relief!'

Jenny dimmed the lights. Malcolm murmured his approval. Prompted by little beeps from somewhere she began pressing buttons on a kind of projection system. He stared at a lengthy succession of blobs of all colours, sizes and configurations, sometimes in single lines at differing orientations, sometimes in bold, jolly, 2-D combinations. Sky blue, jungle green. Shocking pink. She noted down his responses to various questions. How many blobs? Odd or even number? What form do you see: Square? Circle? Other?

The shapes seemed to get more complex. After a while he fancied he could see all sorts: continents, blood cells, bats and butterflies. Faces even. When she finally asked him to change eyes he requested a short break. She smiled and nodded her agreement, but then simply walked off clutching her clipboard, leaving him in the half dark. He'd been hoping for a cup of tea. Or even a neck massage.

He stretched, rubbed his chin, then his eyes. So what were they up to? He'd heard about psychologists. While you thought you were counting dots, indeed while you actually were counting dots, they were secretly noting the number of times you scratched your head or touched your left ear. While you were obediently reading the list of words on a screen, backwards, they could be flashing up subliminal images of a suggestive nature and monitoring your breathing and heart rate. Checking your blood pressure. Stealing your wallet. Or maybe they were trying to place you on some rebelliousness-compliance scale, by giving you a meaningless, or even morally repugnant, task and seeing how long it was before you queried it or refused to go any further. Maybe the right response to such deviousness was an open curiosity. He looked slowly around the room, then got up and made a brief tour of inspection. There appeared to be no mirrors at all. Or at least that's what they wanted him to think.

So what was it all about? He vaguely remembered that the previous year there'd been protests outside the Weiss Building. An occupation even. Wasn't that over animal rights? Yes. Students in rat suits. Or was that a bad dream he'd had? And weren't there rumours of research grants from the defence industry? Yes. Something like that.

Jenny reappeared, still smiling, with clipboard in hand.

'So, what are they measuring. Exactly?' said Malcolm. 'Or even approximately?'

'I can't say.'

'Why not?'

'They haven't told me.'

'What haven't they told you? What they're measuring, or why you can't say?'

'Neither. Both. I think, it's an experimental . . . protocol . . . thing.'

'Ahhh, the old need-to-know principle!' He winked and tapped the side of his nose.

She asked him to put his chin back on the rest and close his other eye. Then on they went.

By the time the visual tests were over Malcolm could see spots before his eyes, even when both were closed. In fact especially when they were.

Then it was the turn of the ears. Jenny got him to don a pair of headphones and lean back in the chair.

'Ready?'

'What for?'

'It's a series of auditory stimuli. At a comfortable listening level,' she added. 'Is that OK?'

'Depends what kind.'

'Pure tones, pulse trains, in mono, stereo . . .'

'Long as there aren't any protest songs!'

She promised him there weren't.

The tones came thick and fast – left ear, right ear and sweeping between; rising or falling, steady or sporadic. More questions: how many beeps? High or low pitch? Press the button as soon as you can hear anything; release it as soon as you can't.

When Malcolm finally removed the 'phones his vision was almost back to normal. The hearing would take a while longer. Jenny thanked him for his efforts. More formally than he would have liked.

'How did I do?' he asked.

'How do you mean?'

'I mean did I do, well . . . *well?*'

'There's no right or wrong.'

He nodded, 'Of course.'

He tried the old tea-and-biscuits line – offering to treat her even.

'I've got to process some data,' she said. 'Anyway, you're an experimental subject.'

'So?'

'We're not supposed to fraternise.'

'Fair enough,' said Malcolm, 'but we could think of it as me, sororitising. It's all relative. I can be *very* flexible.'

She smiled. 'They'll be in touch.' And she was gone.

Chapter 22

Minding the Steps

Malcolm got his philosophy tutor's approval for the dissertation outline without disclosing his own secret working title: *Principia Sandwichia*. Nine o'clock Saturday morning he was at his desk, armed with a mug of tea and hard at work. Section One – What is a Sandwich? Underlining the question had not helped. Nor had adding a second question mark. Except maybe to concede a growing uneasiness about whether he really wanted to ask the first question. He looked across at his image in the wardrobe mirror. It looked back, a little surprised. Mirror mirror. Now there was a phrase!

Sandwiches have simple mirror symmetry about the central meaty plane. But simple symmetry is only a short step away from treacherous degeneracy. And it's steps that trip us up. Or sometimes the lack of them. Coming down stairs in the dark we may remember to count to thirteen. But where did we begin? Was the landing *zero*? Is it thirteen going up, or coming down? And thirteen *what*s, anyway? Should we count the hall floor? It seems odd to bundle such a massive, single area along with the multiple and countable step surfaces. Maybe it would be safer to count the banisters. Or the gaps between them. Safer still though just to put the light on. Is that all we really need – less enumeration and more illumination?

Posts and spaces, treads and risers, trips and falls.

Dead ends. Full stops.

He swapped his oldish biro for a newish one and turned over the page, even though the first side was only half full, seduced perhaps by an unconscious confusion of proverbs and metaphors about new brooms and leaves, clean slates and sheets, and other stuff. The proximity of fully charged pen to empty page would surely create such an irresistible gradient that, even without the favourable gravity, words would just tumble on to the paper. Surely. It was just a matter of time. Few things weren't. In the end.

He tried dangling the carrot of the celebratory drink or two he could award himself if this draft were completed by Sunday night. But deadlines can stimulate or stifle depending on how the task can be spread out in time. There are milestones and there are millstones.

Two full days of slog split by eight hours of unconsciousness was an uncomfortably chunky distribution. The ideal, extreme, would be a continuous, undifferentiated weekend of slow, semi-automatic writing in a state of deep relaxation. A more realistic compromise would be gently alternating periods of snoozing and snacking, thinking and writing, with a disregard for the conventional timing of food and sleep – a manifold, interleaved, club sandwich of a working schedule. Yes, that would be the least painful course.

Had he been able to doodle Malcolm would have doodled. But the doodling facility was yet another one nature had withheld. Along with whistling through the fingers and wiggling the ears. Maybe it was wrong to speak of ability, because the activity was so clearly spontaneous – you either doodled or you didn't. He often did arguably similar things with desk-top paraphernalia – the straightening out of paper-clips, the daisy chaining of rubber bands, and occasionally, in an act of redundancy of Zen proportions, the multiple stapling of a single sheet of paper.

But somehow he felt these were creatively inferior. He would always retain an admiration for those who filled in corners and sometimes whole sides of paper with that curious mixture of squiggly regularity – the artless art, the random design, in spite of, or maybe just because of, the contradictions. According to a magazine article he'd once read these supposedly casual scribbles were straightforwardly revealing of character, betraying you instantly as oblique, caustic, well-rounded, or just plain loopy. In the library Malcolm would obsessively screen his blank notepads from onlookers, for fear he might be diagnosed as altogether lacking in psychological traits.

In private he could afford to fold his arms and contemplate the white space at leisure. In a way he was exercising his right not to draw. An inalienable one, perhaps. But it hadn't always been so. In the

152

school art class it was taken for granted that everyone had the ability. The lessons were merely a chance to demonstrate it. Only a stubborn child would fail to perform well. He stared at the yawning white sheet till it shimmered and spun. Blank portrait became blank landscape. Dreamy arpeggios, plinking heavenwards, tugged him back to those long Friday afternoons, awash with puzzlement and artistic floundering.

The Art Room, like the Music Room, is materially well equipped. Reams of creamy foolscap, brushes by the hundred, primary-coloured paint powder by the vat. But outnumbering and outshining everything are the hoards of gleaming, lidless jam jars. Teacher is proudly protective of this ever-expanding collection, having been brought up in a time and place when they were negotiable for cinema tickets. And having quietly cornered the market over several years he looks forward to a time when this defunct currency will come back into its own. He will then retire into the Robertson's & Chivers Fort Knox which is his store room and dictate the local economy.

The walls and floor are decorated with the accidents of generations of kids, and the high ceiling with their pranks (the brush required a mighty flick to overcome the clinging capillary forces of the bristles and still leave enough speed for the coloured droplets to reach their target). The results are not altogether unartistic, though of course more Pollock than Michelangelo.

To Malcolm the rules of Art seem as vague as those of rugby. Pupils are assigned a tedious annual cycle of tasks, each specified only in terms of the desired result. Guidance is not on offer. Technique, a word never spoken. A little way into the Christmas term they are dealt sheets of foolscap and ordered to "paint November the fifth". Malcolm sits and stares into space for a while, as if mustering artistic forces for a creative coup, but in truth unsure even as to what *kind* of command that is.

It isn't long before a "Get on with it lad!" comes from behind. He queues up at the sink to three-quarter fill his jam jar, returning to the table to chew the end of a balding paintbrush for a while in what he hopes is an artistic fashion. Then, seeing the others dunking their brushes he dutifully dunks his own. The crystal water is irreversibly tainted. Still aware of critical eyes from behind he starts to stir, and continues to stir long after it has reached equilibrium. He lets go and watches the brush revolve lazily in the drab soupy vortex.

'Get *on* with it!' The voice is now uncomfortably close.

'With what, exactly? Sir?'

'November the *fifth*!'

'Oh, sorry, I thought you said *December* the fifth!' Malcolm keeps his face as straight as his paintbrush, and "Sir", satisfied of his complete idiocy, moves on.

Over the next hour Malcolm daubs a big tangerine blob to serve as a bonfire and adorns it with peripheral orange sparky specks. He finally adds rocket trails in thin yellow parabolae – though he'll never be an artist he has already good ballistical intuition. Then, creatively exhausted, he sits back and stares at the one and only product of his brief "citrus" period. When Teacher's back is turned Malcolm makes, with a flick of the wrist, the odd contribution to the ongoing, community ceiling-scape.

The afternoon is rounded off with a familiar, ritual exchange.

'What on earth is *that*?'

'It's, er, November the fifth, Sir.'

'Looks more like a mess to me!'

'Well, I can't paint. You see, I was born like it, actually . . .'

'Don't ever say that.' Sir turns to address the whole class. '*Everybody* can paint!' And that's his last advice for three months.

Malcolm is surprised to learn of his ability. After all he's already tried and failed. Often. It seemed to follow though that there might be other things he was able to do that so far had never even occurred to him. Could he perhaps play the trombone? Speak Hungarian? Neither were particularly interesting to him. But just think of the potential for amazing your friends! Let alone yourself.

And now it is New Year and they are all painting "The Snowball Fight". Malcolm's artistic ability doesn't seem to have improved over the Christmas holidays, in spite of all the food he's eaten. So, he just daubs a big white blob to serve as a snowman, with small black blobs for buttons, adding peripheral white snowflake specks, and parabolic snowball trajectories. This, his "monochromatic" period, lasts till the bell goes, when they're all encouraged to take their works home. Or at least to get them off the premises. Malcolm fashions his effort into a makeshift megaphone and, in a rudimentary rehearsal for sweet nothings, toots the School Hymn in Veronica Dimble's ear, all the way to the bus stop.

Lost youths. First steps. Last posts.

Back in Room 216 he put down his pen. Half a page! OK, half a side. But single spaced! Sandwich time.

Full stops, food stops. Bus stops.

Ah, yes!

Recently Malcolm had been having trouble on the No. 66, finding himself charged sometimes *9d*, sometimes *1/-* and sometimes *1/3d* for the same journey. Different conductors were equally adamant that he was respectively over- or under-paying, or respectively under- or over-travelling, depending, respectively, on whether he specified a price, or the point of alighting, when buying the ticket. Interestingly, when he travelled the route in reverse he came across the same differences with the same conductors, but in the opposite sense. At least, mostly. Clearly each had his own odd, personal perspective on the system, which a careful analysis might reveal. But it was hard to keep track of all the many factors.

A complication was that conductors were sometimes unaware of where he'd got on. This meant that a failure to challenge him didn't necessarily indicate approval of the tendered fare. When directly contradicting one another the conductors always cited as the reason for their own certainty, and for their absent colleagues' confusion, the fact that the bus stops at both ends of Malcolm's journey were so-called "fare stages". He'd checked, and found to his concern that they were indeed so labelled, and formed the edges of a single "fare zone".

So what, he wondered, might be the formula for determining a fare? Presumably you paid only for distance travelled and not for time taken, as in some taxis, (and certainly not for speed, acceleration or any higher derivatives). Maybe it involved the number of boundaries *crossed*. But that could be zero, one or two, depending on conventions. Or maybe the number of zones travelled *in*, which could likewise be one, two or three.

A study of the bus company regulations was unhelpful except for revealing that it was a breach of local bye-laws to "embus or alight other than at an officially designated stop". This meant of course that a zone boundary could have been placed at any point whatsoever in the continuum *between* bus stops without affecting the fare structure or introducing ambiguity. So to place it at the one point which constituted a stop seemed like an act of infinite perversity.

Informal questioning of the various conductors failed to resolve the matter. The system was considered by each as entirely straightforward, as were the perceived misinterpretations of their colleagues. As one of the more helpful ones had put it, 'You see, if you get on where it goes up, you can go another stop.' Malcolm was still working on that one.

He'd even written to the borough transport department, suggesting that a sign proclaiming "bus stop fare stage zone boundary", particularly without any hyphens, was confusing. He got an almost polite reply from a Mr Border, explaining that there was no problem because it was in fact quite unambiguous, and meant exactly what it said, and what's more anyone who travelled with intent to avoid payment of the appropriate fare might be liable, or rather *would* be liable, to an excess, on top of that already paid, indeed, on top of that which *should* already have been paid. Enclosed was a copy of the regulations, which indicated that it was still a breach of local bye-laws to embus or alight other than at an officially designated bus stop.

Now the weather was improving it was hard to ignore the virtues of alternative transport. After all, you could embike and debike with impunity anywhere you wanted. And with the sun on your face and the wind in your hair the corporation's various zone boundaries swept by all but imperceptibly.

In Gray Hall time was sweeping by. Saturday became Sunday. The dissertation grew. Another paragraph. Another slice of bread. Another mug of tea. Though not necessarily in that order. Or any particular order. Step by step these ingredients which made up his weekend began to spread and spill, infuse and overlap, naturally and pleasantly, without rendering one another inedible. Or illegible.

But time and again he felt drawn back to square one. Or should that be square zero? The year dot, even? Whenever that was.

Malcolm lolled back in his chair, hands on head. He'd always found it difficult to imagine a time before his own birth. It had to be conceded, though, that one had ancestors. And that they did too. And so on, and on. Were there any clues in the mists of antiquity, the dawn of man?

For Meta-Malcolm minus one-hundred-thousand, life is simple and hard. A daily struggle to avoid hunger, thirst, disease, rapacious predators; the lashing rain, the icy winds. And, of course, Proto-Peregrine – the local aspiring alpha male, flaunter of the latest line in loincloths, life and soul of the cave, always ready with a musical turn (beating his chest when no goatskin is to hand) or an especially primitive joke. The man is surprisingly podgy, given the harsh conditions prevailing, and distinctly hairy, low-browed and thick-skinned, even by contemporary standards. A Neanderthal's Neanderthal.

P-P is perched on a high stone slab, filling the long winter evening with blow-by-blow accounts of mammoth hunts and fire-making feats. A heap of flaming logs projects a flickering shadow of his ample bulk, grotesquely magnified, on the cave wall behind. The company responds to the saga with sporadic and highly equivocal grunts. That nobody leaves is a testament to just how cold it is outside. Meta-Malcolm whittles an already sharp stick in silence, and eyes the long-maned beauty on an adjacent rock . . .

Come to think of it, a formal historical line could be quite fruitful. *Seven Ages of Ambiguity* would make a hell of a snappy title. Malcolm wrote it down. It did. All he needed to do now was coax the facts into this numerical straitjacket. And come up with ten thousand snappy words to go with it. He gave a long sigh.

So, to begin at the real beginning, wherever that was. Or whenever. What kind of thing, actually, *was* a beginning. A process? An instant? If the former, it was hard to see how we could begin *at* it. If the latter, it was just as hard to see how things like, for example, *The Word*, could have been *in* it. Though we were famously assured it was.

Boundaries seem to have been a source of confusion ever since this alleged beginning. No sooner do we have a distinction between darkness and light than we are told that *the evening and the morning were the first day*. What happened to the afternoon? There follow several more "days", also with parts unaccounted for and out of order. How can we hope for rigour and clarity with such off-hand definitions from such an authoritative source so early in the game?

In contrast, the much later reference to *forty days and forty nights* is reassuringly explicit; it seems to acknowledge the possibility that an unqualified *day* might or might not be taken to include a night. Travel agents could learn from this. There's still a problem however. The *contiguousness* of these said days and nights – essential to any convincing account of self denial – is only implied. The odd bed and breakfast (which must have been high up on the list of temptations) is not specifically ruled out.

In Malcolm's school, History may or may not have been more or less bunk. That's safe to say. But it had certainly been hard going. And it did repeat itself – on Tuesdays and Thursdays. Art may have been long but History was interminable. Perplexing too. Why, for example, when numbering the centuries, did they fail to recognise the zeroth, thus making every subsequent one jar numerically with its first two digits? Could anyone now state that the Battle of Hastings was an eleventh-century event without feeling a hint of dissonance – the ghost of a ruler poised above the knuckles?

Malcolm yawned, gently rubbed his hands together then flipped through his notes. Decent progress had been made. He could call it a day. If not a night.

Chapter 23

Mattingley

As a recent experimental participant you are invited for a follow-up interview . . .

The unsigned sheet was in a sealed envelope left in Malcolm's pigeon hole. As before, a cheque for fifteen shillings was attached. He was intrigued. Was this the organisers, officially winding up his involvement? Was this the final payment – a less-than-golden handshake? Or was that to come? Or were perhaps either (or both!) of the experimenters making further, informal contact? With a quiet, cosy assignation. A surprise party? Either way, he savoured the hint of cloak and dagger for the rest of the day. The next morning, at the appointed time, he followed the directions to a small room on an upper floor of the Psychology Department.

'Mattingley,' was all the man said as he shook Malcolm's hand across the big desk. Was that his name? Place of birth? A favourite adverb? If the first then why no "Professor" or "Dr". Maybe he had no academic rank. But the suit and tie, the athletic build, the trim moustache and crisp manner suggested he might have some other kind. Malcolm thought of enquiring further but in the end just said, 'Hello,' and sat down in the seat indicated.

'So, have you enjoyed participating in the project?'

'Is it over then?' said Malcolm.

'Well, these things are, generally, on-going. You know . . . long-term. But subjects drop in and out.'

'I certainly met some interesting experimenters!' said Malcolm with a grin.

'Ah yes, some of the undergraduates here are very, er, personable.'

'Do you interview all your subjects?'

'Sometimes ones with particular profiles are passed on to us.'

'Are you not in Psychology then?'

'We liaise with them from time to time . . .'

Malcolm felt an urge to ask who "we" was, but was unsure about the grammar, and had a suspicion that that might be just what "they" wanted him to do.

' . . . we take an interest in some subjects – independent thinkers – how they might shape up . . . in the future.

'So you're, what? A careers advisor?'

'Well, yes.' He smiled and nodded thoughtfully. 'In a way!' He flipped open a file on the desk. Malcolm fancied he saw the word *Intelligence* in a page heading, but it could have been *inelegance*. Or *ineligible*. Likewise *Confidential* and *coincidental* are hard to distinguish upside down, and from a glancing angle. Especially when you're pretending to be looking somewhere else altogether.

The man began a friendly interrogation: reading habits, hobbies, family ties. Girlfriends. Malcolm was forthcoming – he had little to hide on any of these fronts. They moved to broader topics: did he read the papers? Here Malcolm was more circumspect: it all depended – sometimes, but often he didn't believe what he read. Was the government doing a good job? Well, they said they were! Was the country strong, the world safe? Strength could take many forms. And safe from whom? One man's safety might be another's peril. And so on.

The discussion began to peter out. The man looked at his watch. Did Malcolm have any questions? A good question. He guessed that, on balance, the less he asked the more likely they were to want him to continue. So he did not demand to know who was who and what exactly they, and he, had been doing. Or whether they wanted him to carry on doing it. He repeated his appreciation of the experimenters – their cool professionalism etc. If *they* wished to test him further, he added with a smirk, he was ready, willing and able. For the usual fee!

The man stood up. 'Fine. We'd prefer it if you didn't discuss your involvement here with others . . .' At this Malcolm risked raising his eyebrows. '. . . we don't want to colour the judgement and expectations of any future subjects.'

Malcolm nodded sagely and performed his nose-tapping routine.

'We'd know how to contact you.'

'Right.' They shook hands again. 'Nice to meet you Mr . . . er . . . Dr . . .

'Mattingley,' said the man.

The sun was shining as Malcolm left the Weiss Building. He took a stroll around the campus lawns in high spirits. It was always pleasing to have the attention of others, if only for a little while. Maybe one day his superior spatial reasoning and reaction times, his visual and auditory acuity, if in truth he had any of those things, would prove to be of special value. To someone.

He wandered into the Students' Union, where it had all begun. Where the "Wanted" notice had been was a poster for next Saturday's disco.

Would he be wanted again? If so, by whom? For what? And when?

Well, good things came to those who waited. So they said. It was simply a matter of time.

Meta-Malcolm 35 is of average height, narrow-shouldered, and a little shy with women. Largely vegetarian, he drinks occasionally, doesn't smoke or gamble, and adheres strictly to speed limits when driving his small, grey, slightly rusty hatchback. He has a limited knowledge of foreign languages, and a strong aversion to pain, discomfort and sudden loud noises. Once or twice a week he takes a gentle jog round the lake in the local park, where he's learned to be wary of the larger geese. He's never parachuted or scuba dived (though he once went snorkelling in Torquay).

In short, he's the perfect spy. The very last you'd suspect – blandly blending into the scenery, merging, morphing. Figure or ground? Post or space? A man of mystery. Meta-mole, pimpernel – they seek him here, and there. At least they would if they ever suspected his existence. Agent Double-O Zero – a triple cipher, a radar-eluding Man Who Never Was. He has no need of high-tech gadgetry, but he wouldn't say no to a trio of female assistants to share his adventures, offer secretarial support, or post-mission massage.

He is out there somewhere, awaiting the call of Queen and country.

Chapter 24

Mr Inbetween

Back in the concrete reality of Gray Hall the last week of term had rather crept up on Malcolm. The dissertation had grown and grown. He was in sight of the critical word count. But the ragged and unwieldy piece still needed a good deal of tweaking. As well as a title.

He flicked back and forth through the notepad, extrapolating the half pages, inserting new ones, interpolating in the double spacing and, more reluctantly but of necessity, deleting. His composite, interleaving work plan (writing between lines, between resting between sheets, between eating between meals) was working well. The idea of betweenness was clearly central to the whole investigation. Come to think of it *On Betweenness* would make a jolly good title.

Or *Inbetweenness* – even snappier! Such a compelling concept. And one intensified by the prematurely Springy air wafting in through the wide-open window, carrying thoughts of nesting, of recursion; the natural urge to plant some item in the inviting space defined by flanking marker posts.

The origin of many a problem. Because while space was essentially singular, flanking was essentially dual. So the twin posts competed to command the space and triangular tangles arose, whichever way you looked. Thus the price label on the front edge of the supermarket shelf which seemed to promise bargain bananas above but referred in fact to extortionate King Edwards below. This kind of ambiguity was repeated endlessly and shamelessly on library bookshelves, matrices of mailboxes and the name-tags on the concertinaed innards of filing-cabinet drawers. Ambiguities that were so commonplace, so resolvable individually by trial and error, that nobody bothered or dared to remove them. Or to count the serious, accumulated cost of the many small confusions . . .

With the house to himself for a few days, Meta-Malcolm 60 has been entrusted with choosing paints for the spare room. Colour schemes for the rest of the place are determined already, by more responsible, discriminating eyes – ones only too familiar with his usual dress sense.

For a full half hour he scans the daunting acreage of colour chart that enlivens the wall of the local DIY shop. The twenty-by-fifty array of little rectangular patches shade smoothly, almost imperceptibly, from left to right and top to bottom, with just the occasional more startling transition between rows. A thousand choices! And hence a million possible pairings, for walls and woodwork. Well, slightly fewer, it's true, if you discount green with green, yellow with yellow etc. Although he might argue that was the perfect match, he's long accepted it isn't acceptable to others.

He steps back and forth, squints, frowns and says 'Hmm' a lot, sometimes rotating his head and crossing his eyes to bring two widely separated samples into adjacency. It's a tiring and slightly nauseating procedure. Some of the names he finds fanciful and confusing. Even arbitrary. Would anyone really be able to say, confronted with unlabelled patches of, say, *Mazurka* and *Fandango*, which was which? Surely numbers would be better. More objective and neutral. Not to mention discreeter, he thinks, wondering if he could ever bring himself to ask, out loud, for a gallon, or even a half, of *Pale Parmigiano*, or *Bolivian Twilight*, in spite of the alluring shades beneath those names. But in the end others will judge his efforts (and may condemn them) on the visual effect alone. By the time the paint has dried the original, mediating word-labels will be forgotten.

He finally settles on cool, slaty *Nantucket*, for the walls, and creamy blond *Madagascan Moon*, for the woodwork. Each looks safe, without quite being bland, contrasting but not conflicting with the other. His choices are not at all bad ones. Visually speaking. At any rate he feels confident enough to ignore the assistant's raised eyebrows as she marches off to the basement to fetch the cans. M-M struts off down the High Street with a carrier bag in each hand, whistling nonchalantly, though looking more Sorcerer's Apprentice than Saturday Night Fever.

He remembers once being told that it was better to do the walls first. Or was it the woodwork? What's certain is that he'll have to do one of them first, if only because there is only one of him assigned to the job. He makes a big mug of tea to help him think and to get into the workman spirit. It occurs to him that it ought to be easier to wipe splashes of emulsion from dry gloss than vice versa, and so he begins with the woodwork. The paint seems rather darker on the door than it did on the chart. And altogether more purplish. But then the lighting was different there, of course. And artificial. What's more it will lighten during the drying. Surely. And gradually fade, anyway. Decoration is for the long term. One shouldn't rush to judgement.

Two days and two glossy dry coats later he is reconciled to the colour. Almost. Over another big mug of tea he decides he must have specified the colour of the gloss when he meant the emulsion, and vice versa. Or, even better, it was the assistant who confused them in this way. Not a problem though. Harmony, or for that matter pleasing contrast, arises from the relationship between *two* colours. If these are interchanged the relationship remains. More or less. It's just like inverting a chord in music.

But he's surprised all over again on opening the emulsion. It looks lighter than it should be. That is, than the stuff that should have been the gloss should, if his theory is right, be. And more yellowish. Much more. Stirring doesn't seem to make it darker, or less yellow. Neither does waiting an hour and drinking more tea.

He returns to the store with the second of the offending cans and heads straight for the chart. At ten yards the individual patches begin to resolve themselves. At five yards the wall colour he really wanted, for all its subtlety, leaps out at him like an old friend. But then his eye is drawn to the patch that sits immediately above it. At first it seems strangely familiar. Then only too familiar – he is holding a gallon of it. Further inspection of the chart reveals that the gloss he has recently applied is, likewise, the upstairs neighbour of the one he thought he'd bought. Before his eyes the format of the chart undergoes a small but shocking shift: the colours are not surtitled, they are subtitled.

He took home exactly the paints he asked for. But what he should have asked for, it seems, were Marshmallow Mist and Buckwheat. He brings the matter to the attention of the assistant. She is unsympathetic. A label, she explains, is a label. No, no-one else has ever been confused. And no, paint which has been opened and stirred may not be exchanged. He leaves, carrying the can, his progress down the High Street now less sprightly, and distinctly unbalanced. He decides the new decor might grow on him, in time. It just might. He had wanted to surprise the others. He certainly will.

Thus are the pitfalls of inbetweenness frozen, long-term, into the fabric of things. The problem has even crept into the language itself. The careless, though popular, expression *between each* is its most telling symptom. Phrases don't come more treacherous, nor grammatical sins more cardinal, than this. How tragic and ironic it is that armies of retired colonels and the like direct their collective rage instead against the innocent split infinitive. Maybe they're just trying to avoid the very real peril which they dimly perceive to surround (or is it *adjoin?*) the notion of adjacency. The aim is worthy, but inaccurate. We can argue all night about whether it's more natural to place an adjective before or after a noun – the world itself is split over the matter, and both conventions clearly work. But how can you resist the opportunity afforded by English to simply stick (ahhh! doesn't that feel good?) a qualifier right in the very middle of the thing it qualifies – delivering an instant, delectable, adverb sandwich? Bull's-eye!

Malcolm stared down at his most recent efforts. Another half a page. Half a leaf! Better than no notes at all. A quick consultation of the stomach indicated it was sandwich time again. But his bread and cheese supplies had dwindled, respectively, to a crust, and a sliver. He put the latter on the former and stuck them under the grill. Symmetry was beginning to pall anyway.

Half a leaf, half a leaf, half a leaf, onward. Quite suddenly the dissertation felt finished. Almost. As close, perhaps, as it ever would be. The last Thursday of term ended and the last Friday began.

For Malcolm it began with the clanging of a bucket in the corridor. Edna was early. At least it sounded like Edna. If it was Flora she'd be whistling show tunes. Inexpertly, it was true. But with respect. What she lacked in intonation she made up for in integrity. With Flora you always got both verse and chorus (including, it went without saying, the middle eight). Edna would just clang the bucket.

She clanged it again. Malcolm opened an eye. The clock said ten past eight. Very slightly later to be precise, as the hands were stretched out dead in line. Like a banking aeroplane. Usually the cleaners left it till gone nine, when many of the students would have departed for lectures, leaving more room to negotiate the narrow corridors, fewer mucky footprints on the newly mopped stairs.

Maybe Edna had slept badly, started early, got ahead of herself. Or Malcolm's clock had stopped. But no, the long, red bristle of a second-hand was sweeping away as it should. Maybe he was only half awake and not thinking straight, or maybe his monocular perspective was causing him to misread the time through a parallax error. Opening the other eye might solve both problems at a stroke. But wait a minute. Wasn't it about now that the clocks went forward? Or backward? Or whatever it was they did about now? It seemed only recently that they'd put them back, or had it been forward? But then time was famous for flying, even without our intervention. It was what it did best in fact.

So, either it was "really" gone nine and the first lecture would have started and since there was nothing at ten he might as well go back to sleep. Or, it was "really" only gone seven and so he might as well go back to sleep anyway. Through the half sleep a dim distant voice told him it was a bit naive, if not chauvinistic, to measure reality with respect to Greenwich mean time.

He was too tired to argue. So, in his own meantime he drifted off again, into a dreamland resonating with all the remnants of his recent imaginings. Clanging buckets became chiming clocks, chairlifts and stairlifts, stop watches and stopped clocks, stop cocks and plug-hole vortices, shower taps that made it warmer when you turned them clockwise (a useful mnemonic for that British Summer Time business, perhaps), hall clocks, wall clocks, watched clocks, that never boiled, round tables, turntables, timetables and spinning barbers' poles kept his sleeping senses busy, until he was woken by a clang so loud and close it couldn't be accommodated in the dreamy scheme of things. He boldly opened both eyes and was greeted by two Edna faces in the double doorway. The images fused. He addressed himself to the single, stereo Edna.

'What time is it? Like, *really?*' said Malcolm.

Slightly puzzled Edna consulted his clock and reported that it was quarter past nine. The plane had levelled out. It was then he realised it would be a week or two before they adjusted the clocks. Whichever way. Edna clanged off down the corridor chuntering about myopia and tax-payers' money. Malcolm turned over again. It was definitely bad form to sneak in late for Nietzsche.

So, the deadline arrived. The repeated sprouting and pruning, combing and shuffling of words was over. All that remained was to sandwich the tidied sheets in the stiff cardboard crusts of a ring binder (he selected a grainy, wholesome brown from the College bookshop), and serve them up with fingers crossed to the hungry, waiting examiners.

And so another term ended, another equinox slipped by. The intellectual tide slackened, allowing more everyday concerns to rise to the surface.

Malcolm's skiing extravagances were still reverberating. But debt can take many forms. It's not always red figures on a bank statement;

it can become absorbed and stored as departures from the proper, comfortable norms of a hundred of life's little variables. His overdraft was only nominal. The real serious shortfall existed in kind. Or lack of kind. By having neglected the services of barbers and cobblers, through the deficits implicit in holey socks and patched elbows, though he'd issued no IOUs and held no pawn tickets, Malcolm was in hock from head to toe.

There was nothing else for it. Over the coming Easter vac he would have to make some money.

Chapter 25

Passing Fancies

On a wet Monday morning just before eight Malcolm reported, as instructed, to the factory foreman. He was dispatched immediately to Central Stores and emerged minutes later, his rather slight figure now clad in XXL overalls of plain white nylon, with a dinky little matching cap. Embossed on both pocket and peak, in a bold lemon script, was *WonderCakes Ltd*. As he shuffled back into the packing plant he was greeted by a wolf whistle. But in the dim-lit barn of a building he could not positively identify the whistler, nor quite, over the hum of fans and conveyors, judge the level of irony intended.

'You're on the belt!' the foreman shouted.

'Oh, sorry!' Malcolm stepped nimbly to one side.

'No, no, I'm puttin' you on the conveyor.' He pointed at the length of motionless black rubber.

'I'd be happy to walk!' said Malcolm, with a grin.

The foreman stared blankly back, then launched into a hygiene-and-safety briefing. This consisted of a few dos, and a lot of don'ts, interspersed with vague pointing at small, distant things. Then off he went, leaving Malcolm to it.

Beside the conveyor hung a large, laminated, wordless signboard. It was covered in schematic depictions of hands, feet, cakes, noses and handkerchiefs, in various configurations, all marked with either jolly green ticks or angry red crosses. Not much to go on. Hanging on nearby hooks were a pair of long tongs and an even longer stick with a thing on the end, like a croupier's rake. Malcolm took one in each hand and prepared for action. It was a while coming.

Having learnt that the prospects for vacation work in his hometown were poor he'd opted to stay on in Hall. With no outside conferences to host the college was offering accommodation to its regular residents at a much reduced rate. In spite of which the place was mostly empty. And delightfully quiet as a result. Enquiring at the employment exchange he'd immediately been offered a position as a "temporary operative, foodstuffs industry". No experience was necessary, no interview required. The pay was minimal.

When the klaxon just above his head sounded Malcolm's feet briefly left the ground and his heart missed several beats. No-one had thought to install a warning warning. There followed a long, uneasy silence, like when the Apaches were about to attack. Then came a distant clunk, and a more local hum. The belt began to move, surprisingly swiftly, and in the opposite direction to the one he, for some reason, was expecting. He stood and stared as yard after yard of the smooth blackness slipped past like an empty motorway lane. Then they appeared. Shouldering their way, four abreast, through the dangling polythene strips. Massed ranks, advancing unstoppably in never-ending line – a crowd, a host, of golden fairy cakes.

By the end of the shift, after some trial and error, odd hints from new colleagues in the canteen, and occasional brusque feedback from the foreman, Malcolm had more or less figured out what his duties actually were. Simple really: keep 'em in line, keep 'em movin'! On emerging from the ovens the products, it seemed, were herded and channelled before being scrutinised by beams of light and midget weighbridges. Deviant cakes were rejected by a mechanical arm. Only the strictly compliant made it to Malcolm's section, where the little ride-through allowed a final cooling and some manual control. Beyond a second polythene portcullis they were machine-wrapped into packets of four, six, eight or twelve, according to type.

On the walk back to Hall he did a rough calculation. Several hours at one or two per second, allowing for the gaps and belt stoppages, lunch and tea breaks, meant he must have witnessed the march-past of around twenty thousand cakes. Probably more than he'd seen in his score of years so far. And enough for one a day for the rest of his life. Possibly. Later they continued their parade across his inward eye, lulling him to sleep. Dainty, toothsome little substitutes for sheep, invading and sweetening his dreams, where finally they broke ranks and frolicked all night in gleeful anarchy.

Tuesday morning was rock cakes. These were unruly by nature – a ragged procession of raw recruits of all shapes and sizes. Malcolm busied himself trying to nudge the many stragglers into lines. And pondering the sudden variety – had those discriminating light beams been turned off? Soon he was bored and the items were just flying by in a golden-brownish blur. But reducing your vigilance can have a pay-off. Some things are best detected with a relaxed, undirected eye. Suddenly a cake stood out from the crowd on account of its peculiar shape: a striking likeness of the Matterhorn. Not long after came a passable Fujiyama (or was it Kilimanjaro?)

And so it went. He watched, entranced, giving each of these flukish forms a token prod of acknowledgement as it passed. What a privilege to be the first witness to such a thing. And maybe the last. Tomorrow teatime someone, somewhere, engrossed in the evening paper or TV news, could, with the first unwitting bite, destroy for ever such a happy accident.

For accidents they surely were. In the end it was just statistics. Take flour, butter, eggs, sugar, milk and currants, subject them to the vagaries of sieving and mixing, dividing up and baking. Repeat many thousands of times, and in due course you'd get a Jungfrau or an Eiger, an Uluru or Popocactapetl. Or even – he squinted at the speeding shapes – a Mount Rushmore. Rock faces, human faces. It was just a question of scale, and degree. Wasn't it? He put his head close to the belt, and panned his eyes rapidly to capture images of the craggy textures zipping past. Eventually there'd be a familiar face. A famous face, why not? It was simply a matter of time.

He took the tongs, grabbed a cake at random, studied it at close quarters.

'Put that down!' The foreman's voice was right behind him. And very loud, if some way short of klaxon level. Eating produce from the belt, he reminded Malcolm, was a sackable offence.

'I was just looking at the pattern on it,' said Malcolm. He held it up to the man's face.

'The *pattern?*'

He turned it through ninety degrees, moved it back and forth. 'Don't you see?'

'See what?'

'W.H.Auden!' Malcolm ventured.

'W.H.*Who*?'

'Well, maybe Charles Bronson then. Look at those eyebrows!'

The foreman strode off shaking his head and muttering.

On the walk home, in a light drizzle, Malcolm considered the day's events. Freak images in food were nothing new. The newspapers often carried little stories of supposed resemblances to various heroes and villains, along with not very convincing, grainy photos. They were still rare enough to arouse interest, though. And fetch high prices. A good few weeks' bakery wages anyway. Or the cost of a ski pass. Ones with religious significance were especially prized. Pilgrims would beat pathways to your door. He'd read of a case where a Virgin in a macaroon had changed hands for a four-figure sum.

That had been spotted by chance, no doubt. Had leapt from someone's peripheral vision into consciousness. And changed a life. But for every such thing discovered hundreds might go unnoticed. That meant a systematic, exhaustive search could be quite profitable. Demanding too. He had just over two weeks to explore and exploit the possibilities. Could it be done?

Malcolm lengthened his stride. It would take meticulous planning. He turned up his coat collar. It would be deeply suspicious if he were linked in any way to the selling of a cake. His employers would assume he'd stolen it from the line. Or even somehow interfered in the manufacturing process. A true "find" would have to be found by chance, authentically wrapped and sealed. And not found by him. He was going to need a partner on the outside. He'd start things off, though, on the inside. Next day he began reconnoitring in the canteen.

Having worked for many years in Packing and Dispatch, Big Brenda was an ideal source, a mine no less, of information. She held forth unprompted and at length on colleagues, old and new – their hobbies and quarrels, their excesses, alcoholic and romantic, their deficiencies, in dress sense and personal hygiene. But in among these revelations were clues as to how the whole section worked. At the most casual query from Malcolm she would obligingly supply the details. Not much, it seemed, got past Big Brenda. Within two days he'd picked up vital information on batch numbering, delivery schedules, van routes, and driver shift patterns. All for the price of a few mugs of tea. It was time to test the system.

Friday afternoon began with custard slices – smooth, featureless oblongs which promised little in the way of famous peaks or profiles. A direct intervention was called for. After a quick check that he was unobserved, Malcolm deftly raked one from the belt and inscribed a neat capital M on the top with his little finger. He then replaced it, noting the exact time, and saluted it on its way, before licking away the evidence.

Working from Brenda's data he estimated that the item, wrapped up in plastic with five of its comrades, would leave the factory around ten p.m., along with a few hundred similar packets. But there the trail diverged.

Early evening he ensconced himself in the phone booth in the foyer of Gray Hall and made a number of calls. Posing as a sweet-toothed shopper he established that a dozen local stores sold the product. He guessed that far fewer would get a daily delivery. But which? There was only one thing to do: follow the van.

Malcolm's wait in the lay-by opposite the main gates was a short one. And although his bicycle was hardly a racer the tailing operation around town proved even easier than in spy films. The quarry was, after all, big, red and slow; its driver unaccompanied, unsuspecting and, in all probability, unarmed. Malcolm was home within two hours, having narrowed down the search to just four stores.

He slept fitfully that night. His legs were tired from all the standing and pedalling. But so too were his retinas. Staring for hours at thousands of those advancing slabs of yellow had left its mark on the system. In the darkness complementary colour and motion came to the fore. Each time he closed his eyes or looked at the ceiling he was assailed by armies of livid purple after-images, slowly retreating, but never quite disappearing from view.

Early Saturday morning he was off again, and struck lucky at the second visit. A careful rummage though a pyramid of packets in Aldersons, and there it was: his very own monogram, plainly legible through the clear wrapper. He dropped the pack into an empty wire basket. And immediately felt the need for camouflage. In went marmalade, cheese and a cucumber, as diversionary items. Then a small tin of pink salmon – a subconscious afterthought perhaps, in lieu of the red herrings the store did not stock. In the covert-operations game one quickly learned to improvise. Mattingley might have been impressed.

Within half an hour he was back in his study/bedroom celebrating the success, indeed, eating the trophy, and savouring a large mug of tea. This was, though, only the beginning. It was one thing to mark an item, and then trace it through the system. But how did you spot the cakes with interesting patterns in the first place, whatever their orientation? And in such a throng, at such a speed? It was the needle in the haystack. The sand grain on the beach. The information was there all right, the comparison operation itself straightforward. One just wanted a thousand times the vigilance, memory and processing speed of a human. One day, he felt sure, it would be easy. One day. It was simply a matter of time.

Meta-Malcolm 55 has at his fingertips all the techno wizardry of his age. Prematurely retired, he briefly basks in his new-found leisure, before casting around for a fresh challenge. He's had a career, a profession. A calling, even. Now, on a whim, he tries a *job* – part-time, short-term, low-paid. Partly to see how the other half lives. But also to test a little idea which has been brewing at the back of his mind for some years.

It's a routine day at the *Marvel* (formerly *Miracle*) *Bakery* (formerly *WonderCakes Ltd., part of Panorama Products*). His old briefcase has been placed inconspicuously on a shelf opposite the conveyor. In the front-pocket flap he has cut a small hole. Through it peeps the lens of his Smartycam phone, pointing at the passing confections. A thin cable runs to a laptop in the main compartment, buried under a plastic mac, some magazines and a couple of bananas, all topped off with a layer of paper hankies of uncertain cleanliness. What better deterrent to any prying eyes and fingers? Throughout the shift, exactly twice per second, a silent, high-resolution snapshot is taken and stored.

Once home he switches the computer into analysis mode. Sophisticated pattern-recognition routines (as used by MI5) are let loose on the mountain of data. Every single shot is compared with a large bank of target images, of famous people and places, at thousands of different orientations and scales, and scored for similarity. The billions of calculations continue while he sleeps. Over breakfast he checks the screen for any high-scoring matches; his program ranks these using asterisks and exclamation marks in ever bolder fonts and louder colours.

Over the weeks he fine-tunes the system, tweaking the various thresholds and criteria so as to minimise the number of false alarms, while not overlooking the longed-for, one-in-a-million, bull's-eye match.

Early results are crude but fascinating. The meringues, for some reason, show strong monumental tendencies, yielding in quick succession a rough and ready Parthenon, a sort of Albert Hall cum Taj Mahal, and several Eiffel Towers manquées. The strudels are more geographic (there being something fractal, perhaps, in that flaky pastry) and afford a fair few Isles of Wight, sawn-off Scandinavias and the like. At least to a charitable eye.

But it's faces he's really after, and these demand still greater patience. The scones and crumpets prove the most promising, producing a string of near misses – among them an unmistakable Mona Lisa, spoilt only by a hint of black goatee, and the second nose. But persistence pays off and the law of averages is upheld. M-M and his secret accomplice begin to enjoy a trickle of modest successes. Items are tracked to their destinations using the delivery data he has amassed. Then they are simply bought over the counter and finally offered for sale discreetly, via the internet. Wealthy foreign eccentrics snap them up. He invests in a higher-resolution camera, upgrades the computer memory and processor. Success breeds success. The two treat themselves, respectively, to fine wines and fashionable outfits; a new car and a new kitchen. Then, more boldly still, they book the same Mediterranean cruise. Separate cabins, of course, but within nightly tiptoeing distance.

Thus statistical principles are proven, and conspiratorial urges satisfied.

But then people start asking questions, and M-M 55 retires. Again.

In Gray Hall, Malcolm finished his tea. It was clear his co-conspirator would need to be carefully chosen. A person he knew well enough to approach, and trust. But not one who could be linked to him by others. He ran through his mental list of acquaintances for someone who had that unlikely combination of qualities. In addition to being smart. And it wouldn't really hurt to be young and female either – enthusiasm and intuition would be considerable assets in such a project. His recent visits to Psychology had been promising in that respect, but were perhaps still too public. A more indirect route was in order. He found his mind wandering back to the early Autumn term.

The little lady behind the reception desk at Dingles was more helpful than he could have hoped. No, she was sorry, they didn't have a lost-property department, but if anyone had found a pen and pencil set, all that time ago, it would have been handed to whoever's party it was. She picked up her bookings book – did he want the phone number? Malcolm managed to keep his cool. 'It's worth a try,' he shrugged.

He rang from Gray Hall. No, sorry, Angela had gone home for the holiday, said a familiar voice.

'Hello Helen,' said Malcolm, 'guess who!'

There was a pause.

'Mark?' She sounded pleasantly surprised.

'No, but you're close. Alphabetically, anyway.' Rather dubious compensation, he felt.

'Marvin!'

'No.'

'Martin? Mervyn? Miles?'

'You're going the wrong way.'

'Ah. Matthew!'

'Back a bit further!'

'Luke?'

'Too far.'

There was another pause.

'Give me a clue!'

'Errrmm, think of ducks!'

'Ducks?'

'Ducks.'

'Bill?' she offered. 'Bob?'

'Nope.'

'Donald, Daffy, I don't know.'

He began to suspect she was teasing him. 'D'you give in?'

She gave in. He enlightened her.

'A-ha. The sandwich man.' She didn't sound displeased. Exactly. Though still wary.

Then less so, perhaps, after his mention of "a little business proposition". But inviting her back to Hall again seemed premature. And her suggestion of the Union Bar he politely rejected on musical grounds. They settled on a meeting in the High-Street tea shop.

She had chosen to sit on the far side of quite a wide table. But it all felt less awkward than he'd feared. They commented on the weather, very briefly (it was unremarkably seasonal), then compared and bemoaned the demands of their differing studies. He said her hair looked nice, and she said his was sticking up. A bit.

He made a vague flattening gesture with his hand. 'Anyway,' he cleared his throat, 'I wanted to talk about cakes.'

'Cakes?' said Helen. She grinned, 'Don't tell me, you've got too many.'

'Well, in a sense. To begin with. But I'm whittling it down. Sort of.' He leaned across the table. 'To a very special few.'

He suspended his account while the waitress delivered their drinks.

Helen took a sip of Earl Grey. He began again. But didn't get very far.

'So, you want me to buy a cake,' she frowned, 'and then sell it again?'

He put a finger to his lips. 'Well, it might be a few, actually. And very profitable too. Possibly. We'd go fifty-fifty, of course.' He gestured equitably with his teaspoon.

She looked doubtful. 'Why can't you do it?'

He glanced around before whispering, 'I work too close to the source.'

In confidential tones he explained his position and outlined the plan. He would provide the intelligence: store location, time of day, product description. She would make the purchase, sell it any way she could. There were, surely, occult or UFO magazines and the like, with small-ad sections. It was well known that people traded in these things.

Helen listened, alternately intrigued, amused, and sceptical, but finally agreed. At his suggestion they settled on a codename, then symbolically synchronised watches, clinked teacups, and drank to success. At length she reached over, patted his hand and got up to leave. 'I suppose this meeting never took place,' she winked. Malcolm spent much of the rest of the evening trying to interpret that.

A week went by and Malcolm began to feel more at home in the workplace. He'd rolled up the sleeves and legs of his generous overalls to a length more consistent with safety and dignity. He was on nodding terms with a good few co-workers, and kept the line running smoothly. More or less.

The dull routine allowed plenty of scope for the imagination. With the cake-rake in hand you could be in charge of roulette at Monte Carlo. Or a Battle-of-Britain Ops-Room WAAF. Just standing there watching the procession you could be the Queen in The Mall, or a heavily medalled Soviet General in Red Square. Malcolm would sometimes get quite carried away and do military-band impressions as an accompaniment to proceedings – Sousa for the doughnuts, Elgar for the muffins. But his eyes were always fixed on the endless stream of produce. And soon he found a nifty strategy for coping with the huge numbers.

It worked like this. The very first "stray" cake that came along, regardless of appearance, he would rake aside and keep as a spare. Thereafter, using the tongs, he swapped it for any passing cake which looked, at first glance, to have special features. He could then evaluate this at leisure, and in due course swap it for any one which looked more interesting still. This ensured that there were no absences in the ranks, and meant he always had, in isolation, just one cake, of ever increasing distinction. With luck, by the end of a session he'd be holding the most promising specimen. If this were judged truly worthy it could be slipped in at the very end of the batch, thus greatly simplifying the tracing operation.

Within a couple of days he had a significant hit. The call he made from the phone box opposite the factory entrance was a model of military concision: *Megasave; from 14.00 hours; iced buns; Alfred Hitchcock in profile.*

'How can I be sure it's you?' sniggered Helen.

'*Ducks,*' said Malcolm, and rang off.

But the store was on the edge of town, the bus late and the traffic heavy. Helen found herself staring at an empty shelf, with undisguisable disappointment. The young lady assistant, sensing perhaps some unhealthy craving for the missing product, was sympathetic. Yes, they had had some earlier. Not to worry, there'd be more in on Wednesday. Did she want some putting aside?

Malcolm took the setback with equanimity and pressed on with his duties, while making every effort to keep his profile low. Whenever some joker further up the belt snaffled a cake, Malcolm went into overdrive with rake and tongs, making frantic rearrangements to conceal the glaring gap. If he himself were suspected of any irregularities he might get removed from the belt, and the game would be over. On the other hand he never intervened when, as often happened, an item passed with a blatant bite out of it. If he was accused, he reasoned, simple forensic dentistry would acquit him.

Some mischief was trickier to deal with. The blatantly rude configurations of sponge rolls or éclairs that sometimes came his way were easily spotted, and rendered seemly by a simple shift or rotation. But he was aware that from time to time his vigilance lapsed, allowing the more subtly suggestive arrangements to get through. This left Malcolm wondering about the spiky-pinkish-haired woman who kept smirking and winking from across the canteen. Was she the upstream perpetrator, courting his attentions? Or a downstream recipient, responding to the one she believed to be the author of these graphic messages? Either way, he was careful not to wink back.

No doubt the foreman, too, had questions. Perhaps why, when he came into this man's work area, he was so often greeted with whistled bursts of *Colonel Bogey* or *The Dam Busters March*. Or cheery cries of *"Rien ne va plus!"* It took, he supposed, all types. And some types were worth keeping an eye on.

Late afternoon, on the Thursday of his second week, Malcolm had cornered a relatively convincing Albert Einstein in a flan, and was examining it with some satisfaction.

'Somethin' wrong?' The loud, familiar voice came from behind. Without turning Malcolm nudged the incriminating item back on to the belt. It was now clearly misaligned in relation to its fellows but within a few seconds was safely through the gap in the partition.

'I've told you before, flans is *SIX*, in a row. ONLY *six*.'

Malcolm nodded apologetically.

'The wrapper's set up for *SIX!*'

Malcolm continued to nod as the foreman went on for some time about blockages and stoppages, breakages and shortages, not to mention bottlenecks and jams . . .

As soon as he'd gone Malcolm dashed round into the next section.

'Sorry,' he shouted to Big Brenda, who was standing, hands on hips, supervising the packing machine, 'I just let an extra one slip through. Hope it didn't mess things up for you.'

Brenda simply shook her head. And patted her stomach.

It all came down to his last day. It was sunny for a change, Good Friday, and Hot Cross Buns were high on the menu. Were they passing at a more solemn pace than usual? Or were his eyes and brain at last adjusting somehow to the flow? By late morning he'd captured a real humdinger. A ghostly outline of a Madonna graced the top-left quadrant. She seemed to be perched on the white piping and gazing down at a similarly spectral childlike smudge, bottom right. Malcolm persuaded himself the swirly, grainy irregularities in the background could be little clouds. Or even wings. When the time was right he sent the two figures on their way with a gentle, reverent shove of the rake.

At lunchtime he made the crucial phone call. During the afternoon he was able to relax at last, just letting the various items go by. And looking forward to the rendezvous.

But when Helen entered the tea shop just after five p.m. she was empty handed and unsmiling. The buns, apparently, were all in special-offer, Easter-bargain packets of eight, and the 2x2x2 arrangement had opaque, corrugated paper between layers. This meant that half of the top surfaces were simply not visible. She'd checked the considerable pile at Megasave but could see no sign of the chosen one. Within minutes Malcolm was on his bike and speeding across town. He'd clocked off for the last time, and collected his wages. No-one could stop him now.

According to the young lady assistant not so many of the buns had been sold yet – Saturday was the big day. Malcolm decided the odds were favourable enough. There were sixteen packets left. He bought them all. The assistant held the door open as he left with a large carrier bag in each hand. 'Happy Easter!' she called after him, rather uncertainly. It wasn't just women, it seemed, who had these odd cravings.

It took the two of them a whole half hour to unwrap and examine each bun from many angles, under Malcolm's desk lamp. 'Guess somebody got there first,' he said at last, philosophically. It took them a further hour to eat several each. 'You do believe me, don't you?' he sighed.

'I have complete faith,' she smirked. 'Is it all right if I give a few packs to Mark?'

'Who's Mark?' said Malcolm.

'You don't know him. He's got a sweet tooth.'

'Anything else?'

'Yes. A freezer. And a motorbike!' She eyed the great pyramid of buns they had built on the desk. 'What about the rest?'

'Ducks?' said Malcolm.

'Ducks!' said Helen, getting up to leave. 'It's supposed to be fine weather tomorrow.'

Chapter 26

Rights to Silence

No sooner had the Summer Term got underway than Gray Hall began to present extra problems. At least to Malcolm. With some others, though, the place seemed to have acquired a peculiar, if short-lived, kind of popularity. Within three weeks Room 304, directly overhead, had had no fewer than three occupants. It was unmistakably three – although Malcolm hadn't got to know any names or faces, their footwear and gaits, their individual styles of snoring and slamming the door, provided three acoustic self-portraits as characteristic as any signature. And each one had spent the bulk of his brief stay experimenting with the positions of bed, desk and wardrobe. The sheer size and weight of these items had clearly been a stimulating challenge, forcing them to fall back on the techniques their not-so-distant forebears had developed for building pyramids and henges – dragging, shoving, levering or rolling the things end over end, throughout the lengthy day and into the small hours. And after investigating the surprisingly large number of permutations possible, each, it seemed, had given up hope of finding the longed-for configuration, and moved out again.

Meanwhile the neighbours to left and right contented themselves with putatively musical offerings. One early morning in early May Room 215 began practising a protest song. The strummed guitar accompaniment was vigorous, and had a harmonic adventurousness which went well beyond the original songwriter's intentions. It wasn't long before No. 217 joined the march – though whether in comradely support or counter-protest was hard to say. Malcolm threw open the windows, letting in the masking throb of a two-stroke motor mower, along with a little Spring bonus of birdsong and the smell of new-cut grass. But his twin tormentors were gaining in confidence with every chorus, and soon outmasked mower, birds and all. Faced with this uncombatable pincer movement he grabbed pen, paper, a half-read

185

article on prime numbers and a half-eaten slab of chocolate, and fled to the calm of the campus library.

The Theology section was an ideal location – easily accessible, yet far enough from the entrance to ensure peace and quiet. As usual it was deserted. He sat there for a full half hour, not reading or writing a word, just soaking up the quiet and gentle routine of scholarly life around him. Miss Angle and her assistants came and went about their librarial duties in soft-soled silence, eyes alert for misaligned spines and alphabetical disorder, whispering and smiling to one another, tidying and tending the little paradise. Mindful of his own slothfulness, as well as a general lack of theological credentials, Malcolm sat up straight each time they approached, suspending the chocolate-chewing action, picking up a notepad and pen and scratching his head in what he hoped might look like doctrinal perplexity, before reverting to a contented slouching and staring into space as soon as the threat had passed.

Paradise. Only trouble was, they closed at 9.00 pm. Well, more accurately, the trouble was they threw you *out* at 9.00 pm. Malcolm would have been happy to linger on, reading, writing, thinking, or just being, while the little team of cleaners hummed around his feet with their suitably muted Hoovers, while the re-shelvers glided past wheeling knowledge by the trolley load.

Paradise. Free light, free heat. Free silence.

Well, almost free. If you divided the total of the modest library fines he'd incurred by the accumulated periods of study, it would come to far less than a penny an hour. In contrast, Gray Hall offered little more than high-price bedlam.

By mid-afternoon both article and chocolate were finished. Malcolm stayed on, musing and browsing, leaving reluctantly only when hunger got the better of him. Tomorrow would be better planned. He would pack himself some sandwiches and an apple or two so he could stay away from Hall till evening. But it looked like being too rainy for the lakeside bench. And food was forbidden in the library. Well then, he'd just have to sneak it in and eat surreptitiously. He wasn't by nature a flouter of rules, but there were higher considerations here. The deception was just a means to a scholarly end. First one must eat, then one may philosophise. Or calculate. In any case, what was paradise without forbidden fruit?

For the smuggling operation Malcolm made use of an old A4 box file, lined with non-rustly paper and prominently labelled "Pragmatism". The sandwiches he cut, cut and cut again, into a platoon of bite-sized, corned-beef soldiers. By 10 am he was back in the seclusion of Theology, enjoying a late breakfast. The sandwich-box ploy worked well – in less than a second you could one-handedly flip up the flap and pop a portion into the mouth, while the eyes never left the book, or the pen the paper. Once the transfer was safely carried out, the subsequent chewing could be as slow and discreet as necessary.

The soldiers were first rate – the relative thicknesses of bread, beef and margarine layers engineered in perfect proportion, although he said it himself. So delectable were they in fact that Malcolm risked taking two at once. He folded his arms, closed his eyes and began a gentle rumination. Paradise. A whole day's nourishment within arm's reach. Not to mention a lifetime of food for the mind within a few paces. What more could a man want? Apart, perhaps, from a glass of chilled, dry cider. And, well, a lithesome Eve wouldn't have gone amiss.

'Have you finished with this?' The stern, familiar voice came from behind.

For a moment Malcolm was back in the third-form classroom, frantically manoeuvring a gobstopper to the side of his mouth in order to field a question on King Harold which had suddenly been shot his way. He glanced sideways to see Miss Angle waving a sizeable volume which had been lying on the table close by. Along the spine in gold lettering he could just make out *Revelation and Redemption*. Denying any responsibility for the book would have meant opening his mouth, and hence revealing the sandwich subterfuge – indeed possibly spraying Miss A. with the evidence, albeit masticated beyond formal identification. So Malcolm could only respond to the question by putting on a sequence of facial expressions – moving from intellectual abstraction, through startled awareness, to exaggerated nods and smiles of gratitude. With a quizzical frown Miss A. slipped the volume back into its place on the shelves above. It was a while before he risked another, single soldier.

Nevertheless he was on the whole pleased with the box-file system. It gave a sort-of midnight-feast, wooden-horsey zest to the operation. There was a certain geometric appeal too. The file neatly accommodated two full slices of bread side by side. This meant that each slice was about A5 in size, and that made each soldier – at a half of a half of a half of a whole slice – a toothsome A8. As the morning progressed he felt a certain escalating excitement at passing through the A7 and then the A6 stages of consumption.

An idea began to take shape. Could it be that the 'A-series' convention for paper size offered a practical, unambiguous way of quantifying sandwiches? It was long established, and doubtless approved by the International Standards Organisation. Even the non-technically minded were used to its repeated halvings and doublings – the logarithmic (or was it *exponential?*) relations were painlessly inbuilt. He picked up a soldier and bit it neatly in half. The resulting two A9s enjoyed a brief, individual existence, before being reunited and then munched into an amorphous lump. Yes, the A-series, with its emphasis on area and successive subdivision, just might be the solution.

Yes, but then . . . He stopped chewing. Wouldn't there always be parties, bent on preserving confusion, who would reject the system? The Dorises of this world, sensing a threat to their powers of mystification, would somehow or other manage to subvert things. Malcolm shut his eyes again and pictured the exchange at some future, HMSO-approved sandwich counter:

'I'll have an A4 of cheese and pickle please.'
'Sorry luv, we've only got foolscap. 'E's not been yet!'
'OK, foolscap it is.'
'Right you are.' Hands are wiped on an apron. 'D'ya want it single-sided, double spaced, or folded in half?'

It didn't bear thinking about.

As the week wore on there was no sign of an acoustical let-up at Gray Hall. Malcolm began to arrive earlier and earlier in his new-found haven. And to leave later and later. Friday morning he was first through the door and settled in before Miss Angle had had chance to ink her little date stamper. The library was in many ways the ideal environment. Virtual silence wasn't just an agreeable fact of life here – it was ordained in big bold red letters on a dozen signboards throughout the building. Volume zero! Or as close as you could get to it. It was a shame he ever had to leave the place.

But then, *did* he have to? Wasn't there some clause in Magna Carta (or was it the Domesday Book?) guaranteeing freedom from auditory persecution? If there wasn't there should have been. Surely there must be some kind of historical right that could be asserted. Maybe he should ensconce himself in Theological Studies, clasp one of those big, black, leathery Authorised Versions to his chest, and claim sanctuary.

But today he had more mundane concerns, if only slightly more: prime numbers. Funny things. Somehow both ordinary and special, they'd exerted a fascination on thinkers through history, from the Ancient Greeks to his own thoroughly modern maths tutor. She'd shown him her shelf-full of books on them, suggesting he might like to do a mini-project on the subject as part of his continuous-assessment requirements. It was safeish ground – well-trodden, but with unresolved conjectures aplenty, and a lingering hint of mystery.

He uncapped a black biro and began to muse. First, with his philosophical hat on. What were these numbers, in their essence? Their defining characteristic was that they weren't divisible, exactly, by other numbers. So, should we regard them as, say, triumphantly defiant and inviolable? Or just plain awkward? They'd often been seen as symbols of solitude, on the grounds that they never occurred next to one another. But then neither did odd numbers. Or even ones. Or for that matter the squares, or the cubes. Splendidly isolated? Or sadly friendless? Prime numbers: a strange community.

Malcolm sneaked his first sandwich morsel of the day – an economical, summer-seasonal cucumber, sprinkled with a little salt and encased in wholesome granary bread. He slumped back contentedly in the chair. Even for limited periods libraries were nice places to be. There was something about them that engendered a peculiar mixture of excitement and security, not unlike the clothes-horse tents or tree houses of childhood. The layout and proportions of this particular bay were somehow perfect, offering an optimum state of enclosure. The three walls were insufficient to surround (with the resultant feeling of entrapment) and yet more than enough to merely flank (with the residual vulnerability). So there he sat, peninsulated from the world, pondering the glorious public privacy of it all. What fun it was to be immersed in scholarship, walled in by knowledge, dwarfed by cliffs of sheer erudition!

He looked up at the bookcases, towering ten or twelve feet above. Sheer they might be. But not unscalable. In fact the inter-shelf separation (dictated in the end by the vertical extent of comfortable eye movement, plus top and bottom page margins, and a bit of headroom) provided large but quite manageable steps. Coupled with the shelf *depth* (horizontal eye range plus left and right margins and a bit of spineroom, which could so easily yield to become toeroom) they just begged to be climbed.

But did he dare? Though he'd never had reason to think about it before, there was definitely something unorthodox, if not actually sacrilegious, about climbing bookshelves. On the other hand there seemed to be no-one about. He peeped into the adjacent areas. Deserted. He looked around again, drew a deep breath, and took the plunge. Or rather the leap. The climb was a matter of a few seconds.

And what a prospect from the summit! A landscape of learning stretched out before him. Serried ranks of wisdom as far as the eye could see. On a clear day you could probably have made out Home Economics.

Peering down into the oaken canyons between the back-to-back bookcases provided a further revelation. The library building's walls and pillars were of a grand, Victorian width, giving rise to generous, hidden, man-size voids. In places there were bracing beams and planking a few feet below the top, providing a platform where you might walk unseen. And the whole area was riddled with interconnecting deadspaces. In the event of Humanities suffering a military siege a handful of snipers could have held back a battalion.

Malcolm's reconnaissance was cut short by the squeak of a door and approaching footsteps. Only by a swift and nimble descent was he able to avoid the embarrassment of having to explain himself. Or, more likely, of not being able to do so. In the end though, was there anything to explain? Could there be any better reason for making the first ascent of a bookcase than simply *because it was there*?

Reseated at the table Malcolm kept his arms folded whenever anyone came near. And he put on an extra-innocent look – one could hide dusty fingertips, but not the incriminating trail of prints they would have left. Over a slim chocolate biscuit he pondered the significance of his discovery. It was considerable. And it seemed unlikely anyone else had realised the possibilities.

Hiding up top would give you a grand, Olympian kind of perspective. Not to mention the potential for mischief. He could become the Phantom of the Stacks – pencil-throwing poltergeist, master of the lightning sortie, annotator of unguarded essays, scuttling back to his vantage point to perch and gloat, stifling sniggers as he watched a fellow scholar, on returning from the gents, rubbing his eyes and scratching his head as he counted and recounted his much-depleted bag of boiled sweets. Hours of fun. Laughter in paradise.

But quick to dawn also was the realisation of a much more practical use. After all, here were acres of unclaimed, convenient, sleeping accommodation – warm, quiet, and above all, free. By relocating his lodgings from Gray Hall to the library he could, at a stroke, save a serious amount of rent money, as well as much wear and tear on the auditory nerves.

By late morning Spring sunshine had broken through and lured most of the students outdoors. They strolled along the campus pathways among budding trees and sprawled on the benches and grassy banks. Their revision books were propped open on laps and their pens poised over notepads, but in the main they showed far more interest in the ducks on the lake, the scudding clouds, and in one another.

So Malcolm went largely unobserved that afternoon as he made a survey of the library building from Aeronautics to Zoology, peering and probing above and behind the many bookcases, like some anxious house-hunter, looking for the optimal site. There was considerable variety.

The Botany bay was secluded, with a view of the college lawns, but had peeling paint, and a permanent and less-than-fragrant smell of something more than books. A more desirable location was Critical Theory. Blessed by the late-evening sun, it boasted an adjacent (though far from modern) convenience, and a handy fire escape. This was just as well since the local users seemed to have the most casual attitude to wastepaper disposal; a brief inspection revealed the hidden recesses to be knee-deep in crumpled sheets of foolscap – the false starts, middles and ends from the essays of a generation.

In some ways the most promising location was Philosophy itself. Having one wall populated entirely with convenient, toecap-wide volumes of the *Journal of Ethics* it was almost insultingly easy to a serious literary steeplejack. Though with the need for speedy ascents and descents perhaps one shouldn't be complacent.

Malcolm wasn't, of course, restricted to free-climbing techniques. Throughout the library various aids to scaling and reaching had been thoughtfully provided. In his home bay, maybe as a reflection of the inaccessibility of the subject, there was a rickety wooden step-ladder which had had the word 'Philosophy' branded on its side – possibly when its *bona fide* users had got tired of retrieving it from the light-fingered, troublesome neighbours in Politics and Economics. But an over-reliance on it might have led nosy folks to his lair. Or he might have woken a little later than intended to find himself marooned aloft for an indefinite period.

Widely scattered too were the "hop-ups" – squat, round frusta with rubber non-slip mats stuck on top, like gramophone turntables. These were handy enough for giving an extra shelf of reach, or as a temporary perch while browsing the higher foliage, but hopelessly inadequate for reaching the summit (even if you managed to fully exploit that internal spring action by jumping on to one from table height).

No, unaided climbing, as well as more challenging, would be more prudent. It would take a sleuth of Sherlockian acuity to spot the significance of the pattern of indentations in the ranks of books – starting with the left foot by Zeno, then the right above, amongst the Stoics, then the left again by Augustine, followed by a bold traverse into Scholasticism. Next, a hand-jam in the British Empiricists (you're nearly there, just don't look down!), and before you knew it you'd be easing past Wittgenstein and on to the silent summit, with not even a ladder to have to kick away.

There'd be a good deal of equipment to be taken aloft – food, clothes, a sleeping bag, a small Union Jack. Plus, of course, a flashlight and plenty of spare batteries – it would be a crime not to fully exploit the location's built-in bonus of a staggering choice of bedtime reading.

The plan seemed irresistible But could he really get away with it?

On his way out Malcolm stopped by a large notice in the foyer, mounted on the wall under glass, where the rules of the house had been spelled out in a small but authoritative typeface and signed by the chief librarian. At the top was a table showing the loan periods and number of volumes allowed for readers of varying statuses, together with the corresponding scale of charges for late returns. There followed the opening hours for term time and vacation, and the procedures for raising the alarm and evacuating the building in the event of fire. Then came a comprehensive list of prohibitions, including the smoking of cigarettes, pipes and cigars, the introduction of consumables, the distracting or disturbing of fellow readers, or any generally disruptive behaviour. Finally, there were stern warnings pertaining to the annotation, defacement, mutilation, soiling or unauthorised removal of any book, thesis, journal or pamphlet. But there was not a single reference to overnight camping.

Malcolm looked back at the towering, booky crags. It needed athleticism, stealth and a little nerve, but it could be done!

Later that evening, in the Union Bar, he began to put together a game plan. A major concern were the turnstiles just inside the library entrance. They stood either side of the issues desk like twin sentries. Each had a hefty vertical spindle supporting solid, shiny metal arms, that clunked round through a whole quadrant at every passing. Did they maintain a rigorous tally of exits and entrances? Would someone remaining after hours be immediately betrayed by a discrepancy in the figures? A simple test would tell.

The following day, towards the end of his study session, Malcolm took up position by the card-index files close to the exit, keeping one eye on the turnstile and one on the counter. Within a minute there came a 'Can I help you?' from Miss Angle. The smile seemed obliging enough but the tone was decidedly unhelpful.

'No, I'm just, er, just going to have a browse.' He could hardly say turn your back for a minute.

He pulled open one of the drawers and began riffling and frowning in an almost convincing manner. It was a full five minutes before his chance arose – the foyer being momentarily empty coinciding with the normally vigilant Miss A. retrieving a heavy volume from a low shelf behind the counter. In a second he'd vaulted over the turnstile bar, unobserved, he was fairly sure. But just in case he put on an expression of impish delight, so that any casual witness would put the action down to *joie de vivre*, rather than some calculated attempt to confound the system.

At closing time he returned to the library and hung around outside for the better part of an hour, nose-blowing, shoelace tying, reading and re-reading the unreadable notice board. But no alarm bells rang, no security staff were summoned, no bloodhounds released.

Malcolm wandered back to Gray Hall in buoyant mood. It was in the bag! Nobody would know, or possibly care, it seemed, about his comings, goings or stayings.

It was only later, over a celebratory cider in the Union, that he realised how inconclusive the test had really been. If he'd been able to sneak out, then someone else just might have sneaked in, thus balancing the body count for that day. One couldn't risk everything on such minimal evidence. A more exacting experiment was called for.

During the course of the following day Malcolm deliberately circumnavigated the library system many times over. To minimise any suspicion he varied the routine, interspersing short periods of study, alternately in Philosophy and Maths, with trips to the canteen for cups of tea, or leg-stretching turns around the newly mown lawns. On each entry he allowed a trailing coat or bag-strap to snag the turnstile bar behind, ratcheting up an extra click. On each exit, having waited till he was unobserved, he thwarted the count, sometimes leaping over or limboing under the bar, sometimes inhaling hard and sneaking past sideways like a cartoon cat.

By evening he'd clocked up a shortfall of a dozen or more in the in-out tally. If anyone were really monitoring the figures they wouldn't have been able to rule out the possibility that a small guerrilla army had infiltrated the stacks.

Again he waited around outside for any signs of an alert. A grey-uniformed porter came along, relaxed and whistling, checked the library doors in passing and wandered off. A green-smocked lady appeared with a spray can and a large yellow cloth, and polished the brass handles and finger-plates. All seemed right with the library world.

Chapter 27

Sleeping on it

Evening found Malcolm again in his favourite corner of the Union Bar. There was a lively crowd in but the jukebox was mercifully low, even lapsing into complete silence from time to time. Having downed a whole half of cider and got halfway through a second (with the prospect of free accommodation for the rest of term a man could afford to splash out a little) he was feeling particularly pleased with the day's work. He took another swig, leaned back, closed his eyes and imagined having the library to himself for up to twelve hours a day. The evening stroll along the cool stone floors, past the shelves of Shakespeare and Aristotle; nodding goodnight to those little busts of Socrates and Darwin, nestling in their wall niches. He would read awhile, then clamber contentedly to bed, drifting off to sleep with not a protest song or slamming door to be heard, cradled in the arms of Biblius (or would that be Librius? Or Literarius? – there had to be a god, or goddess, of books. It was only right). Whoever. Whatever. Silent night. Rock-a-bye Baby. Shangri La!

Except, of course, if the place were patrolled at night! Malcolm put down the glass heavily, slopping cider over table, lap and feet. People looked. What if there were security checks? The faintest glimmer of his torch would be visible in the darkness; the gentlest snoring would reverberate unhindered through those vast panelled hallways. And when, exactly, did the cleaners clean the place? Might they appear at random, forcing him to lie low, or rather high, for hours on end?

He mopped up the spillage with several paper hankies. It was clear further research was needed. But making direct enquiries would arouse suspicion. And he was loath to actually lie. A more roundabout approach was needed. One that took him two more halves of cider to formulate.

The following morning Malcolm presented himself at the porters' lodge armed with the elaborate and carefully worked-out question, amounting, in effect, to: *If I'd left my (rather expensive) pencil case in the library last thing one night recently, would anyone in authority have found it (and taken it to lost property), before regular users (who might have fewer scruples) returned in the morning.* He delivered this in a vague but worried tone – hoping that the hypothetical phrasing would be put down to general scatter-brainedness, and not to any kind of devious intent on his part. He needn't have worried. The porter listened patiently, long accustomed to dealing with the rambling eccentrics of the academic world. He then explained that the cleaners came in on Mondays to Fridays, shortly before the library opened at 9 am, though, sad to say, as far as he knew, no pencil cases had been handed in.

Malcolm smiled gratefully and tried to look philosophical about the imagined loss. He didn't feel able to press on the question of security patrols, but took it as a challenge to establish that for himself. By chance he'd recently picked up some nifty tips on countersurveillance in an otherwise dull spy film. Without knowing it, it seemed, people could be made to leave traces of their passing.

Next Friday evening Malcolm contrived to be the very last in the Zoology section, at the far end of the building, pretending engrossment in a small volume on molluscs when the warning bell sounded, until finally being asked to leave. As he followed the assistant to the exit he planted a series of little tell-tale indicators to record any disturbances that might occur overnight.

Next morning he was waiting by the library at opening time, to ensure he was the first to enter. But all was well: the several hairs were still in place across critical door frames, where he'd fixed them with a dab of saliva; the minuscule tent of paper was still perched on the light-switch, from which the draught of even the stealthiest passing watchman would have wafted it; and, most remarkably, the Staedtler HB pencil was still standing bolt upright on its flat end on the table where he'd balanced it. Malcolm was euphoric. Could you imagine an environment more promising of peaceful nights? Even the best hotels had lifts, passing traffic, unruly guests.

Back in the Union that evening he began planning out the last month of term. Living in a library would clearly involve some peculiar demands and constraints. But there'd be no need for austerity as such. He could still have modern conveniences, and a daily routine. Things would just be redistributed. He would eat in the canteen, or the High-Street tea shop, bed down atop the bookcases in Geology, or Greek, according to whim, and shower in the changing rooms of the campus Sports Hall.

Shaving, though, might invite awkward questions. He would be fancy free, a local nomad, his night sky the vaulted ceiling of Humanities, his pillow a volume of Hegel – padded with a towel, of course. Though not too thickly – who knows, some kind of overnight cranial osmosis might achieve what several months of study had failed to deliver. Malcolm got himself another drink, and began to grow a beard.

For the several weeks of residence he'd need to bring in core possessions and hide them about the place. He estimated there would be the equivalent of several suitcasefuls. The rest of his stuff could go into lockers in the basement of Gray Hall where luggage and bulky items could be left over the summer, for a nominal fee.

Multiple visits to the library with bulging bags would certainly raise eyebrows. But then any searches would be far more likely on the way out, after the tell-tale pyjamas, socks, tin-openers and toothpaste had all been safely stowed aloft. Nevertheless, even with the largest bag he dared use there would need to be many trips. Too many perhaps? Well, not necessarily. Much of the cargo would be clothes. And clothes could be worn (indeed the human body might have been designed for just such a purpose). Malcolm did some calculations – measuring himself up, mentally rehearsing his daily routine, estimating the minimum requirements consistent with comfort and hygiene. Five runs should do it. Monday through Friday. With tight packing. He drained his glass and set off for the little office in the foyer of Gray Hall to give the required week's notice and initiate the process of getting a rebate on his rent.

Was it his imagination, or was the Hall unusually peaceful that evening? Perhaps it was just easier to tolerate what wouldn't have to be tolerated for much longer. No, it was definitely quiet. True, there was some distant music. Malcolm put his ear to the wall. It was still faint, and had that unnatural bassiness of structure-borne sound. But it was quite tuneful. Even stately. Not unlike a Mozart quartet. There were other sounds – more local, though not locatable. Disjointed and sibilant. The water pipes conspiring? More like people whispering. Maybe the neighbours had got wind of his departure and decided to be quiet out of guilt. Or spite.

By bedtime the silence had become disturbing. It was a relief when the radiator began to tick rhythmically, or the washbasin put out one of its occasional, not unmusical, glugs. He would miss that. But doubtless libraries had their own acoustical schedules that one could learn to love.

There would in fact be a whole host of new features to get used to, both good and bad. Life would be fairly quiet and relatively costless. But then again, fairly dark. And totally mattressless. And there might be other snags that came to light only after he'd moved in. It would be wise to do some serious rehearsing. He dug out his old sleeping bag and spread it on the bed. On second thoughts he transferred it to the thin carpet, and slipped inside.

Sleeping on a floor is hard enough. Lying awake on a floor soon gets to be really tedious. He tried his left side, his back, his right side, then back, left, and back again. He repeated the oscillation. Several times. In vain. Bits of him went to sleep in shifts, but never the whole lot at once. Maybe rotating full circle, with a brief spell on the front, would be more natural.

Malcolm wondered what his normal nightly sequence was. A time-lapse film, shot from the ceiling, would have been revealing. Come to think of it, it seemed likely he performed several complete cycles during sleep, since he often awoke wound up like Tutankhamen in those untuck-inable Hall sheets. Remarkable what one could do while unconscious. That amounted to thousands of revolutions in a single year. With a circumference of a good yard, the equivalent of a mile or more. Extraordinary. If unchecked by walls or periods of wakefulness one would reach the coast within a lifetime. He pictured himself rolling merrily along, over hill and vale, across the many decades, to a final lemming fate. There were worse ways to go. Then, altogether less merrily, he pictured himself in his prime, precipitated from a high perch on to a solid library floor. It was clear he would need to find a particularly deep, safe recess for the bivouac. Or else rig up some restraining system with ropes and pitons.

At 3 am he was still wide awake. And silence still reigned in Gray Hall. He tried the rotation method, over and over, losing count of how many times. Creeping waves of alternating numbness and tingling circumnavigated his body. Maybe he should be revolving anticlockwise. Or was he doing so already? It all depended on whether you viewed from the head or the feet. Maybe one should go clockwise only in the Northern hemisphere. Like water in plug holes was supposed to do.

Sheep-counting might be worth a try. But it, too, was fraught with decision-making. Should the animals be counted from the first, or zeroth; be free-running, or synchronised to the heartbeat; move from left to right, or right to left (or even, lemming-style, top to bottom)? And what would be the optimum inter-sheep spacing? Someone should conduct experimental trials on the relative efficacy of the various approaches. Maybe someone had.

It was beginning to get light when a door was slammed in the room above. Shoes were flung, one by one, then something heavier. There was a pause, and another, and then Mr D. began singing. *How many times?* Malcolm sighed, turned over a final time, and fell into a deep sleep.

Next morning a still-yawning Malcolm examined his mild but extensive bruising in the mirror with some concern. But also a dash of pride. The venture was clearly underway, and new experiences always came at a price. Doubtless one would toughen up in time. Meanwhile he added some form of cushioning to his mental packing list.

Over a leisurely breakfast of tea and toast he pondered the day ahead. At some point he was due to wrestle with differential equations, and a chapter of Leibniz. Not to mention those pesky primes. But all that could wait a while; given the lingering stiffness and staleness, now might be a good time to test out the Sports Hall showers.

The building seemed empty as he strode in, whistling nonchalantly and trying to look athletic. The holdall in his grasp carried none of the usual, unintelligible sporting names or logos, but was reasonably grubby and battered. Any porter or bona fide sporting user would have assumed it contained boots or racquets, or sticks and dubbin and things, instead of a change of clothes, a slide rule and half a packet of peanuts.

The sweaty, steamy atmosphere of the changing rooms stirred uneasy memories. It was years since anyone had had the authority to make Malcolm run, jump or throw things just by blowing a whistle. But he still felt a little vulnerable – an interloper in a preserve of fitness and unquestioning obedience.

With the showers to himself his confidence grew. There was no competition here, no scrutiny, no points to be won. You just needed to play the part. He began to make hearty, soapy, slapping and splashing noises as the hot jets hit the shoulders. His voice reverberated pleasantly from the shiny tiled surfaces, its rough edges further masked by the myriad droplets drumming on the plastic panels and trickling into the drains. Overall the effect was not unmusical. He launched himself into a medley of manly snippets from sea shanties and other heroic genres, here and there slipping in a melodic nod to *Háry János*, a nifty allusion to *Hall of the Mountain King*, the odd piratical *Yo Ho Ho*. The water temperature, pressure and flow rate were perfect – by the time he'd shampooed, soaped and rinsed, the residual stiffness from last night had quite melted away. Lingering under the soothing stream he closed his eyes and began to hum a tune altogether vaguer and more serene.

Then a voice came through the steam.

'Good game?'

Malcolm opened his eyes but didn't look around.

'Er, not bad,' he turned off the tap and began to towel vigorously. 'Who won?'

' . . . Er, *we* did.' He returned the soap to its plastic box.

'Good score?'

This was an altogether trickier one. You got very different numbers of points in different kinds of game. He knew that much. Cricket, for example, was always much higher than football, for some reason. Maybe because it went on longer. Or was that croquet?

Malcolm put on a tone both modest and confident. 'Let's just say a fairly convincing margin.'

He grabbed towel and soap, and made a dash across the duckboards towards his clothes without looking back.

Chapter 28

Room at the Top

On the following Monday morning, mid-May and warm already, an unusually bulky Malcolm arrived at the library just as it was opening. In addition to the usual pencils, penknife, handkerchiefs and string, his pockets were packed out with the little extras his new lifestyle might call for – safety pins, rubber bands, playing cards, matches, a combination corkscrew and tin-opener. Under his ski anorak he was wearing several jumpers, on top of several shirts. Under his trousers he was wearing trousers, and under his socks, socks.

There was no sign of library staff as he crossed the foyer and pushed against the turnstile bar. It advanced a sort of half-click and then stopped, as did Malcolm, pinioned in the fork of two chromium arms. He pushed and pulled, fumbled and wriggled to and fro for a time but, bolstered by so many layers of clothing, it seemed impossible to move the arm in front forward or the one behind back. Or to crawl under or clamber over either. He'd come to grief at the first hurdle. It was embarrassing, but he needed help.

He began a series of sighs, discreet coughs and throat clearances. Without result. It seemed he might be in for a long wait. Alternatively, if he was going to get free unaided the only way was to reduce his bulk. By crossing arms and pulling upwards on the waistband he managed to get the body of the anorak over his head, but it remained fast at the neck and wrists, which were tightly elasticated against the ingress of snow.

In the sudden darkness he became quite calm, like an enshrouded parrot. Or perhaps, more worryingly, an ostrich. Whichever, the situation did invite reflection. The problem of trying to get help without drawing attention to yourself was philosophically engaging. And anyway, help from whom? He was stuck at, or perhaps *in*, the very entrance to the library proper. In literal limbo. An asylum seeker frozen in the searchlight on the barbed wire. Given this borderline status the porters and the library staff might well argue over whose jurisdiction he fell under. He could become the subject of a tug-of-war. Or, as a stateless, non-person, be left to rot as an example to all. On the other hand, it could be maintained that anyone who . . .

'Having problems?' The familiar voice came from alarmingly close.

He forced himself to remain calm, but raised his voice to compensate for the muffling effect of the jacket. 'Seem to be a bit stuck. Actually.'

Miss Angle reached under the counter and pressed something. Malcolm just heard the other half of the click (or it might have been a backward unhalf-click) and suddenly was able to move forward out of the machine's embrace, re-adjust his clothing and restore his vision.

'Thanks!' He was aware of Miss A's gaze, following his abnormal form as it shuffled past the desk. Looking straight ahead he smiled nonchalantly. 'Turned chilly again!'

During the course of the morning he made several visits to the gents in Critical Theory, one of the least frequented in the building, divesting himself layer by layer. The various articles he folded tightly and hid on top of the bookcases, whenever he could climb unobserved. Anything small and unbreakable was simply lobbed aloft. Other items he slipped opportunely behind or between books, wherever a thick layer of dust testified to no recent disturbances.

He made a point, though, of distributing his things over a wide area – taking great care to note what had gone where, according to best squirrel practice. The discovery of a cache of clothes would have been sure to provoke a manhunt. Quite apart from unnerving the female staff. But an isolated item could easily be put down to undergraduate mischief (intimate garments did from time to time come to light around the campus, flapping from flagpoles or substituted for blackboard dusters). Or indeed to donnish eccentricity. For example, it was rumoured that a certain professor of Classics, in the fever of scholarship, would mark important literary passages with anything vaguely laminar that came to hand. Library staff regularly extracted gas bills, beer mats, packet soups, insoles, half-eaten Ryvitas and the like from the volumes he left on the returns desk.

The day had gone well. On the whole. A good volume of stuff had been brought in and secreted. But as closing time approached Malcolm grew anxious, aware of a big discrepancy between his respective appearances on arrival and departure. This was not a good time to be attracting attention. Apparent dramatic weight fluctuations, especially coupled with frequent trips to the toilet, could be misdiagnosed. He just might get reported to Student Welfare and grilled about eating habits.

But with minutes to go a solution suggested itself. On his way to the exit he paid a final visit to the gents, and emerged somewhat transformed. Miss A. still watched with some concern the figure which breezed past the desk. This was partly because it seemed a little less bulky and more mobile than earlier in the day, but mostly because its every movement was accompanied by a strange dull, rustling sound.

Safely back in his room Malcolm removed several dozen scrunched-up paper towels, almost half a dispenser-full, which had been padding out the arms and shoulders of the anorak. De-crumpled and flattened under the mattress overnight they could be re-used a number of times.

Each day for the remainder of the week he shuttled between Hall and library, transporting the necessities of life. He took pains to vary the times of arrival and departure, as well as the balance between items concealed on his person and ones packed in the bag. As every successful smuggler knows, it pays to keep 'em guessing.

Saturday night was for last-minute packing and finalising tactics. Timing would be crucial, especially first thing in the mornings. Oversleeping could lead to disaster. Even if he didn't give himself away by snoring there might be no opportunity to climb down once other library users had arrived for the day.

He reached for his trusty alarm clock. It was a rather magnificent old machine, built like a tank, though sporting many chips and dents – battle scars inflicted by generations of indignant wakees taking their revenge on it for doing its job so well. And it could be heard through a brick wall. Heavy muffling would need to be applied. Though measuredly – just thick enough for the sound to be audible from close range and no more, and just flexible enough to allow winding, and for the 'off' lever to be felt and operated quickly with eyes still firmly closed. Malcolm spent the next two hours experimenting with a variety of absorbing materials and wrapping methods.

The answer turned out to be socks. Two and a half pairs to be exact: first the green and yellow stripy ones – once warm, bright and soft, now holey, drab and shrunken from countless wearings and laundrettings; then the thick woolly ones from skiing; plus, finally and outermost, the larger, left one from the putative pair his auntie had knitted him last Christmas.

Sunday was D-day. It began warmish, with intermittent rain and sun. A late Spring day. A day for garnering resources, for building nests. Lightly loaded with final bits and pieces Malcolm arrived around mid afternoon, in good time for early closing at 4 pm. He welcomed the long night ahead – time to get settled in, time to explore. The extra-large helping of sandwiches would see him through. Monday morning he would do some serious grocery shopping.

The library was surprisingly full. It seemed exam panic had set in early. He turned his attention again to the prime-number project, thinking it would be a useful distraction – something pure and austere to calm his own nerves.

So, how should we view these things? The name suggested they were somehow foremost, superior – as in prime ministers, or movers (or rather *mover* – given its job there could hardly be more than one of those). But also vulnerable, as in prime targets, and suspects. Euclid had shown there were an infinite number of primes – from any candidate "highest" one you could always generate one yet higher. Computers were now playing a big role in the study – no sooner had a preposterously large prime been discovered by some calculating colossus than it was knocked off its perch by another. Such fleeting fame. Did they bask in the brief spotlight? Did they bicker and pout in their infinite ranks? Primes – metaphors for so much in life.

Malcolm sensed his philosophical hat was getting a little too comfortable. So far he'd managed only a general, wordy introduction to the project. Something his tutor would appreciate, he felt, as far as it went. But she would want to see some theorems and proofs; some calculations, some . . . well . . . *numbers*.

It was hard to concentrate. As time ticked on the presence of the other students began to disconcert him, as if they were dinner guests who'd overstayed. Windows of opportunity for hiding and re-appearing were limited. Malcolm needed at least one empty bay, to allow unseen ascent or descent. At the same time there had to be enough comings and goings to provide general cover, so he would neither be suddenly missed nor seem to spring from nowhere. Luckily many had drifted away by 3.30 pm, allowing him to make his move. He was safely aloft when the ten-minute bell went, and stayed put for a good half hour after the last light had been extinguished and the last distant door bolted.

The first night in any house or hotel is traditionally a restless one. If it's not lumpy beds or creaky floorboards, it's some other kind of strangeness. Or perhaps some strange kind of otherness. During the long evening the library revealed a gentle rhythm all its own: the half-hourly automatic flush from a rank of distant urinals, at ten past and twenty to the hour for some reason; the half-minutely advance of the several wall clocks within ear-shot. It seemed that all the clocks were triggered by some central synchroniser, but the sounds arrived slightly staggered from their varying distances – a ricochet of clicks in the cavernous hall.

Hot-water radiators have their part to play. Malcolm was surprised they were still active in that season. And the pipes were in fact permanently cold. But water seemed to ebb and flow according to some ancient rhythm, in unfathomable patterns of trickles and gushes. The bookcases, too, took time to settle – issuing continual faint creaks and groans as they accommodated the changing temperature and humidity, plus the odd resounding snap when some mounting tension was finally overcome.

Only the books themselves remained silent. Alphabetic adjacency makes strange bedfellows – Leibniz and Locke, Nietzsche and Ockham, jacket to jacket, reconciled to their comfortable shelf lives, nestling down for the night in mutual tolerance, like ageing spouses. Alone, aloft and supine in his sleeping bag Malcolm lay wide-eyed for a good while, taking it all in. A night owl in a forest of oak.

Spread out around him, a world of knowledge. Or perhaps a brave but rather imperfect map of a world. Inside his own skull, an extremely imperfect map of that map – his personal, microcosmic library. Unsystematized. Uncatalogued. Fragmentary. Exams are round the corner and there's a good deal of work to be done on the mental re-shelving and acquisitions front. A tide of tiredness draws him out of his home bay of rationality towards more ancient, unfrequented shores. Metaphors proliferate, and mix. Sirens of unreason call from the mist.

Malcolm is racing through a maze of shelving, in pursuit of something unclear. He goes *left, left, right, right, left, left, right, right*, and so on, until he feels he knows exactly where he is, without realising he doesn't know where where he is is. He sets off back to where he was, now pursued by something unclear, but soon realises he doesn't know where where he was is. Or even was. The bookcases (or is it the gangways between them?) broaden and heighten to Manhattan proportions, then soften and buckle into giant, navigable cortical folds, before reverting to shelves and spaces. He runs on. *Left, left, right, right.* Suddenly he is outflanked by a mob of baying peasants. The ring of flaming torches closes in. He starts to climb, hand over hand, shelf after shelf, the summitless stack of human knowledge. A foothold gives way. He grabs wildly at a shelf-full of metaphysics, before plunging backwards, a flock of Aristotles fluttering after him into the abyss.

He opens his eyes and half recognises the surroundings. But the subject labels signposting the area are gone. Classifications falter. Categories dissolve. The books mingle, swarm and pulsate in a vast Dewey Decimal dance. Covers disintegrate, leaving a monstrously thick club sandwich of learning. Then pages, paragraphs, words, letters merge. And all is soup.

Meanwhile, in another part of the library forest, Malcolm is on patrol, foraging, communing with nature, indeed naked, though unashamed (luckily this is not a conventional, busy-Saturday-afternoon-in-the-High-Street dream). He wanders into Humanities, where recently he's seen fleeting shadows, heard footfalls and beguiling woodland calls. Scaling the heights of Literature he finds a footprint in the dust – high-arched and promisingly unshod. His own size-ten, plonked alongside, reveals its relative daintiness. Lacking a box of milk chocolates he leaves a handsome volume of Keats and retires to the shadows.

Patience is rewarded. She emerges into the moonlight, all hair, eyes and limbs. A fellow feral. She senses his gaze and covers herself with the Keats. He grabs a Times World Atlas in reciprocal modesty. They circle one another, wordlessly, while time stands still. The silence is broken by the approach of authoritative footsteps. Hand-in-hand they make for the seclusion of Horticulture.

Chapter 29

Quest for Fire

From out of nowhere came an insistent rattle – distant, dull, yet brassy. Like something heard through the wrong end of an ear trumpet. The sight of the unfamiliar ceiling quickly brought home to him where he was. He switched off the alarm and checked his watch. 8 am.

Or rather, O-eight-hundred hours. Malcolm had resolved to adopt the military-style format to help keep up the discipline so vital to his success. He'd always found it an exciting designation – conjuring up tense, sweating faces huddled around a periscope, synchronising watches while the *asdic* pinged away. Pity that the "hundred" rather conflicted with the actual sixty minutes in each of those hours, especially given that the whole scheme was intended to remove the ambiguity between base 12 and base 24. That must have cost a few lives and limbs over the years. Still, libraries are more forgiving environments, and all that really mattered was that there was ample time to dress, descend, wash and reascend before the cleaners appeared. All went smoothly, though the hot water was cold.

When the cleaners hadn't shown up by 08.55 he wasn't unduly concerned – they must have days off. Or just off days. But when, a quarter of an hour later, no students or even staff had arrived he began to worry. By quarter to ten he was trying to convince himself that it was one of those Greenwich-Mean- versus British-Summer-Time things. By ten past he'd decided it was a Bank Holiday.

Or was it? He hurried to the issues desk. Through the window of the little office he could just make out a page-a-day, rip-off calendar with bold black digits. It indicated the previous Friday. Not much to go on. He reached over the counter and picked up the date stamper, feeling it might hold some clue. But it was too dim to read those little rubbery numbers (and in any case, wouldn't they be backwards? Or at least upside-down?) He rested the thing on the back of his left hand and pushed the handle down hard. The sound was familiar enough, but the accompanying sting came as something of a surprise. The result was a date, two Fridays hence, outlined in neat, blue-black figures, with a pink oval weal beginning to form around it. Again, not a great deal of help.

He stared down at the imprint, feeling as if he'd just branded himself a prisoner. It would certainly provoke embarrassing questions if not removed. But, given its official purpose, wouldn't it be indelible? He could cover it with an elastoplast. Or, more daringly, return himself to the desk, for official cancellation. That took him back to the question that had brought him there – when would they be open? Clearly a more direct approach was needed.

Malcolm picked up the telephone behind the counter and dialled the main college number. During the many rings he had time to place a handkerchief over the mouthpiece.

Then a voice said, 'Porters' Lodge'.

'Hello. Yes. Can you tell me what time the library opens. Today. Please.'

There was a pause.

'It's Bank Holiday. They're closed till tomorrow morning.'

'Oh. Right. Of course. Like, all day?'

'All day, I'm afraid.' The voice was friendly, and vaguely familiar. 'Not lost another pencil case, have we?'

'No, no. I just needed to, er, look up some, references. You know. And more general things. It's not important really . . .'

'Well, you can revise out on the lawns. It's a lovely day. Do you good.'

Malcolm put the receiver down, only just managing to resist the urge to wipe away his fingerprints.

He wandered back to base, the general mental anguish which had been building now focused entirely within his stomach. It would be almost twenty-three hours before he could get to the canteen.

Malcolm had eaten the last of the cheese-and-tomato sandwiches before retiring. A real midnight feast. The generous fillings of unusually mature Danish Blue may well have contributed to the liveliness of his dreams. He emptied the plastic bag which now held only the gleanings from his food cupboard, salvaged as he left his room for the last time. It didn't amount to much: eleven and a half cream crackers, a sachet of brown sauce (being a bequest, or oversight, of the previous occupant) and four packet soups. *Instant* soups. Or so it was claimed. He examined the instructions – *Just add boiling water!* Just?

He checked the washbasin in the gents. The hot tap was still cold, though the cold one was tepid. But even warm soup would have been unthinkable. Undrinkable. And who knew what was lurking in those ancient pipes? Very hot would be the very minimum for health and palatability.

He nibbled on the half cracker and tried to recall a little thermodynamics. The aluminium mug would clearly be a better conductor than the only alternative, stoneware one. He three-quarter filled it with water. It took him a further, whole cracker to decide on and locate a source of heat. In the seclusion of the Domestic Science section, well away from any windows, he plugged in an Anglepoise lamp and bent it over backwards as far as it would go. Little twangs of protest arose from its tortured springs, but it stayed put, like a champion limbo dancer, bulb and shade pointing at the ceiling.

A saucepan, if he'd had such a thing, would have sat comfortably on the rim of the shade, but the mug was much too small. Some kind of supporting grill was needed. Malcolm sorted through his extensive armoury of pencils and pens, finally selecting a matching pair of HB Staedtlers for their general sturdiness and anti-roll, hexagonal cross-sections. He laid these across the rim of the shade, forming a bridge of parallel chords, then sat the mug of water on top, an inch or so above the glowing sixty-watt bulb. From the shelves opposite he pulled out a book on nutrition and sat down to monitor the proceedings.

After fifteen minutes a dipped little finger revealed that the water had crept above room temperature, but after half an hour it was still no more than warmish. On reflection this was not surprising – the pencil arrangement was pretty inefficient, allowing the bulk of the heat to escape around the sides. With the mini saw-blade on his Swiss Army knife – its first ever use in fact – Malcolm removed the A4 lid from a boxfile and cut out a roughly circular hole, slightly less than the mug in diameter. This replaced the supporting pencils and ensured the heat was concentrated on the base of the mug.

After another half hour the water had clearly reached equilibrium – it was hottish, but a good deal less than boiling. Malcolm was however by now a good deal more than hungry, and resolved to give it a try. He pondered the four soup packets in turn, shuffled them, then pondered them all again. Finally he opted for mulligatawny, in spite of never knowingly having had it before, and even being unsure exactly what it was. There just seemed to be something hot and nutritious in that strange string of syllables.

The aroma that emerged when he cut open the foil packet was not disappointing. But when poured on to the hot water the brownish powder just sat there on the surface. Vigorous and protracted stirring seemed to make things worse. Defying all centrifugal expectations the stuff just gathered itself together in a conical heap and rotated lazily at the hub of the vortex. It was clear that the water would have to be brought close to boiling point before those grains would dissolve and thicken into anything remotely soup-like.

Malcolm consoled himself with another cream cracker while he tried to think up alternative methods of heating. The hot-air drier in the gents was far too feeble (though it might have allowed anyone with a couple of hours to spare to defrost a small chicken – that dirigible, insertable nozzle could almost have been designed for the purpose). He seemed to recall that the Romans (or was it the Greeks?) had used glass spheres filled with water to focus the sun's rays. The water bit was easy – all he would need to find was a large, hollow glass sphere. And some Mediterranean sun. There were no candles in his camping kit, but there was an almost full box of Swan Vestas. He might improvise a mini brazier with a metal-waste bin and some paper towels. But there was something deeply discordant about libraries and naked flames – the names of Alexandria and Gormenghast flickered disturbingly around the edges of his mind.

No, the light-bulb technique was safe and sound enough. It just needed more power.

Malcolm turned his eyes heavenward. From the high ceiling a whole series of pendant lamps were swinging ever so slightly in a breeze from somewhere. It was hard to judge from down below, and far too risky to switch them on, but from their size and ample bulbousness they would have to be at least 100 Watts. Naturally enough they hung mainly over the reading-table areas, a good twenty feet from the floor, and hopelessly inaccessible. There was however just one, in the reference section, that seemed to be hanging close to the top edge of a bookcase. An enticing pear, ripe for picking.

But from the summit, even at full stretch, it turned out to be a good yard above his fingertips. He looked around for anything that might provide extra reach. There were, of course, chairs aplenty. But the spans of those rather flimsy, spindly legs were too wide for the top surface of the bookcase. And anyway, he would have had to build an acrobat-style pyramid of them to reach far enough. In the absence of a safety net something altogether more solid and dependable was called for.

Occupying much of the bottom shelf was a set of ancient encyclopaedias – dusty, shabby, but still mechanically sound, and substantial. So much so they needed two hands to lift. Malcolm dragged a wooden ladder from several bays away and after many clamberings had transferred the twenty-odd volumes aloft.

He rested a while, did a bit of mental arithmetic, then began to fashion a staircase.

Step 1 was built up from Aardvark to Bedlam, supporting Bedouin to Camembert, and so on for several volumes, up to a height of about eighteen inches.

Step 2 (Ectoplasm to Freemasonry, Freesias to Godalming etc.) took one to a precarious three feet or so.

Step 3 became so wobbly as it neared completion it had to be re-built from scratch. But even with greater care in the alignments there was an unmistakable lean. The ever-so-slightly thicker spines subtly curved the stack progressively, and perilously, away from the vertical.

Malcolm began once again, this time rotating every second volume through 180 degrees, so that on either side of the column the alternating thicker and thinner edges neatly compensated for one another. He felt a distinct air of ceremonial as he laid the culminating volume, Wildebeest to Zurich, and stood back to admire the work. Solid as a rock! Another short rest, then up he went.

From the summit, a good four feet six above the bookcase top, he could just read "150 W" on the bulb, even though it was dusty and unlit. Surely a powerful enough source. It was just touchable with the fingertips, but to remove it against the bayonet-socket spring he would need to grasp the glass shade above with the other hand. Another few inches of height were needed. Malcolm made one more trip to ground level, returning hot and sweaty with a Who's Who, a large Latin dictionary and the local Yellow Pages. One final ascent, and the pearly prize was in his grasp.

Who dares wins. Per ardua ad Mazda.

Hunger focuses the mind wonderfully. Within a couple of minutes the heating apparatus, with its new, souped-up power source was reassembled, and the mug of would-be mulligatawny placed back on top. Malcolm switched on, in hope, but not at all certain of success. Empirical evidence was lacking – in the entire history of cooking there was probably no exact precedent for the experiment.

He had plenty of theoretical misgivings too. First, the desk lamp was doubtless running beyond its power rating (but then, didn't manufacturers always have generous safety margins?) Second, that famous flammability figure of 451° Fahrenheit, though it referred to paper, was likely to be similarly low for cardboard. And third, the incompatibility of electricity with water would extend, in all likelihood, to soup, of whatever flavour. All in all a dicey set-up. After the exertions with grimy books he very much needed to wash the dust from his hands and face. But leaving the scene, even momentarily averting the gaze, was unthinkable.

He stared exhortingly at the water in the mug. Within five minutes there was definite movement on the surface. The brown particles began to separate from the mass, dancing in little eddies until they dissolved. He stirred gingerly, half afraid of disrupting the magic processes of convection. Tiny bubbles appeared, then bigger ones. He stirred more vigorously. Within half an hour, in spite of being in possibly the most watched pot in history, the brown liquid had thickened to a convincing, homogeneous, soupy texture, and was steaming invitingly.

Not before time. It was already thirteen-hundred hours. The atmosphere had become distinctly chilly, and so had Malcolm since his exertions. He pulled on a thick sweater and started on the minimal and much-delayed breakfast. One hand he kept clutched around the mug to conserve heat – the other held a cream cracker directly over the soup, ensuring that any falling crumbs were not wasted. Captain Scott would have been proud.

And so the day progressed from soup to soup. Mid afternoon was Country Vegetable – most welcome on a still almost empty stomach. And as satisfying in the preparation as the tasting. Malcolm watched in awe as the unpromising ingredients, having somehow survived the rigours of dehydration, quickly blossomed on contact with the water, into recognisable shapes and colours. Like desert flowers after a rainstorm.

By comparison the tea-time Beef and Onion was a huge disappointment. In less extreme circumstances it would have been consigned to the plughole after the first sip. But Malcolm shut his eyes and drained the mug like a hero.

Returning to Domestic Science after a post-prandial stroll round Humanities he was struck by the lingering pungency of it. It was strong enough to make the eyes water. Strong enough, more worryingly, to provoke the authorities into a search for vermin. Or a corpse. Something had to be done, but it was far too risky to open windows. By propping open two internal doors and fanning violently with a third for several minutes he managed to reduce the concentration, though only at the price of a much wider distribution. Doubtless the smell was still detectable, but no-one would know where to begin looking.

Supper was set for twenty-hundred hours. Beef and Tomato, with croûtons, and a cream cracker. That would leave a very long gap with nothing to fill it except the last three, now slightly spongy crackers, enlivened perhaps with a smear of brown sauce. He would rather have left the last soup until bedtime, but the high-power bulb had to be back before dark – the climb was perilous enough in daylight.

It was duly replaced, and Malcolm began to dismantle the staircase, step by step, volume by volume, in roughly reverse alphabetical order. Down they came. Trappists to Vesuvius, Schrödinger to Stilton. In the fading light he moved slowly, the long day of sherpa-less climbing beginning to take its toll. Nietzsche to Popocatepetl, Matterhorn to Myopia, Goebbels to Hogmanay – a whole new angle on the history of ideas. In spite of this rich fantasy fodder when he later crawled into the sleeping bag he fell into a deep and dreamless sleep.

Tuesday morning Malcolm was out of the library building just as soon as he was able. Pale and blinking, sporting a now week-old stubble and carrying a small bag, he looked like a young old lag off on parole, as he headed for the High Street for the heartiest of breakfasts.

Chapter 30

Books at Bedtime

The month progressed from day to day. A succession of cloudless nights sent temperatures plummeting, making Malcolm grateful for every extra pullover and sock he'd brought in. From his perch in Humanities he was treated to a parade of magnificent dusks and dawns.

And he became aware of the moon as never before. Dangling in the late-evening sky with an implausible, story-book shape and shininess, it helped him navigate around his new quarters. It reassured him too, like a child's night-light – a friendly, if inconstant, face. Night by night he watched it shift and grow, at times weaving its way through the trees, at times eclipsed by the cold rectangle of Gray Hall, looming on the far side of the campus.

He found himself waiting eagerly for it each evening. Waiting, too, over the days, for the exact halfway point, when the terminator would split the circle with a diametrical, surgical, razor slice. He'd never seen that before. Or at least never noticed it. But what was the big deal?

A back-of-an-envelope sketch confirmed what the underlying geometry of that hour would be: the earth, moon and sun forming a giant right-angle triangle in space. Where else? What could you expect at this lunar half-time? A whistle blast from some cosmic referee? A thumbs-up from a squinting Pythagoras surveying the scene, signalling the moment of right alignment? The times of total newness and total fullness should have been just as special, and just as fleeting. But total halfness had something extra. A moment of poise and ambiguity, of bitter-sweet balance; a knife-edge division of silver and shadow. And he longed to see it – this equitable pie-chart in the sky. Just for the sheer oxymoronic, bang-on, Yin-Yang duplicity of it all.

But he was thwarted. One night the moon was distinctly less than half, the next, distinctly more. It seemed the magic moment had passed by below the horizon. Whatever that meant. Unable to face the three-dimensional geometric analysis, which would have extended to the backs, and fronts, of several envelopes, he remained unsure as to whether geography or season, or both, were to blame. Did he just need to wait another lunar cycle, or did it all depend on some creeping precession of the earth's axis? Could he expect to catch it next month, or would it take ice ages to appear?

Whatever. Every day the moon was bigger, brighter, later to rise. From gibbous onwards the light was so bright Malcolm could read and write by it. And he had to keep a low profile after dark. To a passer-by he would have cut an eerie figure, ambling along behind the mullioned windows with a leathery old tome tucked underneath his arm.

The need for caution was, in fact, ever present; although he was feeling more comfortable with the unorthodox lifestyle, discovery was always just one mistake away.

'Been climbing?' said Miss Angle one morning, as they edged past one another in the narrow corridor between Philosophy and Folklore.

Malcolm froze and swallowed hard, but managed a look of puzzled innocence.

'How do you mean, exactly?' He began a frantic mental preparation for bluffing or rebuttal. She merely gestured at his zipped-up anorak and bulging knapsack. He began to regain his composure. The ruddy complexion, the incipient beard, the perhaps unnecessarily stout boots must have added to the outward-bound, *al fresco* impression he was radiating.

'Well, no. Not exactly.' He swallowed again, then brightened. 'I've just been struggling with the categorical imperative. Actually.' He waved a volume of Kant and managed a grin.

'All work and no play . . .' She wagged a finger and returned the grin. It was the first one he'd ever seen from her.

It was true he was having problems with Kant, having just got back an essay in which he'd set up, then shot down, a rather oversimplified version of the famous dictum – that you should act "as if you will everyone to do likewise . . ."

It can't, wrote Malcolm, be deduced that you shouldn't do something, simply from the fact that if everyone did it it would be a bad thing. A single counterexample would prove this. He gave three. If everyone on Earth behaved like, say, his Uncle Ernie, (a) it would precipitate a world mango shortage (for he's very partial to the fruit); (b) there would be annual mass asphyxia on the beach at Bognor Regis in the first two weeks of July; and (c) Auntie Ethel would be, shall we say put under considerable pressure. But Ernie is a decent man, he went on. Indeed, everyone who knows him thinks there should be *more* like him in the world.

He got a B-minus.

The night of full moon was something of an occasion, marking as it did the halfway point of his stay. Seated at a safe distance behind one of the largest windows he cracked open a flagon of dry cider and a packet of chocolate biscuits, and had eaten and drunk rather more than half by the time the disc had cleared the trees. It was as big and round and silvery as anyone could have wished.

Beside him was a considerable stack of books. Being utterly spoilt for choice he was fast developing eclectic tendencies. He read a few verses of Keats, a page of Eliot, a chapter of astronomy, and an encyclopaedia entry on the Cubists. Finally he spent a dutiful half hour on his prime-number project.

This was coming along. He'd homed in on the so-called *Goldbach Conjecture* – that every even integer greater than 2 can be written as the sum of two primes. First made in 1742 it was still unresolved. Proving it would have brought him worldwide fame, of course. And at least a B-plus grade. It would have been equally impressive to disprove it. And seemingly easier – you'd only have to find one counterexample.

He'd written a philosophical-historical introduction and devised a short computer program which did a token search of a limited range of numbers. Though there was little prospect of any revolutionary results his tutor seemed happy with the modest progress, pleased that he was engaging in this area she herself found so beguiling. He'd been half hoping to come up with a *Malcolm Conjecture*, to round it all off.

But most of the obvious, snappy ones seemed to have been bagged already. Perhaps he'd claim to have an ingenious proof of Goldbach, one that he couldn't include without exceeding the official project word limit.

Meanwhile, exams were half over, and going not too badly. The tide was turning.

The cider was refreshing and relaxing, if a bit on the warm side. He took a long swig. The moon crept onwards and upwards. By keeping his head stock-still Malcolm persuaded himself he could actually see the motion. Or were those tiny, oblique lurches the result of atmospheric turbulence? Or maybe his own, alcohol-enhanced, eye tremors? Wishful thinking, even? He closed one eye and stared, then opened it and closed the other. Could he really see it moving? He could definitely see it, and it was assuredly moving – everybody knew that. But that wasn't the same thing, of course. He took the penultimate swig of cider and leaned back contentedly.

Funny thing, the moon. The gravity there was so feeble, they said, that you'd be able to leap twenty feet in the air. Except there wasn't any air, because the gravity was so feeble. So you would have to wear several-hundred pounds of space suit, which would presumably reduce your leaping abilities back down to more mundane levels. Pity. Anyway, they reckoned you could see the Great Wall of China from it. Or was it the Pyramids of Giza? It might, of course, be hard to tell them apart from such a distance.

Whichever. It would be many years before Malcolm saw either of these sights, and then it was from a tourist bus – also largely airless, though firmly on the ground.

But tonight he could see the moon. Could *it* see *him*, he wondered? Probably not. Quite apart from *it* being a several-billion-year-old piece of rock, with the concomitant lack of sentience, Malcolm was altogether smaller and less well illuminated. He waved at it anyway, took the final cider swig and wiped a hand across his mouth. The stubble on his chin, which for a fortnight had been undergoing its own silent waxing, had softened and begun to curl. He slumped further back in the chair and allowed himself a *sotto voce* howl of celebration.

During the next week, as the moon began to wane and rise much later, he moved base camp into Geology, just to have it in view as he went off to sleep. After a hard day's revision, it was a sight for sore eyes.

The sun was no less compelling, providing spectacular, and sometimes rude, awakenings. Morning by morning he noted its more subtle advances against the leaded crosswires of the window panes. These provided a kind of extended, Cartesian grid, and provoked in some primitive part of Malcolm an urge to track the movements and positions of the heavenly bodies which now featured so prominently in his new world. Wasn't this, ultimately, how we made sense of things? From observation, measurement and analysis came an understanding of nature, and then a power over it. By reading the language of angles and shadows you could chart the oceans, find out when to sow and reap (and even, perhaps, the dates of Bank Holidays).

It was a pity he was having to live in secret. A pity, too, that the place was invaded each day by fellow students, and monitored by such vigilant re-shelvers. Left alone he could have stacked up books on tables, chairs and window ledges, carefully aligning them to mark the progress of sunrise day by day. He would have been the architect of a monumental literary calendar for predicting and celebrating the summer solstice. The author of the first Bookhenge . . .

'Have you finished with this?'
Malcolm surfaced rapidly from his little reverie. Miss Angle looked rather sunny this morning. The dress may or may not have been new, but was decidedly springy. Or summery, perhaps. Leafy, anyway. She waved a volume of Sartre.
'Oh. Yes. Thanks.'
She smiled. 'It suits you!'
'What, Existentialism?'
'The *beard!* You look like an explorer.'

'Any particular one?' He twitched his eyebrows mischievously but she was off again on her re-shelving rounds, humming a vague tune. It was a tune he'd heard from her on a number of occasions recently. Quite an intriguing one. The rhythm was consistent. *In*sistent even. A sort of *Tum tum ti tum tum*. But the melody seemed to vacillate. He couldn't quite place it. Or rather she couldn't. Was it *Climb Ev'ry Mountain*? Or *Roll out the Barrel*? Who could say?

On warmer days he lingered by the lake, befriending the more confident ducks, and acquiring something of a vagrant's suntan. There was no disruption of the revision schedule – the wooden bench became a bookshelf, his knees, a desk. Fluffy clouds and balmy breezes eased him through the more daunting chapters of Kierkegaard. Even Machiavelli seemed less dark and threatening when read *al fresco*.

The High-Street teashop, too, was an agreeable study venue – at off-peak times as quiet and relaxing as any library. (It was several years after the demise of the Palm Court trio and several more before the introduction of piped music). And it had the advantage that eating and drinking were not forbidden. Indeed they were positively encouraged: Malcolm's little intellectual struggles were for ever being interrupted by offers of more tea and scones. All that frowning, pencil chewing and space gazing couldn't fail to trigger a nurturing response in the proprietress – a greying, ageless woman who had made a career from doling out tea, and occasional sympathy. She'd ministered to them all over the years – truants, the unemployed, the bored, the lonely, footsore flag-sellers, blocked writers, brief encounterers, cakeaholics, and now, without knowing it, solvers, or, rather, a, would-be solver, of inhomogeneous differential equations.

'Haven't you got a home to go to?' Her voice was kindly but firm.

Malcolm closed his book thoughtfully, slipping in a dainty serviette as place marker, then capped and pocketed a red biro. It was a good question. For ten minutes or more she'd been looming gradually larger in his perception, sweeping her way to his table by the window, emptying ashtrays and re-filling sugar bowls as she went. She flipped the sign hanging on the back of the door, thereby officially declaring the shop closed. Simultaneously, but with more dubious authority she had, in effect, declared the world open. Malcolm smiled gratefully and went out into it.

The very next day he began a phased withdrawal from the library, mirroring the move-in of a month before. Starting with the least vital, items were transferred to the Gray Hall basement lockers. After some agonising, and a whole morning of reconnaissance, he filled out a residence application form for the Autumn term, specifically requesting Room 801. As the topmost, northernmost and easternmost of the array it had only one neighbour, in the room below. Otherwise there was just the kitchen and utility room; and Malcolm felt he could cope with the sounds of cooking and ironing, however furious or extended. With luck the remoteness and lack of sun would mean that there'd be few competitors for this particular tenancy.

Tum tum ti tum tum.

That strain again! So symmetrical – even sandwich-like – in structure.

The humming was coming from an adjacent bay. It was the last day of term and five o'clock was approaching fast, though, strictly speaking, no faster than the usual one second per second. Malcolm was the only straggler as the ten-minute bell sounded, echoing through the stillness with an extra finality. It tolled, or at least buzzed, just for him.

Tum tum ti tum tum.

What *was* that? *Moonlight and Roses?* Or *Boiled Beef and Carrots?* It was hard to know. And perhaps unwise to ask.

There were other unaskable questions. For instance, what did librarians do in the summer? Fly off to meet their fellows at vast bibliographic jamborees? Compete in international re-shelving or date-stamping tournaments? Or something more recreational. Even frivolous? Eleven months a year of institutionalised silence would surely build up intolerable tensions. They would deserve specially tailored holidays which allowed them to vent their peculiar frustrations.

Malcolm sensed a niche in the travel market: *Librarian Breaks* – themed package tours to special venues where they could let rip – the very antitheses of Trappist retreats. On the evening of arrival you'd be given a welcome drink and briefing, then take a vow of vociferousness for the duration. The all-inclusive price would provide a full range of transgressive paraphernalia – facsimiles of priceless texts to deface, sticky and slurpable drinks, crunchy sweets in rustly wrappers and packs of extra-tenacious bubble gum. There would be day trips to local libraries for a brisk march around the reading room with megaphones, klaxons, bugles and big bass drums . . .

'Haven't you got a home to go to?' The voice was right behind him.

It was still a good question. A not unwelcome one either. Or unanswerable, for that matter. Single negatives he could handle any day.

'Yes!' said Malcolm, turning, smiling.

Was that the ghost of a wink?

Questions remained as he made his way to the exit.

What was he to make of the Collected Poems of T S Eliot (Faber, hard-bound edition), discovered earlier, on his favourite table, propped open at a conspicuous angle, at page 222 ?

'We shall not cease from exploration . . .'

And all the rest.

Finally, what would *she* make of the box of Milk Tray, resplendent on a trilithon of Britannicas in the furthest corner of the reference section?

And all because . . .

A post-ultimate question. What do poor students do in the summer? An easy one for Malcolm. A man constrained by distressingly simple economics.

Throughout a year of battling for solvency he'd been eager and grateful for the tiniest token gain. Every little bit counted. For example, the lack of a February 29th, though unremarkable, was helpful. Even the recent one-hour shift to British Summer Time marginally hastened the next grant cheque (as it was due before the reversion to GMT) without increasing hunger.

He'd already sold several second-year textbooks – Spinoza's *Ethics* and Pascal's *Pensées* being early victims, traded, in effect, for a basket of supermarket groceries and three fish-and-chip suppers, respectively. Food for thought. A regrettable but pragmatic exchange. The old adage still applied: First one must eat, then one may philosophise. Malcolm minimised the residual guilt by promising himself to buy them again when he became rich or overweight, whichever came first. (He was destined to become neither, but did in fact re-acquire, though not reread, both, as bargain book-club introductory offers, thus partially redressing the earlier insult to continental rationalism.)

Before long he'd be overtaken by the Autumn term of the third year and the need to buy even weightier and more costly books. That left the intervening three months to make good the deficiencies and begin the build-up of a skiing surplus. It was certain that by Christmas those Alpine cravings would have become insurmountable, again.

What might be suitable vacation work for a quiet, studious type? Something not too demanding intellectually. Or physically. And perhaps not confined to a workplace, rather out and about in the fresh air, with a chance to engage with new people.

> Meta-Malcolm 25, between stints of study again, stops to adjust the thin leather straps, which have begun to chafe. Tomorrow he'll put on a thicker jumper – although he already feels rather warm. His burden consists of three plywood panels – a double-sided one held above his head by lengths of two-by-two timber, plus two covering his torso, front and back. These are attached to a kind of yoke which fits, almost, round the neck and shoulders. Thus rigged out he's been walking the High Street.

With dignity, if not pride. Carrying messages for all. Today, if you meet him head on, he reads, top to bottom:

PRENDERGAST

something
for everyone!

From behind it is:

MURGATROYD

simply
the best!

M-M had been concerned to discover that while the subject company names at the top are readily interchangeable (indeed he's responsible each morning for ensuring the two he's issued with are firmly velcroed in place) the corresponding predicates below were permanent. Read from either side he presents no contradictions. But if you'd met him yesterday it would have been **Blenkinsop** that was so universally bountiful, and **Fothergill** the indisputable top dog.

There are a few benches in this pedestrianised zone, but encumbered as he is he doesn't try to sit down. Mainly for fear of staying down – like an unhorsed knight in armour. He turns to look at himself in the darkened window of a travel agents, mops the sweat from his forehead.

'Why aren't you walkin'?' A voice from behind.

He turns back. 'Sorry?'

'Why are you standin' still?'

'It's the only way to stand!' says M-M, with an almost amiable grin.

The man is not amused. He flashes a badge of sorts.

'Ahh! Are you from, er . . .' M-M tilts his head right back as if to read the sign, which however simply tilts back with him, '. . . Prendergast?'

'No.'

M-M twists round to read the back of the sign, which likewise evades him. 'Murgatroyd then?'

'No. Peregrine Placards and Promotions. You're supposed to be workin' for us.'

'I've covered a mile or two already today,' says M-M defensively.

'Where?'

'Up and down the High Street. Well down and up, actually – there's a bit of a slope. Never noticed before I had this thing round my . . .'

'We pay you to keep movin', not to stand around.'

'Well how fast would you like me to move?' His tone is one of innocence.

'Fast as possible.'

'OK. Why?'

'So you cover more ground!'

'True,' M-M frowns, 'but what's the advantage of that?'

The man rolls his eyes. 'So you see more people. Or more people see you, rather.'

'Surely that's only the case if they're all standing still.'

'How come?'

'Well, if I'm walking, then for every extra person I pass coming towards me there'll be one coming from behind who won't pass me, but would have done if I'd been stationary.' He hitches up the rig into a slightly less uncomfortable position. 'It's like running in the rain – your back stays drier but your front gets wetter.' M-M feels he's on thinner ice with this last assertion. The man just stares. 'It's all relative. To a first approximation the number of people who see me is independent of my walking speed. He gestures at the milling crowd. Now if you could get *them* to walk faster . . .'

'And how would we do that?'

M-M scratches the top of his head, just reachable between the two-by-twos. 'I'm not sure. Loud martial music?' He raises his eyebrows. 'Sprinklers . . . ?'

'We're not payin' them, we're payin' you. Anyway, movin' things stand out – everybody knows that,' says the man triumphantly (feeling that his Psychology O-level is finally paying off.)

'But if everything else's moving it's the *stationary* things that stand out from the crowd. Get lots of attention. Think of those mime artists. And human statues! You didn't seem to notice me 'till I stopped.'

'I can assure you I've been watchin' you for some time. Anyway, I'm not gonna argue. Do you want this job, or don't you?'

'Yes,' says M-M and sets off down the street. After a hundred yards or so he makes an ostentatious turn. The full three-sixty. The man is still watching him. M-M starts to call out repeatedly with increasing volume and conviction "The end of the world is nigh!" The crowd gives him a wide berth. Nobody so much as looks at his signs. It begins to rain. He continues on into the distance, his enticements and warnings falling alike on stony ground, a walking demonstration of communication failure, an increasingly soggy human sandwich, earning a crust.

Real Malcolm would have preferred something more cerebral. Trouble was openings for casual philosophers were scarce, and would no doubt have paid poorly. He'd rather lost his appetite for cakes. At least in large numbers. But food was an issue here. And home cooking the most attractive and economic option. So home he headed. Presenting himself at his local employment exchange he was forced into something altogether more manual and muscular than philosophy. It paid poorly too. But they couldn't stop you moonlighting in your head . . .

Chapter 31

Getting On

Malcolm's reverie was broken by a violent tap on the shoulder.

'I've been wavin' at you for the last five minutes!' The foreman's face was contorted with indignation.

'I'm sorry. I didn't see you.'

'But I was right *behind* you. And I've been shoutin' as well.'

Malcolm removed the wax earplugs slowly and deliberately. The foreman regarded him suspiciously. He had done for some time now. In fact ever since the day Malcolm had refused to dig a trench in the towering shadow of a precarious ton of bricks – on the grounds that, while they might owe a good deal to poetic fantasy, most figures of speech were founded on concrete experience. Of the kind he'd no wish to share in.

'What've you got *those* for?'

'Because I'm using *this*.' Malcolm let go of the handles of the pneumatic drill and it fell slightly closer to the foreman's toes than he'd intended.

'Well, all right. If it helps you concentrate. Come with me, I've got a *job* for you.'

'So what d'you call drilling through three feet of concrete with a blunt bit?' muttered Malcolm to himself as he followed the foreman to a far corner of the site. They stopped by a small mountain of pinkish grit. Newly tipped from the lorry, its planar faces undisturbed, it lacked only a crowning Union Jack on a stick.

'Well, don't just stand there, lad!' He called everybody under thirty "lad". It allowed him to think of them not as people, with names and brains and things, but as amorphous, greyish lumps moving around the site at his bidding.

'What would you like me to do in addition?'

'Go and fetch a *shovel!*'

Malcolm went and fetched a shovel from the shovel shed. It was shiny and old, and classically shovel-shaped. Not unpleasant to the grip. He stood to attention with it, in a stance approaching satire, but looking just earnest and prepared enough to stave off further criticism, and waited for instructions. Or inspiration. The tea-break hooter. Death. But none was forthcoming. Fragments of his earlier reverie began to reassemble.

Fate, in the form of alphabetic adjacency on the register, has placed Malcolm next to Angela Gimble in the A-level physics practical group. In the drab and lengthy Thursday afternoon lab a ray of sunshine bursts through. And when he learns they've been assigned optics experiments it's rainbows all the way. In the discreet gloom of soft sodium lights they peer through prisms and tweak the knurled brass knobs on well-oiled verniers. All in hot pursuit of the fleeting yellow lines – fugitive images, showing the natural reluctance of any quarry to linger in the crosswires. Heads are bent, and close, heavy black curtains drawn against intrusions. The ageing Vent-Axia fan is unequal to the cheap and potent perfume which, in the confines, will soon creep above the low and seemly concentration allowed by the headmistress (sadly for her she can't monitor such things with the ease and precision of a wooden ruler on a hemline). Witnessed only by racks of eyeless lenses on dusty high shelves the two conspire. So closely, in fact, that they'll have to shuffle their lab notebooks in the hand-in pile, in case the similarities suggest their scientific objectivity has been somehow compromised in the darkness . . .

'Well, get on with it lad!' The voice came from a passing fork-lift truck.

'With what? Exactly?'

'With the *grit!*'

'Could you be a bit more specif . . .' But the foreman was gone in a puff of exhaust.

There was nothing for it but to get on with the grit. He dug a tentative half-shovelful from the South face and moved it about three feet westwards. It didn't seem to mind.

'Not there, *there!*' The fork-lift was now speeding in the opposite direction.

Augmented by the contrasting intonation of the two *there*s the foreman's gesture narrowed the field of operation to about an acre. Not wanting to appear stubborn Malcolm adjusted his shovelling action to be significantly different from before, now moving the grit a slightly greater distance, and south-eastwards.

The summer sun was pleasant on the back of his tee-shirt. In fact, with the modest exertion, the morning was already warm enough to go topless. His shirt afforded little protection from falling brick stacks, and had the word, or, at least, the letters "A N G L E" emblazoned inexplicably across the front. He'd asked the salesman what it meant and was told he could always wear it inside out, though that had been known to cause an allergic reaction. However, he was loath to discard the shirt, simply because it hid his unique lack of tattoos.

Tattoos, exhibited proudly as souvenirs of hard and lengthy service, naval, penal or other, though in truth more often the product of one-off episodes of drunkenness or plain stupidity, were the *de rigueur* symbol of site credibility. He once asked Big Paddy why he had so many.

'Well,' said Paddy, spitting into the cement mixer, 'you can always have 'em removed.'

Expectorating was one of Paddy's more endearing habits, one that extended to wheel barrows, water butts and once, through a combination of a freak gust of wind and a tragic trajectorial miscalculation, to the inside of his own left Wellington. Its origins were lost in Hibernian mists and myths. But so frequent and extensive was his practice that future archaeologists, unearthing the building they were now building, would have been able to clone him from any fragment of doorstep, wall or window ledge. Maybe it was simply a form of territorial marking. It certainly ensured that workmates kept a respectful distance. And that he was never asked to make the tea.

The reverie floated back to the surface. Malcolm began to get on positively well with the grit. It had just enough cohesion to form practical clumps and yet yield silently to the shovel, and just enough *ad*hesion for the shovel to hold on to its load, and then part with it at the flick of a wrist. It really was the most amenable grit.

'Go easy on that. You're not layin' a drain!' The foreman was passing on foot this time with a roll of blueprints under one arm and wearing a tin hat (partial defence, perhaps, against incoming bricks) with the word, or, at least, the letters, "G O L P" on it.

'I'm not laying a drain,' Malcolm repeated to himself, and tried to further refine the shovelling movements to be, within the limits of his skill, maximally un-drain-laying-like.

Soon the outside world was receding again to the smooth and soothing rhythm.

> Cuddly Caroline Strimble is struggling with her trigonometry, and the class of the fire-breathing Miss Cusp is drawing near. Enter Sir Swotalot, brandishing a mighty slide rule . . .

But the delicate and promising image was dispelled by a vaguely familiar form, looming larger by the second in Malcolm's peripheral vision. Looking up he recognised the car sweeping through the site gate. It was grand enough to sit comfortably in the broad-gauge ruts left by lorries, and had a leisurely suspension. Its wide wheels radiated a mud wake. It belonged to the owner of the firm.

Through his side window the boss eyed him suspiciously, as in fact he'd been doing ever since Malcolm had said 'Good morning' to him on his first day, from the depths of a hole he'd been asked to dig. It had been the straightforward, dispassionate tone of the utterance which had so disturbed Mr Big. Obsequious greetings he tolerated, obscene mutterings he had a certain respect for, but simple, neutral, 'good morning's, devoid of irony or affectation, were deeply disturbing. He clearly wondered who the hell Malcolm thought he was.

The boss stepped out but left the engine running. 'What are you doing?' It was much more of an accusation than an objective enquiry.

'Oh, I'm just getting on with this grit.' Malcolm kept his face as straight as his shovel handle and his eyes lowered around the level of the boss's Wellington tops – an attitude which gave the illusion of respect, with the bonus of avoiding the spectacle of the man's beer gut.

'All right.' The tone was begrudging. 'Make a good job of it. They'll be here in the morning.'

Another cloud of exhaust, and then silence. Malcolm returned to the task in hand.

Fate, in the form of a poorly finger, elastoplastered tidily by his mother, augmented by himself to heroic proportions with a few metres of gauze (one couldn't be too careful where hygiene was concerned) and rounded off with the odd, well-timed grimace of martyrdom, has gained him a reprieve from the playing field and a tidying sinecure in the sports pavilion. He enters whistling stoically, pupils widening smoothly from pinpoints as glare gives way to gloom and then overshooting at what greets him, before settling to an aperture suited to the light level. Between a quiver of javelins, whose soiled and rusty points might have infringed the Geneva Convention, and a tangle of hurdles, eyes wide in wonder at his over-sized digit, sits the winsome, and less overtly indisposed, Amanda Trimble. Her perch is a large metal drum. Unbeknown to either of them it is half full with the narrow miles of next season's sporting white lines. She drums against its resonant sides with the backs of her plimsolled heels.

Outside, reassuringly distant shouts, whistle blasts and leather-timber impacts signal the continued occupation of their classmates. The magic potential of the hour is quick to dawn. This is not the windy bikeshed of cliché, wreathed with the tell-tale smoke of lesser transgressors, but a sporting sanctum, albeit with a whiff of linseed oil and creosote, where they've each been ordered to spend the afternoon, alone and unrefereed.

They begin. The random harvest of beanbags littering the floor is soon safely gathered into a tidy corner. They quickly turn to the jumble of gym mats. Though minimal and austerely padded individually, they will add up to unforeseen luxury when neatly piled in bulk. There's comfort in numbers. Enough indeed to insulate the most sensitive princess from the bumps and splinters of a rough timber floor . . .

'What doing you, Malcolm?' The turbaned voice issued from a nearby hole. In under an hour Singh had transformed himself, unaided, from sixteen stone of most palpable Punjabi on flat ground, to an occasional spade blade glinting in the sun.

'I'm not laying a drain!'

Singh laughed heartily in his resonant subterranean lair. He'd lived in the country for a decade and become a most valued worker – tireless and built like a bull. But he'd never lost his understanding of incomprehension. He and Malcolm often formed an enthusiastic, if bewildered, partnership, desperately trying to fulfil some ill-specified whim of the foreman.

'What doing *you*, Singh?'

'Same like you.'

'Need any grit?'

'No. Not needing grit for not laying drains!'

And they laughed till lunch time.

In the cramped wooden hut on the edge of the site Malcolm was just over halfway through a rather gritty batch of cheese and tomato sandwiches (of his very own, quantity-controlled manufacture) when his reverie was interrupted by a familiar cry.

' *'ere, you went to university . . .*'

He was always alarmed by the tense (didn't they know this was just a vacation job? Did they feel he'd finally found his level in life?) but he looked forward to a little brain teaser.

'*. . . what's a river in India?*'

'Depends how you mean . . .' began Malcolm.

There was a general jeer followed by a specific, scornful remark about tax-payers' money, from a source who was most ill qualified to comment.

'Ask old Singh,' said Big Paddy, 'he comes from over there.'

'*Pakistan!*' protested Singh.

'All the bloody same!'

'Not bloody same. Bloody different!'

'Pyrenees?' came a helpful voice.

'Too many letters!'

'Write little.'

'If you can!'

A timely hooter blast brought the sparring to an end, and something akin to professionalism descended on the group. Dregs were drained, tin hats donned, shovels shouldered. Out there there were barrows to be wheeled, holes to be dug and filled. And grit with which to be got on.

Chapter 32

Counter Intuition

And so it had gone. Muscles tautened, skin toughened. Summer passed. The great worldly wheel of fortune teetered on its axis. And then it was back to the daily rounds.

But just how many?

'Yes dear.'

Malcolm took a deep breath, and spoke clearly and slowly. 'I'd like two, complete slices of bread, each buttered on one side, with those sides facing each other, and a slice of corned beef between.'

Hilda just stared.

'And cut into four, roughly equal, pieces. Please,' he added.

'Sorry?'

He let two seconds go by, then repeated the order, word for word, and even more slowly.

Hilda stared for a while longer and then said, 'You mean, like, a *sandwich*?' Her accompanying gestures were a masterful précis of the manufacturing process, right down to the salt-sprinkling coda and the final cross cuts.

What else could he say except, 'Yes.'

'A corned-beef sandwich?'

'Yes.'

She looked relieved. 'Right,' she smiled, 'fine! How many do you want?'

Malcolm managed to suppress the welling scream just long enough to order, and get clear of the building with, a rather limp, but well-defined, pizza slice.

This was more than a regular language problem. This was obtuseness of the acutest kind. The oxymorons were taking over. Here were canteen staff engaging in conduct above and beyond the call of everyday perversity. You could only maintain that standard of communication failure through intense personal commitment (topped up maybe by attendance at special day-release courses).

And there had to be a logical solution. In the strict, rational sense. Something which rose above the contingent difficulties, went somehow beyond the particular confusions.

He felt increasingly like one of those mathematical-puzzle-book explorers lost in a jungle, among a tribe of habitual liars and their indistinguishable, truth-telling neighbours. Malcolm, the intrepid seeker after sandwich specificity, was at the fork in the path. And there had to exist some carefully contrived, resolving question. A question whose scope embraced both parties and their differing conventions, or lack of them. One which could be asked of either party, and would result in some kind of neat, internal cancelling out of their respective interpretative habits. Something like *'If I asked your colleague for* n *sandwiches, how many do* you *consider she'd give me?'* Then all you'd have to do was order, from the first lady, the geometric mean of the two numbers. Or maybe the arithmetic mean. From the second lady. Well, something along those lines anyway.

Then again, maybe he should reconsider the use of pictures – design his own flip-chart lunch menu of scale drawings showing the range of all conceivable sandwich numbers and configurations, in plan view and side elevation. But he felt a certain uneasiness about that too. A deep-rooted reluctance to give up on words.

For the school trip to Calais some years before Malcolm had bought a set of flash cards covering likely emergencies. His favourite, which he kept on top of the deck, at the ready throughout, had been **J'ai perdu ma valise!** This carried a schematic depiction of a missing suitcase (not unlike his own, in fact, but with a dashed outline and halo of question marks acknowledging its doubtful ontological status). But would he have had the nerve to use it in the event of such a loss? Who was to say that the gendarme he presented it to wouldn't simply have gallically shrugged and then produced a corresponding card carrying a schematic smirking face and the words **Tant pis! Pas de chance!** ? These iconographic approaches were still thwartable.

Quel dommage.

In Malcolm's experience neither deliberation nor alcohol nor any combination of the two had helped to bring a solution, or even a diminution, of the sandwich problem. Nevertheless, evening found him sitting thinking in the Union Bar. And it was getting late. Again. Though at no greater rate than previously, if that was any consolation. And even if it wasn't.

One second per second. That was the inexorable, non-negotiable, going rate – the current (and past, and future) cost of living. One minute per minute, or hour per hour. However you chose to look at it, and even if you chose not to look at it at all, there was that same inescapable cancellation of both the quantity and the units, leaving you adrift, bereft of any real purchase, in an endlessly long division. Simplifying everything to silence as it proceeded. Closing behind you like a cosmic zipper. Was that what consciousness was, perhaps? A flowing of pure, dimensionless unity?

Malcolm took a slurp from his cider, and returned it to the table more noisily than might have been expected, given that there was a spongy wet beer-mat to absorb the impact. This was partly due to a genuine co-ordination problem – there having been many a slurp already that evening. But it was also an unconscious reaction to the *lady's* glass they'd given him at the bar. This smooth, round, stemmed container held every bit as much as the chunkier, windowed, handled variety, he'd expected, but failed to specify. What's more, the contents, though seen by many as sweet and innocent, were actually very dry and potent. There was nothing namby-pamby about *Scrumples*, even in half pints. (CIDER WORTH STEALING! claimed a deep, rugged voice on the current TV advert.) But the all-too-dainty image of the drink somehow prevailed, and the only way to combat it was to endow the drinking act itself with some extra informality. In the absence of sawdust to spit in and mates to swear loudly at and with, one was reduced to slamming down the glass then smacking the lips, wiping the back of the hand across the mouth and exhaling audibly in a satisfied, manly fashion.

Slurp. Yes, it was getting on. It and he both. Though no faster than anything or anyone else.

One year per year.

It had been a tiring year, the last one. And one had certainly just passed. Although it was neither December nor January, nor near his birthday, nor close to the start or end points of any conventional twelve-month time span, it was, as always, the case that a year had just gone by. And wasn't such a period a lot for a man to cope with? After all, fewer than eighty of them proved more than enough for most people.

Slurp. Malcolm felt he might be destined to do better than most. In numerical terms at least. But numbers weren't everything. What counted was the integral of pleasure over time. That's what you had to maximise. But how should you play it? Try to grow old slowly, eking out the heartbeats, drawing out the pleasure? Or quickly, before you had a chance to die? Extended, arctic twilight? Or precipitous, tropical nightfall? By the time you found out it might be too late to choose:

> Meta-Malcolm 99 rarely speaks, and hardly walks. Though he's often spoken to. And much wheeled. But for all his weaknesses on the motor-function front, his sensory systems have survived almost intact.
>
> It is evening. From the terrace he smells the freshly cut lawns and the residue of supper, sees the darkening pines, hears the clank of dishes from the kitchen, the cluck of mallard from the lake. His eyelids droop and he drifts off, to dream of Wordsworth and Wittgenstein, woolly socks and the Matterhorn, Schwarzwälderkirschtorten, snowflakes, girls in white dresses (and in truth a good deal more. And less – in deference to age we list here only a very proper subset of his favourite things).
>
> Fading in from behind come undainty footsteps and the creak of a starched uniform. Nurse Kimble delivers reality aplenty for all his five senses: Chanel and antiseptic, a tuneless but not unpleasant humming, a firm professional hand on the

shoulder. 'Come along Malcolm,' she croons, 'time for your entertainment.'

It's Friday again, which means that a local volunteer has driven from several miles away to perform a two-hour-long medley of 1960s popular songs. The old rosewood upright house piano is ill tempered (tuning, surely, being wasted on the elderly) and ill named (it's been an unequivocal *forte* ever since the soft pedal was decoupled by an impact from Major Pringle's speeding wheelchair).

As Nurse K. wheels M-M in through the French windows the other residents of Dingle Court Manor (formerly Dingle Croft Lodge, and now owned by Manor House Lodges, but in fact all part of the Panorama Care Management Housing Group) are already singing along, arrayed in a rough semicircle focused on the piano. *How many times?* A good few. But many here are beyond counting. She parks him in a thoughtfully left gap, firmly applying the brake before departing.

Although manifestly artificial the lights in the Union Bar seemed to be slowly fading along with the evening. And even Mr Dylan was beginning to sound tired of his own voice. Maybe there was hope for mankind after all. But then how many times should you be able to sing the same song, which insists that times are changing, and remain fresh and convincing? (Sound recording has a lot to answer for. Our facility for experiencing boredom presumably evolved to stop us repeating an activity to the point where bits of our bodies start to wear out and fall off. But nature hasn't had time to adjust to recording technology. So the original artist may walk off after the session and never again experience the natural inhibiting effect of having to hear himself over and over again, while blameless listeners in pubs, restaurants, shops and lifts may become bored to an unlimited degree.)

One year on. To the day, you could choose to say. Was he sitting at the same table? A tricky question. Because on the one hand it was, as before, the furthest from the jukebox, in that little alcove with the slightly plusher upholstery and more kindly lights. But then the tables themselves had become shuffled during the Summer when temporarily removed to allow carpet shampooing in the aftermath of an informal, end-of-term drinking contest. The distribution of the scuff marks on the legs and the knots of vintage chewing gum on the underside would, in fact, have revealed it to be different.

He was, though, pretending to read the same book (that is, it was the same book he was pretending to read, as opposed to it being a different one he was actually reading and he pretending it wasn't, however you might do that).

Was it in any sense the same cider he was drinking? Heraclitus would have said not, insisting that everything was in a permanent state of flux. Or was it a fluctuating state of permanence? It was over a year since Malcolm had done the Pre-Socratics. But then they were unlikely to have changed in that time. Whatever, it was the same brand, and so from the same orchard, or the same variety of apple at least. (And perhaps one should take account of those worrying graffiti allegations above the new urinals, concerning the bar manager's re-cycling policy). And the two drinks would be linked in the much diluted, statistical sense of Caesar's last breath. It's often been pointed out that we're each harbouring many air molecules from the great man's terminal exhalation. This is simply because there are many more such molecules in a given lung than there are lungfuls in the whole atmosphere, assuming that those privileged particles have been randomly distributed about the globe. Given the routine diffusion and stirring storms of two millennia, they surely have been.

A similar argument, then, would apply to Caesar's last pint, or for that matter anybody's pint or half-pint of anytime, assuming the requisite churning in the world's ocean currents. Were there such things as cider molecules – conglomerations of apple-shaped atoms, joined by twiggy bonds? Maybe not. But something in the stuff he was drinking was working its effect all right – potent little microscopic templates were snapping into matching brain holes and diverting the flow of thought.

Malcolm loosened his new tie – a greeny-yellow number he'd acquired in the High Street that morning. It still felt funny to be wearing one, with neither a wedding nor a funeral in sight. He'd intended it as a cheap, quick, sartorial fix, to offset and distract from the ever-problematic trousers. The resulting image, he hoped, was a neat combination of rebellion and compliance. A kind of healthy, balanced formal tension which might intrigue without offending. Brand-new tie, dingy old jeans. What could be more smartly casual? But as far as he could tell no-one had yet given him a second glance.

He went and got himself another half.

Chapter 33

Costs of Living

The bar was getting busier. Conversations buzzier. Rhubarb was proliferating.

A year older. Undeniably. And wiser? In a sense, of course. But how much? It was hard to estimate the value of a year's acquired wisdom. You couldn't just subtract the wisdom of infancy from that of old age and divide by three score and ten. The acquisition was probably most irregular – the rate quite possibly peaking somewhere around the middle of a degree course. And come to think of it, the cider, even in extremely moderate doses, would have its effect, being mentally detrimental, according to received (though possibly itself impaired) wisdom. And time itself would be taking a toll. How many brain cells was it you lost every day? There was a time when he'd known.

Malcolm carefully drank the first half-inch from the brimming glass without lifting it.

So, why was he here, exactly? That is, why, exactly, was he here. Indeed why even approximately was he here? Was it coincidence? Hardly. He'd been there, that is, here, on at least a dozen Friday nights over the last year.

With the backs of his fingers he stroked condensation from the glass. It began to form again immediately.

What does it mean anyway to describe something as a coincidence? Are we making a claim of eerie unlikelihood? Or dismissing it as unnewsworthy? On the whole we tend to be a bit casual in using the term. Strictly, we should identify some first *incidence*, and then get excited only if a second one shows up. If you arrange to meet your girlfriend under the town-hall clock at 8.00 pm, and you're there at eight and she arrives within a minute or two, that would hardly be a coincidence. Even if you both arrive on the stroke of eight, however convenient and pleasing, it wouldn't raise the eyebrows of any passing statistician. But if it's your wife who happens to be passing the scene at eight ... Now *that* would be a coincidence! He shifted his glass slightly to the right.

In a similar way the old claim to have been *at the right place at the right time* needs a careful analysis. This gets reported suspiciously often – at least for an event rare enough to be noteworthy. And it sounds doubly fortunate, but is really only singly so. Probabilities combine multiplicatively only if the events are independent of one another. That would require there to be at least one place which was permanently *right*, in some sense. If such a place existed it would be populated to bursting – the locals, by definition, content to be there, irrespective of time and the events any given time would bring. We might, without undue scepticism, doubt the existence of such an eternally happy venue. The right place can only be defined by reference to where it is that something happened at the right time. Likewise there can't be a right *time* without reference to where you are – a moment of universal felicity. For any time there'd be a right place and for any place a right time. The two are tacitly defined with reference to each other and so the implied rarity of the conjunction is undermined.

He shifted his glass back to where it had been, and wiped off some more condensation.

So, he was free to claim this was the right *place*, or, at least, *a* right place, since anybody who could monitor the location for all time would be rewarded. Sooner or later. For example, by finding a stash of bank notes, or witnessing exquisite sunsets and meteor showers. Or by meeting the right person, in the *here and then. Or* (but not of course *and*) he could claim this was the right *time*, because somewhere, there was momentary bliss, in the *there and now*. But for that elusive rightness *here and now* he might have to go and wait. Where to? And how long? Wasn't that life all over? Jam over there, and more jam over there too, but rarely jam over here. Maybe tomorrow.

Malcolm got himself a refill. He'd stopped pretending to read the book, even to himself.

So, a new year was beginning. Not, of course, *the* New Year. But what did it matter? Was there ever a better time to take stock than *now*? Assessments were as likely to be right, and any resolutions more likely to be kept, if volunteered out of the blue, rather than triggered by some convention of the calendar.

Over a sixpenny bag of **Tangles** ("crispy little polygons with a savoury coating!") aimed at provoking a thirst which would justify the drinks he'd already had, Malcolm considered the year's tally of gains and losses. A useful rehearsal perhaps for some final reckoning, at the pearly gates. Or the fiery trapdoor.

For offering unsolicited road-crossing help he'd received the gratitude of three little old ladies, but the scorn of one rather bigger, much younger and, it had to be admitted, perfectly able-bodied one.

He'd gained a singular tie and a pair of putative trousers, lost a vest at the local "Launderama", when it had clung limpet-like to the roof of the drum, and broken even on socks – six (gift wrapped and intact) received, and six (holey and repellent) dispatched to that big laundry basket in the sky.

He'd forfeited a mile of hair to the local barber (if you added all the little bits together) and a few grams of nail clippings, skin flakes and sundry material, distributed more casually, to the general world.

He'd submitted a mile of blue biro in essays and the dissertation, wound up loopily on to a few-score pages, and received only about ten yards of red in return, from his tutors. This was evidently an acceptable exchange rate, as he was deemed to have passed his continuous assessment. And, in the year's least comfortable transaction, he'd exchanged a few cubic millimetres of decayed tooth for a similar volume of amalgam.

Other inputs included half a hogshead of cider and a flagon or two of custard (imbibed, sensibly, at many, separate, sittings), a brace of gnats during a late-evening bike-ride yawn, and a controversial number of sandwiches.

All in all a rather modest transfer of material, for what was a small but not totally insignificant fraction of a lifetime. And what of the future? Another two-score years and ten, according to ancient authority. A bit more, according to current actuarial tables. What would that require? What stock of supplies would sustain a marooned twenty-year-old long enough to have a fair chance of death by natural causes? A back-of-a-beermat calculation showed the necessary survival pack to be quite basic. Assuming that the subject knew his predicament and was accordingly frugal:

- a small swimming pool of drinking water,
- an Albert Hall of air (give or take a foyer),
- a less-than-thirty-by-thirty-by-thirty matrix of vitamin pills – allowing life to be factored geometrically into the daily element, the monthly row, the biennial layer,
- a few cowfuls of milk,
- a few cubic yards of sandwiches.

For any given non-edible commodity – paper, ink, matches, candles, tubes of toothpaste or cakes of soap – a whole century's supply could be carried with one hand. How disturbing. That these measures of a lifetime were so countable, containable and, finally, exhaustible.

Malcolm got himself a re-refill. Half a pint, half a pint, half a pint onward. He was feeling the creeping effects. Little drops of cider, coalescing, mounting up subliminally, provoking little protests from belly, brain and bladder. The latter now most urgently.

He eyed his drink. There was danger in leaving it on the table unattended. But a proper risk assessment was tricky, involving a fair few psychological factors. As well as just how much liquid was left in the glass. The greater the amount the greater, of course, the potential loss. But the actual chances of removal were also dependent on that amount. A full half pint would invite outright theft, as the Scrumples slogan warned, while anything less than an inch might be taken as dregs and whisked away by the bar staff. Half full seemed an obvious compromise, but had ambiguous echoes he could do without, and brought to mind the tedious cliché about optimists and pessimists. He finally opted for the half compromise (or would it be a double one?) of drinking only the first quarter (that is, the highest and most accessible), reckoning that a half-half-empty glass, being not only significantly depleted but also tainted by an unknown mouth, would be doubly unattractive to would-be scrumpers.

He hung his old ski jacket prominently over the chair arm and placed the book open and face down between glass and half-empty *Tangles* packet. Glancing back from the door of the gents he felt satisfied with the impression of his absent self which the little scene conveyed. Here, it seemed, had been sitting a moderate, literate and not totally unathletic body. The image was one of calm, scholarly recreation. Unthreatening, but with just a hint of *Marie Celeste*.

Human ingenuity is a never-ending and universal cause for celebration. Well almost. As the parade of triumphant inventions grows apace we must keep one eye open always for the blundering counterexample. We can only marvel at the simple functionality of the paper clip, the safety pin and the zip fastener. And all of these are, in turn, outshone by that toast of the highway, the trail-blazing, life-saving, leading light: the cat's eye – jewel in the crown of innovations, crouching watchfully in the tarmac, housing the magic little mirror, so cunningly shaped it throws back the light beams whencesoever they came.

A neat and appealing principle. But not appropriate to all situations. The gleaming stainless-steel urinals recently installed in the Students' Union were meant as a resounding affirmation of swinging 'sixties design. But the venture into trendy geometry had backfired badly. The hyperbolic-paraboloidal (or was it parabolic-hyperboloidal?) shape, inspired maybe by the Sydney Opera House, or le Corbusier's pavilion at the Brussels Expo, ensured that whatever your attitude, elevation and angle of approach (and Malcolm had tried 'em all) reflected spray was focused back along the incident path. You entered the Union gents with apprehension, and exited a marked man, only the improbably perfect symmetry countering the impression of gross incompetence. Those with contortionist leanings would adopt an exaggeratedly evasive stance, allowing the floor to become wet. This caused the next caller to stand yet further back and the whole situation to deteriorate ever more rapidly, in a kind of vicious parabola.

Malcolm washed his hands with extra-special carelessness to help dilute and camouflage any unfortunate traces. Then he spent an extra-long session on the 'Sirocco' hot-air hand drier. But he still had reason to be grateful for the bar's low lighting when he re-emerged.

Chapter 34

End Games

There was a new arrival at the adjoining table. She was reading a book, or at least pretending more convincingly than Malcolm ever managed to. His little delay in returning had allowed her the few vital minutes to establish herself. In fact, to a third party she might have been there for hours. *Was* there, perhaps, a third party – a companion getting drinks at the bar? Evidently not – beside her was a small empty glass with orange-juicy traces in the bottom and around the rim.

Her choice of seat seemed a little bold. By the usual convention newcomers complied with a kind of "minimum-energy configuration", sitting in a position which maximised the sum of the squares of the distances to all other occupants of a room. Perhaps, being absent at the time of the calculation, Malcolm had simply been left out of it. Or perhaps, misconstruing the *lady's* glass, she'd gravitated towards his empty place for the sake of sisterly protection. He slipped back into his seat in a less than ladylike manner, feeling now both an intruder and impostor, but her eyes stayed firmly on the book.

Malcolm took a silent, but not unmanly, swig, leaving around five-eighths of the half left. A whole range of potential opening lines suggested themselves. But each he swiftly dismissed.

Do you play ping pong? – too abrupt.

Dark in here isn't it? – too threatening.

Reading a good book at the moment? This might rehabilitate the old cliché by adding a twist of tense. But it left him open to the retort: 'I'm *trying* to!'

He picked up his own book and started pretending to read again, hoping to minimise suspicions by trying to find a part he had not already pretended to read, but finding it difficult, in the event, to be sure about the matter. Meanwhile he continued to struggle for a suitable overture.

What do you think of the tie? – too vain.

I bet it's not your birthday tomorrow, is it? – too weird for words.

Then suddenly it was she who was conducting the overture.

'Pardon?' said Malcolm, having to pretend to stop reading.

'I said, do they do sandwiches in here?'

'I'm afraid not,' said Malcolm, not at all sure that he really was. 'Do you like *Tangles*?'

'Well, it's a quite while since I was in one . . .'

He waved the half-empty packet to clarify, but she was grinning broadly.

'I think I need something more, substantial. Really.' She was pale and slim, and looked like she really did.

'Like a sandwich?'

'Yes, I would. Several, actually.'

He laid the book face downwards and leaned toward her. 'But how many, *exactly*?'

'That's rather difficult to say.'

'You can tell me. I'm a man of the world!'

'No, it's just that,' she frowned, 'it's sometimes a bit hard to quantify these things.'

'Give it a try.' He leaned a little closer.

She made a rather neat and fetching, three-fold gesture, carving out a considerable pile of notional sandwiches just above the table, in orthogonal planes, with her parallel palms. 'That many.'

Malcolm stared intently at the imaginary feast. 'So, cheese & tomato then.'

'Actually, yes!'

'I could make you one.'

'Really?'

He executed a two-handed *abracadabra* gesture. 'You're a cheese & tomato sandwich!'

A soft shoe dealt his shin a glancing blow. He pretended to ignore it. Neatly splitting open the rest of the *Tangles* packet, right along the seam, he offered them across.

She poked around with a lithesome index finger. '*Someone*'s had all the rhombuses. They're my favourite.'

He affected an air of innocence. 'I'm a trapezium man myself. They have a sort of . . . irresistible . . . piquancy.'

She looked doubtful. 'Don't you find they stick in the teeth?'

'Not if you swallow them whole.' He threw one in the air and caught it in his mouth before flushing it down with a slurp of Scrumples.

She resumed her examination of the dwindling collection. 'Tell you what, I'll have the isosceles triangles and you have the squares.'

'I can't see any squares.'

'Maybe it takes one to spot one!' A winning grin.

In the half-light, with the added cover of distracting cider sips, Malcolm could risk regular sideways glances. The mouth was especially compelling from this viewpoint. The complexion would have been peachy from any angle. In any light.

The Union barman signalled last orders. Two long flashes. A Morse-code M for Malcolm. It was a heaven-sent hint.

'Can I get you a drink?' He managed a smart-casual tone.

'Mmm, please. I'll have whatever you're drinking.'

Malcolm squinted at his own glass. 'What, three-sixteenths of a cider?'

'Well, maybe I'll go the whole hog, and have a half.'

'OK. Won't be a minute. Don't let them take my drink away!'

She mockingly measured the depth in slender horizontal fingers, and nodded reassuringly.

Malcolm stood up. 'And I've counted the *Tangles*!' He narrowed his eyes at her.

'But how could you tell if someone ate, say, just half of a rectangle – turning it into a right-angle triangle and conserving number?'

'Teeth marks along the hypotenuse. Always a give-away.' He ambled off barwards and returned with a plain, cylindrical, unisex glass. It was still surprisingly full of cider.

'Cheers!'

'Cheers!'

They limited themselves to waving the drinks in the air from their close but separate tables. Glass-glass contact would have been a little premature and in any case mechanically unwise given the disparity in masses and shapes, and the unequal co-ordination of the two parties.

Malcolm took off his tie and rolled it up.

'What are you doing?' She was smiling.

'Oh, I was just a bit warm . . .' He perched the tie on his book, safe from cider spills.

'No, I mean, studying.'

'Have a guess!'

'Give me a clue.'

'What are *you* doing?'

'I asked first!' She wagged a finger at him.

'How do you know that wasn't the clue?'

She looked at him sideways. 'So, you're studying, what, deviousness?'

'Only indirectly.' He took a sip of cider. 'What's your name?'

'Have a guess!'

'Rosie?'

'Nope. Have another!'

'Eve?'

'Nope.' She took a sip. 'Have another!'

'Rumplestiltskin?'

'Nope, but you're getting warmer. Have another!'

'Nope. Let's just savour all these unknowns.'

They sat and savoured. The jukebox was murmuring a mellow ballad, well suited to the hour. It was the nearest they would get to a last waltz. The rhubarb had reached a new high. But Malcolm was thinking of peaches and cream.

'Hey look!' She was rearranging the last of the *Tangles,* 'If only we had another one of *those* . . .'

'Hmmm?'

'. . . we could prove Pythagoras' theorem.'

Malcolm swallowed guiltily.

'Oh well, just a thought. You can still make a little house. Look!'

Together they assembled an instant, prefab dream home on the table top and watched it a moment in silence. Then hunger prevailed and they began a demolition, converting it first into a bungalow, before razing it to the ground.

The barman called time.

Malcolm drained his glass. 'Still hungry?'

She drained hers. 'Still hungrier!'

'Well, back in Hall I've got the ingredients for an unlimited number of cheese & tomato sandwiches.'

'An unlimited number?'

'Well, large but finite.'

'But how large, *exactly*?' She leaned toward him.

'As a matter of fact that does bring up a serious question.' Malcolm paused. 'If you like I can show you my dissertation on it.'

Her face took on a quick succession of expressions, reflecting enthusiasm, hunger and curiosity, but well tempered with the ghosts of old maternal warnings. It was a virtuoso performance. She picked up her bag and book. 'Just going to powder my nose.' She was halfway to the Ladies before he had a chance to say how amply matt and cute it looked already. And as for the mouth!

So what now? He could wait at the exit. The only exit. Or he could sit and savour the uncertainty. He sat. Someone arrested the last non-waltz in mid bar. The rhubarb underwent a swift diminuendo, leaving the cider to ring in his ears. Someone took away the glasses. The lights flashed, flashed again, then hovered at a twilight level. The room retreated. A kind of criticality reigned.

A distant voice called *TIME*. And *TIME* again. The word reverberated, losing its conventional, cheery, landlordly resignation, gaining in a kind of cosmic loneliness, like the call of a humpback whale, meaning everything and nothing. Malcolm closed his eyes and floated on time and tide. What kind of thing *was* time? An infinite number of infinitesimal end-to-end instants? Or just one monumental, monolithic moment? A great healer, allegedly, and perhaps truly. But then, too, a great carcinogen and clogger of arteries. A great consumer of life. Come to think of it, what kind of thing was *life*? Really? An

254

interval between two instants? – a finite filling sandwiched between the big bang of birth and the weeny whimper of extinction? Or an instant between two intervals? – a vanishingly thin and fragile incarnate slice between eternal crusts of insensibility? Who knew?

TIME. Again, like a tolling bell. The fourth time. Or was it the fifth (or even the third)? How many *TIMES?* It was hard to say (but wasn't there a song about it?) Maybe he shouldn't have had that last cider – but then again it's hard to avoid having the last one, if you've had one at all. And he certainly had. Maybe he shouldn't have had the first, at least – that would be the one now affecting him most. But stone-cold sober the world could still be confusing, when it counted. Perhaps one day the world would learn to count properly, and all would be well. And the first would be zeroth and the last, merely penultimate . . .

There came a last, resounding and most timely, *TIME*. Malcolm opened his eyes to find her watching him from across the now uncrowded room. He raised his eyebrows enquiringly and performed a butter-spreading mime on an outstretched palm. She responded by grasping the imaginary, promised snack with her delicate but manifestly real, promising hands and making an enthusiastic teeth-sinking gesture. He gathered together tie, jacket and book and got to his feet with a studied steadiness. Cool air and coffee were called for. By the eager lungful and the steaming mugful. No half, rather double measures all round.

Malcolm felt a year end

And begin.

For many years Mike Greenhough lectured and researched in physics and the science of music at Cardiff University. He has long had a little toe in the arts, and has served on the judging panel for *sciart* awards – funding for collaborations between established writers, musicians and visual artists, and scientists. He has numerous awards for comic short stories and poems, winning the inaugural All Wales Comic Verse Competition, the Percy French Award for Comic Verse and a Canongate Prize for New Writing. A poetry collection is in the offing. He sails and skis. *Malcolm* is his zeroth novel.

mikegreenhoughwriting.co.uk